Last Stop Ladakh

Also by Steve Tolbert

Channeary

Settling South

Eyeing Everest

Stepping Back

Escape to Kalimantan

Tracking the Dalai Lama

Dreaming Australia

Surfing for Wayan and other stories

Packing Smack, Talking Wombats

O'Leary, JI Terrorist Hunter

Playing Lady Gaga, Being Nan Pau

Steve Tolbert

Last Stop Ladakh

Last Stop Ladakh
ISBN 978 1 76109 149 0
Copyright © Steve Tolbert 2021
Cover photo by Sourav Verma on Unsplash

First published 2021 by
GINNINDERRA PRESS
PO Box 3461 Port Adelaide 5015
www.ginninderrapress.com.au

1

Moonah, Tasmania

'Next to a children's swing set in a Lahore fun park,' Joe went on in the low rumble that was his septuagenarian voice, 'a gathering ground for families, especially Christian ones on Easter Sunday. Ironically, most of the seventy-two killed and over two hundred injured were Muslim women and children. An offshoot of the Pakistani Taliban claimed credit for advancing God's work… Me – I've always preferred the reprisal practices of Santa Claus to that of God's. What's a withheld toy or two for bad deeds done compared to a God-inspired suicide bomb?'

Borderline, Ahmed thought, taking the last suck on his rollie, stomping it out and dropping it into a plastic bag at his feet. Still, Joe was careful to use the word 'God', not 'Allah', and who other than the perpetrators would disagree about the horror and depravity of such an act? He thought to say, I hate as much as you do the Muslims responsible for making people hate Islam. He didn't. Joe already knew that.

With regular media coverage of the 'enemy within', of extremist efforts to incite hatred between Muslims and non-Muslims, an agreement of sorts had been struck: over cards, no talk of jihadist militants blowing themselves up in crowded marketplaces or neo-Nazis slaughtering mosque worshippers during Friday prayers, or anything else that could spark religious debate, particularly extremist-linked debate; though the distinction between debate and discussion was hard to draw sometimes.

A crowd roar burst from Ahmed's wireless, sparing him his right of reply. 'Three for ninety-five,' he said instead, 'second six for Khawaja.'

'Australian of the Year material.'

Ahmed nodded, raking fingers through his beard as if to dislodge any attachments – ash, food, insects. 'I reckon he's got some Lebanese in him,' he said, probing for a response, but failing to get one. There was also the issue of his personal enemy within. But for now Ahmed focused on his cards.

As Joe waited for Ahmed to pick up the discard or take from the pack, he looked out of the alcove and scanned Main Road, the over-hanging newsagency pennant flapping in the hot north-westerly, the traffic, the signage – Banjos, Hamze Bros Fruit Shop, Top Slice Pizza – and in the distance a smoke cloud mushrooming up from the Derwent Valley and stretching their way. 'John Ruskin once said there's no such thing as bad weather, just degrees of the pleasant sort.'

'Card player?'

'Nineteenth-entury English poet.'

The last over finished before lunch at the SCG, so Ahmed switched off. 'An optimis', yes?'

'In his youth he was.'

'Ex-teacher know things like that.'

'Ah yes, the esteemed Wikipedia Broughton here, avid consumer of the intellectual life that I am…' He stood, bowed lower than his back was comfortable with and made an attempt to curtsey. '…with my pro-found knowledge of all things old, useless or nearly so: like this thermos for instance.' He opened it with a flourish. 'See how I did that? Now, is your taste espresso, long black, flat white, latte, chai latte, mocha or cap-puccino?' Before getting an answer, he topped up their mugs. 'Right – flat white it is.' He sat. His voice dropped. 'However, a sad fact, my friend, although a marvel at cards and coffee brewing, sir ex-teacher is built on a much smaller scale than his brain likes to admit sometimes.'

They raised their mugs in unstated toast, sipped their coffee and watched locals pass before Ahmed picked up from the pack and lay three jacks down on the portable table between them.'

'Later, Ruskin changed his mind big time,' Joe added to the earlier topic.

'Climate change?' Ahmed asked.

'Back then? Possibly. By all accounts, he was a prescient man. Or more likely he got old and cranky like the rest of us, making the journey from everyone being his friend to everyone being a rip-off merchant until proven otherwise.'

'Then I think he need more to believe in.'

'Mmm, probably Santa Claus.'

'A faith-lift is what Andrea at the fruit shop says.'

Joe chuckled. His great friend and neighbour across the table, still *Lawrence of Arabia* film-star material; his baritone voice, coal-black hair, beard and wrinkle-free skin making a mockery of his sixty-seven years on earth. Like the roll-your-owns, strong coffee and dim sims he consumed either side of lunch were the keys to eternal youth. At his rate of ageing, he'd still have the poster boy look for hair colour and skin care ads when blowing out the candles on his hundredth birthday cake; except when he winced, which he did now, his face a fist as he shifted in his chair.

'Spasms?'

'Not so bad.'

Joe gave him some time. 'By the way, where were you yesterday afternoon when I wanted to talk to you?'

'About what?'

'Salvation and the prospect of happiness in our next lives.'

'Asleep…fortunately.' Ahmed lifted his eyes again and stared into the distance as though his cards barely had a place in his thoughts. Something was gnawing at him.

'You know when you're finally getting old, Ahmed?'

It took him a few seconds to reconnect, respond. 'When you can't shuffle the cards any more.'

'Yeah, that, or when you can't get through another taxing day in the alcove without a nap.'

'Or when your birthday candles cost more than your cake, Andrea at the fruit shop says.'

Joe grinned. 'The older the violin, the sweeter the music, the saying goes. That being the case, we should be about due for our premier Federation Concert Hall performance. I've been fine tuning Lee Marvin's "Wandrin' Star" for the occasion. You?'

'"Time To Say Goodbye".'

'Wonderful song, right up there with "Wandrin' Star" and the rest of the best. I've got the DVD with Bocelli and Sarah Brightman singing it twenty-five years ago in Tuscany. Tomorrow, you bring the words and I'll bring along my song-arranging skills. We can work on it in between hands. I'll be Brightman.'

A siren sounded in the distance. They listened.

'Hear that?' Ahmed asked. 'They're coming to get you.'

'They've got no chance: like trying to chase down Insane Bolt in full flight.'

'Usain.'

'What?'

'Ooo-sain. That's that champion runner's first name.'

'You got a wax deposit in your ear? That's what I said. I can see myself in the next few weeks having to rework our table positions so I can sit closer to your hearing aide.'

Ahmed didn't appear to hear. His attention was drawn to a sky-blue niqab coming into view, a woman inside it, Joe presumed, pushing a stroller with a brightly dressed toddler strapped in. With just her eyes bared to the world, she turned towards the alcove and gave a finger-wave, obviously to Ahmed. She must have smiled too, surely.

'Fatima, hello,' Ahmed greeted her, appearing untroubled again.

'Of course, Fatima,' Joe muttered, once the woman had passed. 'Like us, part of the country's adopted, though with a distinctly different fashion sense.' ('Shuttlecock' fashion he'd heard it called, though he kept that to himself.) 'I must have missed the name tag on her dress.'

Ahmed shook his head in mock disappointment before discarding. 'She pass yesterday, Joe, and last week too. Lives across the road.'

'Your road or mine?'

'Ours Joe, ours.'

'For how long?'

'Maybe one and a half, two years.'

'Great smile, obvious dental brochure material. Love the hairstyle. Postmodern in its departure from the short back and sides and spiked summit look. Can't understand how I could have missed her.'

'Hot today, hot all week,' Ahmed diverted, eyes moving off again into the distance.

'Yeah. Makes you wonder what sort of internal cooling system Fatima must have in her…'

'Never pay attention to rain when we first come to Tasmania,' Ahmed interrupted, understanding all too well Joe's penchant for stirring, 'unless roaring southerly wake me up about to smash the windows. But now I do. Last month, rain eleven mill'metres… Very dry.'

'What is it about old men's obsession with the weather?' Joe asked, taking the discard and slapping down three kings.

Their eyes met; they shared smiles.

'Make the garden grow, Joe.' Ahmed nodded westward in the direction of Elderslie. 'And we do not run so fast any more when fire come.'

'Don't run at all.'

'Andrea at the fruit shop says he is too old to run and too young to slow down.'

'Well, life doesn't slow down much more than this: the two of us here slower than octogenarians in leaded underdaks with ankle weights for socks.'

'Slower than a passing kidney stone, Andrea says.'

'Does this Andrea actually sell fruit, or just talk?'

'More talk than sell, I think, 'specially when my Nima is there to serve customers. I go to listen more than to buy. Can make a dog laugh, that man.'

Joe barked a low 'woof' as he discarded. 'Still, I've met one or two octos who make reaching the eighties seem like something we don't want to miss out on.' Gone squint-eyed, he located Fatima again, her niqab billowing out around her as she waited for a break in the traffic then pushed the stroller across Main Road. It was the stroller that sparked his memory; though nowadays most anything could.

Fame, power and money might have eluded him in life, but not Sara – at least the young and middle-aged versions. Made Scottsdale – town of flat trays and pub living – more than just bearable, she did. Her first teaching post at the primary school; his first Tasmanian one at the high school. First swapped looks at the Lords Hotel's country band night; her in a purple blouse, jeans and leather-strap sandals. A snake fits into its skin no tighter than she fitted into those jeans. No thoughts of long term after she asked him to dance; he asked her to a golf club social the following night, and in weekly intervals after that to a barbecue and a comical round of golf. Probably an inkling of longer term, though, when – golf clubs returned – she suggested a drive out a dirt road past outbuildings, three-strand wire fencing, gnarly ghost-gums, 'No Shooting' signs perforated in bullet holes. One of those rare and memorable times when his life and imagination merged. That Olivia Newton-John song 'Let's Get Physical' was in vogue, and they did.

Relaxing in the afterglow, thankful he'd worn his newest pair of underdaks, he commented, 'I don't often get taken advantage of like this.'

'Really? That surprises me.' She placed a hand against his cheek and kissed him. 'I imagine you'll get over the shock.'

'The next few minutes will be critical.' How tender he felt towards her, head nuzzling her breasts, in no hurry to get dressed. Her silver-rimmed sunnies, silver rings on her index fingers, studs in her ears; the hot metal keeping them pressed together in the flat tray's meagre cab-shade until the shade lengthened enough for them to disengage. Whether the relationship progressed or not – and he very much wanted it to – he'd have no trouble storing the afternoon away for lifetime recollection.

'Should do this at night sometime so we can watch the stars,' she said, smiling lightly, 'if the shock doesn't prove too much, that is.'

'I've no plans for tonight.'

'How quickly you adapt.'

His head shifted to her belly, hearing it gurgle; her laughter when it did. He lifted his head, looked around. A fair few empty tinnies and bits of packaging about. The location and the fact they were local teachers made the sex feel slightly illicit, the thought of the repercussions if sprung adding intrigue to the afternoon. Certainly a major upgrade from his awkward hug and mug encounters of the past, he thought, when he dared think about them at all. He had no idea if she'd been hankering for an ex-pat Canadian/American with questionable putting skills and fashion sense, but he had for her. And she'd felt right from first touch.

'Slow hands,' Sara had instructed, like he was still on his L-plates and needed mentoring. That and the novelty (for him anyway) and a sense of time slowing in keeping maybe with the primordial landscape, pinioned the upgrade; though admittedly her laughter puzzled him at first. Was it mocking, or the 'pleased to be with you' sort? He couldn't tell, nor was he inclined to ask. But he did say, 'If you feel like taking another ride out here sometime, I'd like to have first option at being your driver.'

'I'll make note of that.' As sulphur-crested cockatoos shrieked a conversation, she rubbed his back and kissed his face, saying, 'I liked how you befriended my bits.'

He chortled, issuing a warning, 'Careful – I could re-sprout.'

'Really?' She laughed. 'Now that you know the effect a game of golf has on me?'

And when he did, going poorly poetic with, 'Pleasure experienced once is pleasure meant for a replay,' and sliding between her legs again, it was a pity he hadn't lathered himself in suncream first, for which he would pay a price later on, albeit a small one in the context of the afternoon's events.

Over the next few weekends, tent and camping mattress rolled and wrapped in weatherproof bags, riding in the flat tray's cabin together was like an aphrodisiac that strengthened the further they got out of town, the closer to the north-east coast. And the fact that their relationship continued both indoors and out, as did her easy laughter, put an end to his puzzlement: he had to be more than a mere curiosity for her; a country town fill-in until someone more interesting came along. He was who she wanted to be with it seemed, regardless of new arrivals.

Their first Scottsdale Christmas season; her amused expression as she handed him a self-designed voucher inside a card that read, 'Redeemable any time, anywhere for a deep muscle massage at a place of your choice: suncream application included.' He made copies, and for the next seven nights, in his room, or on his flat tray at the end of the track, or beside the old reservoir, he sang –

> On the first night of Christmas my true love said to me,
> Deep muscle massage,
> Place of your own choosing,
> Prefer a soft surface
> Annnytiiime, anyyywhere.

He handed over a voucher. 'Tonight – yes? he queried, drawing her to him.

Next night:

> On the second night of…

No shortage of laughter and afterglow that Christmas.

Quirks revealed; tenderness, trust and books soon partnered getting physical. For her, D.H. Lawrence, Christina Stead, Janet Frame and Thea Astley. For him, pre-Tim Winton and Richard Flanagan, so still Jack Kerouac, Wallace Stegner, Canadians Michael Ondaatje, Timothy Findley and Malcolm Lowry. Easy cooking recipes for the both of them. And once Tosser, their failed sheepdog saved from execution, had been fed, patted and praised, they often lay together, drinking tea or cask wine, books close, legs entwined. On offer as well, Sunday nights' best-ever BBC productions in glorious black and white: *War and Peace, Anna Karenina, Bleak House.*

And it wasn't long before they added travel to their activities: working on their skin cancers while body surfing at Bondi and the Gold Coast, surfing and beach walking in Bali, Dalai Lama-spotting in India's Dharamsala, touring Vancouver with his mother and half-sister, hunkering down as bottom-of-the-world exotics in midwinter North-west Territories, his father sharing his family and remoteness with them.

He noticed how Sara – smallish, hazel eyes and milky skin, faint freckle splashes across her cheeks only visible to the close observer that he was, wavy mid-length auburn hair, rare product of a Battery Point upbringing and public school education – exuded all the self-assurance of someone used to being listened to; wherever she was, whatever door she led him through. With her country-casual dress sense, dancer's poise and power station brightness, eyes followed her room-sweeping smile as she asked the right questions, reached for a drink here, sparked a conversation there. Voices became more genteel around her, poor language muted or barely used at all while she worked the locals politician-like (though hardly for the same motives): gentle, but unstoppable. Then – as though her whistle-stop visit had reached its end – she'd exit waving, him in her wake.

Times like these she was the light to his shade.

'Thoroughly modern woman,' quipped spud-farmer Zac – near-permanent nightly resident of the bar stool nearest the pub's back door and dunny – as he partnered Joe one night in another losing round of darts.

'Yeah, true,' Joe answered; two beers past his limit. Feeling playful, there came an idea. 'Though it's tough to keep her out of the Hobart pubs when we're down there, I can tell ya.' He sighed, shaking his head and lowering his voice to keep-a-secret level. 'Word of advice, my friend. If ever you want to get seriously domestic, avoid getting involved with a former lap dancer.'

'Oh…right.' It was like Zac was told his pleasure stick had escaped his trousers. His eyes flicked from Joe to the floor. 'I…I didn't know.' His drinking hand reached for his new beer. He sampled it – and again. In his discomforted silence, the clattering overhead fan and clanging pokies from the far side of the pub made inroads. Zac's turn at the board. He lifted himself off his stool, ordered a Bundy and Coke and accepted the darts. 'But yeah, Joe, I'll remember that – I will, most certainly.'

Next day, Sara blew in from school on a mission of considerable urgency. Lips pursed, steely-eyed, she dropped her bag, folded her arms across her chest and delivered., 'Seems in a former life I made big money,' she began. 'Doing what, do you think?'

First time he'd seen her so snarly-faced. 'Don't know, queen of my heart… Selling ice cream?'

She slowly enunciated each syllable, 'Lap-dan-cing.'

'Yeah? You never told me.'

She wasn't listening. In a world that could encourage women to stay small and quiet, there was Sara, looking as though she'd put on twenty kilos and sounding dangerous. 'And you have to think in people's minds here what such an activity is a lead-in for. Would fucking for gold be the right call?'

He shrugged, considering his shoes while deciding not to comment on her unfortunate choice of verb. 'Not necessarily. But if a few pinheads are intent on thinking that way, I guess they just have to be endured.' He picked up *The Thorn Birds* from a pile of books on the table and pretended to read the back cover. 'Did you lap dance to pay your uni fees?'

'Look at me, Joseph!' she yelped, scowl deepening, eyes scorching him with an inquisitor's stare.

Had he been one of her students, he might have yelped back, squealed and squeaked. As it was, his blood pressure approaching its upper limits, he gave in to her heated prodding and confessed, adding, 'What enters the ears here gets embellished and soon exits the mouth, wouldn't you say?'

In answer, she grabbed a cushion and belted him over the head again and again, feathers flying.

She kept her pouts that night then scuttled them the next day when he brought home a new cushion and two return plane tickets to Sydney, saying, 'Just thought we could use some time away from this loose-tongued town. The Wentworth Hotel and dimly lit restaurant meals are part of the package also.' Holding the cushion tight against his chest, he couldn't help adding, 'After some lap dancing, we might cool off with an ice cream up at the Cross.'

It took only seconds for her to wrap an arm around him, kiss him and say, 'If I want an ice cream, I'll go there on my own. No telling what else I might take a liking to.'

Small town Scottsdale, everyone connected by blood, gossip or activity. Times when he craved to break from the mould; walk down the main road in a budgie smuggler, Santa Claus hat and cowboy boots. Gay and Lesbians' Mardi Gras arrives in the north-east. A mould-breaker certainly: a career-breaker as well. Teachers must set an example, though darts and 8-ball hangovers were permitted, even encouraged. Still, cohabitating uncertified drew looks, fired gossip amongst the right-minded 'spudtocracy'. Easy to remedy, though it meant an end to transiency, to next town, next girl nirvana. Still, in Sara he knew he'd reached girlfriend summit.

One day on a bench in Apex Park, he mentioned that to her before saying, 'Let's take the next step and go conventional,' though conventional he'd rarely been. He passed her a yellow daisy.

Sara went to stone. 'Conventional?' she asked eventually, as though the word was from another language. 'You mean more than just sharing a bed or a holiday together?' When he smiled, she added, 'I don't believe what I think you're thinking.'

'Maybe this will help. I'm prepared to throw out all my Kerouac books and stop hero-worshipping Dean Moriarty. As well, I'll not insist on you attending Wife-4-Life school to brush up on the finer points of maintaining a perfect home for a hard-working husband.' As her eyes narrowed, he quickly added, 'No – promise, only joking. My nerves are up and jumping around because, well, I've never done this sort of thing before and…and anyway paired for life – though I'm ten years older so odds on it'll be longer for you than for me – I know we'll make a good fit and…and most of all I don't want to stop being with you, now, next year, in fifty years' time.' He went down on one knee, took a second, semi-crushed daisy from his back pocket and handed it to her.

She sniffed the remnants of it, visibly softening. 'Probably worse reasons for going conventional.'

'Probably are.'

'But why do this to yourself?' she asked, her elusiveness cranking up again. 'Why not just leave things as they are?'

'It's just sometimes I think that for you I'm just a chapter in your life, a good chapter maybe, hopefully, but still just a chapter followed by a different one that I'm not in. Whereas for me you're the book, prize-winning and complete.' He stood. 'And…and it's important to say this too, I think, Robert Heinlein in *Stranger in a Strange Land* wrote, "Love is that condition in which another person's happiness is essential to one's own." You should know yours is essential to mine.'

She gave him a long, curious look, maybe trying to catch up with everything he was saying.

He sat back down beside her. 'Oh, and this too: over the long haul, I could love you more than breathing.'

'You can stop now, Joe. I've got the message.' She shook her head slowly. 'And I doubt anyone would prefer love to breathing. It would be a very short relationship if they did.'

'Yeah, well…I'm trembling like a skinny dipper in a snowstorm. So maybe a small amount of hyperbole is creeping in. Not copybook, is it?'

'I've nothing to compare it with.' Her voice became soft and measured. 'What about all the things you were going to do, the places you were going to go: Tibet, Siberia by the Trans-Siberian Railway, Patagonia, the Amazon?'

'They're just escapist places. They're nothing compared to you.'

'You're the freest person I know in Scottsdale, maybe the state. Why give it away? Chances are I'll be here when you get back.'

He took a deep, stabilising breath. 'Tell me to back off, sleep on the couch tonight and try again in the morning or in two years' time if you like.' He went quiet, eyes fixed on the ground.

Long seconds passed.

'Okay.'

'Okay what?'

'Okay, I'll try going conventional.'

Getting the answer he wanted at a point he didn't expect it, he took a moment to realise he had, a mix of disbelief, relief and quiet pleasure working a smile onto his face. 'Yeah?'

'Yeah.'

'You could maybe sound a bit happier.' He kissed her anyway. Tension gone, playfulness crept in. 'Cold nose, healthy dog.' He kissed her again. 'I should tell you I've had three brain concussions, so from tomorrow on early-onset dementia is a distinct possibility. On second thought, going conventional might not be such a good idea, would it?' He ducked, laughing, a perfect target for a good uppercut, a kick to the teeth, a fourth brain concussion. 'Joking, joking – yes, it is a good idea! A brilliant one! Best idea of my brief but memorable life!' He wrapped an arm around her. 'What about a hamburger tonight to celebrate?'

She smiled. 'With chips?'

'A box of them.'

Later that afternoon, he visited the jewellery shop with one of her old rings then went and had a word to the pub's kitchen staff. That night they did better than hamburgers, at least in her estimation. They had a two-course roast meal at the pub, her chocolate ice cream dessert topped with a wedding band.

Not much to organise after that. Lucy, Lords' sergeant-at-arms and wife of the publican – a wedding celebrant to boot – voiced a willingness to perform the ceremony. Pinned open invitations to the pub's and schools' noticeboards and extended what they had to a clapped-out house rental, self-written vows for the Apex Park ceremony, pub reception; much of the town's population – scrubbed up and slicked down

– in attendance, including old Zac as best man. Sara's parents and older brother there too – to be expected as the parents were footing the bill – a carton of Tasmanian champagne in tow, though a slab or two of Boags Premium Lager would have roused greater interest. Warm and friendly they were, but no denying the aura of private school about them; a look their daughter had missed out on. And that made Sara all the more alluring for him.

Honeymooned with their loopy dog at the Gardens and Bicheno.

Five years later, over their morning's cereal bowls and coffee mugs, she said, as though reluctant to, 'There's something I suspect you should know about… I've been careless. It appears you've breached my defences.'

'Are you talking, child?'

'I doubt it's a rabbit.'

Soon confirmed by a blur of tissue on an ultrasound screen, the pumping of an aorta like a yapping mouth in a tiny skull. And him in awe that two hearts could be beating simultaneously inside her.

The blur grew, took shape, until at five months – after the foetus's womb-supported trip to Bali and foolishly to Lombok – a very feverish, shivering Sara was admitted to the district hospital, the burning question: can malaria pass through the placenta?

'No,' a medical expert in Sydney informed the hospital within days.

'Earth to Joe.'

'Geez, give a man a heart attack.'

'Know where you are?'

'On the far margin of the universe: Moonah, Tasmania, wonderland of the southern hemisphere and nearing lunchtime.'

Ahmed grinned as though that response was worth waiting for. 'We could play for pebbles if you're worried the stakes are getting too high.'

'The bank manager has me covered.'

They watched people pass.

'Don'tcha just love being redundant, disqualified by age from deadlines, responsibility, back-stabbing and the week's exciting new work initiatives?'

'You planning to take a card, teacher?'

'Heard this one? Teachers deserve credit. If they were paid more, they wouldn't need it.'

Ahmed's scowl, like something was wriggling out of Joe's nose.

'A joke,' Joe informed him. 'Not the greatest, I'll admit, but just shows the effort I'm prepared to make to provide you with your daily entertainment needs.' He sang Kenny Rogers's 'The Gambler' as though giving a performance. 'Know who sang that?' Joe asked.

'Andrea Bocelli.'

'Ah,' Joe nodded, 'maybe he did. Must look out for the CD.'

'CDs: yes, I remember them – popular around the turn of the century, weren't they?'

'Still are, Mr Ultramodern, if you know where to look.' In fact, Joe had no idea where to look. He picked up from the deck: deuce of clubs. Sara's voice: 'About as useful as an extra toe.' He discarded, Sara again tugging at his memory.

So, to birthing classes, a circle of protruding bellies next to gents' timorous I'd rather-be-farming or at-the-pub faces. Learned a lot there until the belly-dweller decided to breech. Still, breeching had its advantages. Delivery was like conception. A specific time at a specific place involving a specific body region: twelve noon, Tuesday 29 October at Launceston General Hospital to be exact. And in little time at all, new life emerged between two expert hands and a bevy of smiles, the mystery of ultrasound scans and malaria fears revealed. Heart-shaped face, startled look, eyelids batting in the light, certainly in need of a good clean-up.

'A beautiful girl,' said an attending nurse, lifting up the newborn prior to swathing it in cloth.

Sara looked between thighs and knees. 'Looks regulation,' she said to the doctor, wanting confirmation.

'Regulation she most certainly is,' he replied after inspection.

She turned to Joe. 'Share and care starts now, yes?'

One of the rare moments he detected vulnerability in her. Only one answer: 'Yes.'

The nurse handed him his clean, wrapped daughter and to share her he stepped up to his wife.

'A small brandy later to celebrate?' she suggested, relieved enough to smile.

'That's it!'

'What?'

'Brandy Broughton – a name.'

Thumbs up from medical staff, and he stood there at mid-Sara position never more proud and delighted, almost expecting his daughter – tiny wheels and rods already rotating in her earthly brainbox – to reach out, take hold of a finger and say, 'Rough few months, Daddy, but I got here. When's the next trip to Asia?'

'Liked the fact my lady garden remained undisturbed,' Sara said, back in her room cradling Brandy in the crux of her arm while still enjoying the effects of the epidural.

Their first laugh as parents before Joe commandeered two glasses and poured a capful of brandy in each of them. 'Epidural portions for two might not reach the backs of our throats. But let's find out.' He passed over a glass and raised his in a toast. 'To the girls Broughton: gold passes to contentment, the essence of my world, always.'

Typically, Sara smiled while raising her glass and time slowed.

Later, as he shouted the bar, Zac came up and handed him a roughly wrapped present. He opened it to reveal a pair of tiny red booties, white socks and the smallest frilly red dress he'd ever seen. 'Daughter of a lap-dancer and a hopeless boofhead darts player deserves a good start in life.' Zac said, unable to check a grin.

Next day, he drove Zac into the hospital for a visit.

Those early days leaning over the cot as Brandy slept – the pulse, breath and look of her. Missed the ABC news and *The Two Ronnies* sometimes just to watch her. Ah, but those awake times, the nappy changes, her colic screams, face turning beetroot and crumpling. Hard to believe such a high, piercing sound could come from something so small: the size of her voice box rivalling that of a nearby silo, it seemed.

'Lungs like camel bladders,' Zac said, face screwed up after hearing Brandy one day.

Into her papoose: 'Your turn, Mrs.'

Sara: red-eyed, hair gone stringy, 'No, your turn, Mister.' That's what they called each other when tension revved up, words sharpened. Occasionally she dropped in, 'Ms to you,' when she was running especially hot.

In reply, Joe made the mistake – just the once – of reciting from *Hamlet*, 'What a piece of work is a man, how noble in reason, how infinite in faculties.'

Like fire fed pure oxygen, she responded, fierce in voice, face and eyes. 'Oh go bury your head, Mister Ph-fucking-D!' Sara needed her sleep: as nuanced as a hairdresser with a blowtorch when she didn't get it. 'And by the way, you left the toilet seat up again.' Always best to allow her the last word, or her f-word artillery, that she knew he struggled with, would get a prolonged encore.

'Round and round the garden, like a teddy bear,' would later become one of Brandy's favourite storylines. But before that, it was round and round Scottsdale like an F-111 at rooftop level; doors slamming shut, windows closing.

'Who's going to want to partner you when you grow up If you scream like that?' he'd ask her.

'Living the dream here, aren't we?' Ahmed said, shifting again in his chair.

'Wouldn't want to be anywhere else.'

In earlier times, besides gardening, climate change, sport, population sprawl, 'Leb' vilification and the even trickier topic of what form God took in the eyes of man, they'd discussed travel and taking a trip somewhere together while wracking their brains to come up with exactly where.

'Wadda'bout Melbourne?' Ahmed asked one day, looking eager.

'Naw. You'd be bored rigid. Besides, they'd not give you much of a welcome.'

'Waddaya mean?'

'They've got enough wind up there already.'

Ahmed tilted his head like a perplexed sheepdog and said, 'I'd report you to the discrimination office if I wasn't filling my wallet with your money.'

Payback, Joe continued to think of it; that he was still getting his own back after the walking stick Ahmed presented him with for his fiftieth birthday, the set of false teeth ten years later. 'Stirring' or 'taking the piss', down-under indicators of acceptance, were as spontaneous with them as they were for the native-born.

They'd talked as well about joining an old crocs' support group, or a bowls, chess or table dancing club. Something groupie, anyway, to vary their days.

'Whadda'bout a knitting club?' Joe asked one day, prompting stop-gap deafness in Ahmed. Yet to happen, though, their trips done solely by maps, club involvement by suggestion only.

Joe took from the deck, mind slipping back.

Tough pregnancy, tough three months post-delivery: never to be repeated. Not sure if Brandy's name set a precedent in Scottsdale, but it was rich in alliteration and they were too tired to care how it was received. One thing after colic ended, though, and peace was restored, Brandy's lively manner and bright red stroller, with string-attached balloons, often prompted smiles and talk.

'Got your eyes, she has, Joe,' acquaintances (he liked to think the most observant ones) said. And beaming before he was aware of the repercussions, he was slow to steel himself for Sara's response.

'Voice box and table manners too, don'tcha, love?'

He gaped. He thought. 'But ahead of her in toilet habits.'

'Only marginally.'

Joe slapped down three nines and discarded. Sometimes the past returned so clearly he felt he could write a memoir in a matter of days.

A former home class and English student, deemed by some the detention king of Belgrove High – Joe's and Ahmed's car mechanic now – walked by and looked in. 'Ow're ya goin'?' he called out in a megaphone voice no softer than a street explosion.

'Yeah, fine, Ari, fine,' Joe answered.

Boom went his voice again. 'That's the way! See youse!'

Watching Ari, Joe recalled the day he asked him to stay behind in home class.

He showed Ari the note. 'This absence excuse of yours is written in perfect English,' he said, pausing to watch Ari's eyes flick from floor to windows to school grounds. 'Did your mother or your father write it?' He waited for a response that wasn't coming. 'Because whichever one did, I'd like to ask them to come into school so we can have a chat about it.'

Nothing from Ari, not even movement.

'Well, the look on your face answers my question. Know this, Ari. You're in my home class. You're important – extra important. But unless you're honest with me, I can't do my best for you. And that's what I want to do. You should view me as the start of your second family – your Belgrove one.'

'A friend's sister wrote it.'

'Right. You might tell her it was very well written. We'll talk some more later. Get yourself off to class.'

It occurred to him back then that he expended more energy trying to shape the lives of his home class students than he did his own daughter's. But soon came the retort; energy had to be expended on a needs basis, and Brandy's were being well catered for.

In truth, Syrian Ari was illegally working in a bottle shop at night and was just knackered. So Joe set about familiarising himself with the inner workings of social services, before Ahmed mentioned a friend who had a friend who ran a gardening business and was looking for a reliable, weekend employee. Cutting, raking, sweeping – yes; but also the opportunity to work on small engines, as it turned out. Morphed quickly under the influence of rake, broom and mower repair, did Ari. Gone from the half-dead to a purposeful student and friend of the school, he never missed the opportunity to greet Joe, often from half a suburb away, or so it seemed. 'Sponge,' a colleague once good-naturedly called Joe for affording students like Ari the time needed to unburden themselves of a problem – and there were more than a few who needed to.

Seeing Ari, talking to him, always took Joe back to the days he'd been given the opportunity to teach well. One of the success stories of the school that year was Ari: a balancer perhaps for those Joe couldn't reach, especially during 'the year he nearly slashed his wrists', to quote Sara.

A lady even older than them– also familiar – wearing sunglasses, a cane in one hand, shopping bag in the other, hobbled cautiously by like the footpath could suddenly open up in front of her. She stopped, turned and nodded before continuing on, each small step shortening the distance to somewhere. But not quickly enough, it seemed. She sat on a bench further along, bent down, adjusted her support hose and straightened. 'Got another one for you,' Joe quipped. 'Albert Einstein once said, "You don't really understand something unless you can explain it to your grandmother."'

'Difficult when she is under the ground.'

'Needs to read "living" grandmother.'

'Aphorism?'

'I believe so.'

'I will miss them.'

More people passed as Joe mulled over what Ahmed just said: three adolescent girls in hijabs, eyes only for their phones; followed by three boys of similar age practising their ghetto-gangsta poses – hoodies, baggy pants, blue and white runners, full of swagger and snigger and sucking hard on cigarettes – and moments later an edgy, scraggly-bearded man in a skull cap, pale blue tunic, sandals, long white shirt and trousers, his lips moving as if holding a conversation with himself.

'Head down – incoming,' Joe said, 'incoming' their code word for someone out-of-the-box interesting or controversial moving into range.

Naturally, Ahmed did a heads up, his eyes guided by Joe's.

'Contact at three o'clock,' Joe continued. When Ahmed didn't bite, Joe asked, 'YouTube preacher, you think?'

'Sends messages to Allah, passes answers to our young people look-ing for somewhere to go, something to do.'

Two ways to reply to that, Joe thought. He avoided the contentious one. 'Other than watch soccer and listen to rap music, you mean.'

'Glenorchy Knights and Pitbull for my grandsons.'

Joe watched the passing 'preacher', saying, 'Always considered it a big turn-off having moralisers of the cloth, of any style or persuasion, stationed between me and that rose garden in the sky calling out the entry requirements.'

Ahmed looked at him with furrowed brow and curious eyes. 'When's last time you were in church?'

'I suffer from a candle allergy, so it's difficult for me.'

'I think convenient is the word, teacher.'

'Listen. Have I told you I went on a whiskey diet a couple of weeks ago?'

'Did you lose anything?'

'Two days.' Joe chortled, while Ahmed eyed his cards, unamused.

'Imam, priest, preacher. What they talk about is philosophy, yes, Joe?'

'For the learned Leb and Canuck-born like us, yes. Harder to pro-nounce than religion.'

'You full of philosophy today, Joe.' Ahmed said, probably just so he could repeat that word, linguistic show off that he could be sometimes, or so Joe liked to point out to him anyway.

'Walk first through the fire, then philosophise,' Sara would say to combat his commentary on the state of the world. She was the more articulate one and well and truly a goer, with brains and energy to burn; as likely to meditate in a Buddhist temple as punch a speed bag in a gym. Tougher and much more practical and ambitious too. Assembled flat-packs, which only she bought, as though she'd been raised in a flat-pack factory, written the instructions herself. Applied for promotion just the once, got the position and from that point on lauded the advantages available for an only child.

Ahmed grabbed a card from the pack, laid his hand out on the table, emitting a satisfied sigh. He counted up his points. 'One hundred fifty-five.'

'Against my minus thirty-five.'

'You owe me seven dollars and eighty cents. Pay now, run away, or continue the game?'

'Tell me again about Islam's position on gambling.'

'Fourteenth greatest sin, but not if winnings go to charity.'

'I hadn't heard about that charity bit before. Besides home, here and the mosque, are you going anywhere else in the next month or two?'

Ahmed looked away. 'Just the hospital.'

Joe watched him, recalling that Ahmed made mention of a doctor's appointment days earlier. 'Right. Best continue playing then.' He shuffled the pack and dealt; picked up his hand. 'So, what did the doctor have to say?'

Ahmed took a while to arrange his cards. 'That I won't live to a hundred.'

'And?'

Ahmed eyed his cards, considering. 'That you have a year to pay me.' His air of calm absorption was barely disturbed as Joe felt the world stop inhaling Ahmed's words.

From behind his silver-framed glasses, he searched for the emotion on his friend's face, but couldn't find it. Though the news wasn't a complete surprise – there was the occasional twitch of discomfort and

Ahmed's deep, head-back laughter had been missing the past few weeks. Still his eyes filled. He resisted expressing his shock, how much his great friend meant to him – to blather on about the obvious. 'Then we'll have to make the most of our time together,' he said gently.

Before he could decide whether to use the back of his hand or turn his head, Ahmed glanced over the table at him. 'He who weep when losing at cards.'

'Must be the smoke in the air.' Joe lowered his eyes. 'Chemo?'

'Start tomorrow.'

The sun moved overhead, burned down through the gap between shop buildings, edging closer. They donned their sunnies.

Compliments of the Education Department, they got transfers to the 'wrong side' of Hobart with its shortage of flat trays, bull bars and over-size tyres. 'Though a popular place to start if you come from somewhere else,' Ahmed said one day. Brought their V-Dub Beetle with Tosser, a few museum bits of furniture in a trailer and a collection of books in the back. Moonah Primary for Brandy, Campbell Street Primary for Sara, Belgrove High for him.

Home had taken him a while to find. But, with patterns set – no more searching and restless transits – he surrendered to domesticity on a standard block. Ignored travel ads for the next few years and lived the Aussie dream – a partner, a kid, a house, a dog, a mortgage – paying off the weatherboard and brick place admittedly short of mid-century perfection. 'Modest' was the word he used to optimistically describe it. Carpet worn thin, cracks in the walls, no internal doors. ('Unrivalled charm and possibility,' the fast-tongue agent banged on. 'Encapsulates the 1950s minimalist style that is certain to prove an investor's dream.') L-shaped kitchen and dining, lounge, original fireplace, two and a half bedrooms, small bathroom, separate toilet, small shed, regulation front and back yard with a circular clothes line.

'More than just a square box,' Sara observed, surveying the place, 'though not much more. Like something an elderly relative might live in.'

In hindsight, an exercise in hope over experience before good fortune smiled and they met their renovation and gardening enthusiast neighbours, Ahmed and family. Still, it felt right at the time, as if they knew good fortune would come along in some form. Yes, it was pinched and old, but it was theirs to share with the bank. And Sara was always up for new challenges, and he'd grown up in such austerity boxes in such prestige-free places. And as a one-time devotee of living a life less ordinary, it surprised him just how easily he slotted into programmed suburbia. He got used to Moonah, to being squeezed in the middle of half a million souls; to the melting pot of people and cultures compensating for the lack of open horizon – or so he told himself and Sara, and later Brandy.

Thirteen years of paying off the box, establishing friendships, of the peaks and troughs of high school teaching, Ahmed-assisted renovations (trellis-bordered decks front and back thick with heavy-scented jasmine the feature), Nima's Brandy-minding and gardening advice, and holidays in Asia or at the outlaws' shack at Orford. Good wife, good daughter, good neighbours, good life until the onset of Sara's deep tiredness, swollen gums, chills like she had a permanent flu. 'Feeling a bit off,' is how she worded it, smiling grimly, before finally dialling up Doctor Ridgeway's office.

'A touch of cancer, I've been told,' she said, coming out of the consulting room for the second time in a week after insisting on going in alone. 'Probably best to think of it as my midlife crisis.'

The sense of 9/11 freefall as the ground dropped from his feet; stomach flipped, sickness swirled. He worked to breathe.

'Anyway, might need to keep to the short-termed. And talking short term, that Bruny Island lunch cruise we've been talking about seems in order now while my taste buds are still fully functioning.' She sounded indomitable.

She wasn't. Doggedness can only go so far. From normalcy to a kind of terror as her flesh succumbed to the cancer's advance: the sunken eyes and cheeks; the scans, syringes and tubes, blood extraction and transfusions, unpronounceable tablets and chemo; and with her hair taken, a batik scarf to cover her head. Hope and all their future plans succumbed as well: little sense trying to hold on to them or rework them into delusion.

Reconciled, she said to him and Brandy one day, 'Not unprecedented, so best not to make a fuss about it. Happens to everyone without exception and saves me getting stooped, wrinkly, pop-up veins, my neck stuffed down between my shoulders.'

He and Brandy cooked: him – pasta, steak, eggs on toast; Brandy – chicken cacciatore, lamb casserole and grilled seafood for a catch-all-salad, though Sara had little appetite. After tea, they sat her on a plastic chair and helped her shower, get dressed and ready for the infidels' arrival, or go over to their place a night or two a week. Back home, they washed and kissed her face, helped her to the toilet, to undress, don her pyjamas and make sure she was warm and tucked into bed just right.

Shortly before going into the Whittle Ward, her dark-ringed eyes occupying much of her face, Sara said to him alone, 'I've thought a lot about getting a supply of Nembutal smuggled in and doing a Marilyn Monroe… Read a book about her once. But the good morphine tablets have decided the issue. They'll do… They'll do.'

'More meat on a dog's paw,' she said the next day, glancing down the length of her outstretched arm. 'Were I a contortionist, I could use my hipbones as foot rests.' Still a woman of words despite the rasp and lack of punch in her voice. 'Remember when we first tried each other out?' she'd asked. Her hand, every bone and vein visible, held his with a bird's strength. 'Let the record show how much I enjoyed the ride… that day when you first touched me just so…and ever since.' She paused for a long moment. 'You know I had visions of becoming a Sydney gangster's moll before I met you.' She found a way to smile. 'When it's your turn – and if you're not with someone else – come and find me, okay? Take me down that track again. Follow it up with more of the same.' The effort drained her. She wilted back into the pillow.

Two weeks short of her 16 January birthday, she died in her sleep.

Short funeral service; or at least in reading the program it seemed so to him front-rowed in numb bewilderment, eyeing her coffin, attaching the word 'gone' to it: a woman he'd shared more than three decades with. In all those years, he could never get enough of her; now he had no choice. Ten years older, he should have been the one in that coffin, not her – which informed him again that if life was unfair, death was more so.

Glancing around, it appeared most of the northern suburb's primary teachers were there; the overflow standing at the back. Everything arranged by Sara down to the last detail and conducted by her close friend Ellen Larkin, her mother, Brandy and Nima. Turning loss into words, Ellen Larkin read Kenneth Slessor's 'William Street', Nima from Kahlil Gibran's *The Prophet*. His own role, as requested, to simply occupy a seat.

Then came Brandy's eulogy – hands gripping the sides of the lectern a family trait, it seemed – photos on a screen augmenting her words: her poise and fluency the features before she paused and absorbed him with a look. 'To end,' she said, 'I'd like to read the last stanza from Bruce Dawe's poem called "Accountancy". You know the book it's from and where it's kept, don't you, Dad?'

He nodded and she read,

> This universal law abides:
> The coin of life has just two sides:
> One side is love, the other, loss,
> Though many auditors fail to agree
> That this is our basic currency.*

'Best poem reading I've ever heard,' he said after she sat back down, resting her head on his shoulder. He lifted an arm and put it around her, asking himself, was he too busy or just indifferent to the whoosh of her growing up and emerging fully formed to get a tax file number, the start of a HECS debt, and with a talent for speaking so beautifully?

* From Bruce Dawe, *Border Security*, UWA Publishing

A range of music like Sara's range of interests and friends: Eva Cassidy's 'Songbird', Pachelbel's Canon, Gorecki's Symphony Number 3', Paul Kelly's 'You're 39, You're, Beautiful and You're Mine', and, after all the words had been said, her favourite Karen Lovely numbers 'Knock Knock Baby' and 'Sunny Weather'; both full of bounce and bite, for certain meant to tell everyone to get back out there and get on with things.

There's high risk in setting out to explore the feelings of that desirable someone newly met, getting to know who they really are, of striving to make yourself a focal point in their lives. The risk: attraction is danger; desire can beget scars, death creates a great void. By the time people reached their thirties, few would be unaware of that. But what were the options? Get a pet? Stare at goldfish? Do crosswords? Play cards?

'Everyone has a plan until they get punched in the face,' Mike Tyson said after he had.

Funeral over, Joe stood at a place he didn't recall getting to, dazedly thanking people, mind distant, words awkward. The thought of what he was meant to do without her – toughen, thicken, live in a state of distraction, get to the next day – made all else inconsequential. In the aftermath that night, he slept in patches, waking and listening for Brandy in the next room. The same thoughts circled, ended at the same point and started over again. He tried to read but his novel might as well have been written in Swahili. When Moonah dawned again, he got up, took his broom, went out and swept his driveway and the footpath – not something he'd done for a while. The same people as always retrieved their morning *Mercury*, the same cars passed before Ahmed took shape beside him, placing a hand on his shoulder and saying. 'Mine could use the same treatment when you're done here.'

How could he not smile? 'Don't know if I've got enough hours in my day to rediscover yours.'

'My bet is you have. Come on, we can work on a quote over coffee. Nima's got the pot on.'

After every death, every war, there's the clean-up – but not at his place. He bumbled along. Not even in the navy had time passed so slowly. He felt Sara's absence as much as he had her presence. Unable to get involved in anything for long, he had to get outside, find a way to keep the world looking a little bigger. He walked for distraction, as a filter so as not to feel. Feet divorced from brain, it mattered little where he ended up. There was always a bus stop and a bus to get him home, whatever the time.

He went back to Belgrove and the distracting busyness of relief teaching and volunteering other days to instruct slow readers. Numb to petty annoyances now, of adhering to a class management bar, he came home, glanced up at their wedding photo on the wall and talked about the positives in his day. Later, he spoke to her in fevered dreams, her warmth next to him, sound of her breathing, the soft snoring that in hay fever season thickened and rose, 'rivalling that of three truck drivers or a solitary moose', as he'd say to her in early days, teasingly; and the irony of her reply – 'Put a pillow over it. Your mouth, I mean.' Little sense pointing out his mouth wasn't the issue.

Those long, raw months, hardly a parachute ride, though Ahmed and Nima, monitoring them like ASIO, did their best to make it so.

Gradually a pattern developed that slightly differentiated Monday from Thursday, Wednesday from Saturday, but not by much. Small steps, and over time the walks, increased gardening and vacancy settled into him, regulating his solitude before Brandy returned home from uni and waitressing work. There were times when Ahmed and Nima were busy or away that the postman's arrival, or taking the bins out for collection, were the biggest events of his day. And he told himself life was like having two files in his brain: one for the way things were before her death, the other for after. The question of how different the files were he resisted thinking about.

Brandy – by default staying close to him when she could – came home from uni one late afternoon holding a half sheet of paper with handwritten words on it. She plopped down in her mother's armchair beside him, looking composed beyond her years. 'There's a place called Aleppo in Syria.'

'Uh huh – was once a culture centre. Nothing much left of it now but the heat, dust and bombed-out buildings.' With his girls, it had become habit to add a bit more to their original statements if he could.

'The tragedy of Aleppo, people say.'

Like her mother, she carried the big world inside her.

'They do.'

'A humanitarian disaster.' She showed him the paper, saying, 'I copied this from a magazine. What it says is…' And she recited, 'Often when a thing is unbearable to imagine or accept, we do the opposite of what we should do: we turn away, shielding ourselves in order to protect our own peace.'

'Good words best saved.' He waited, convinced the paper was a prelude to something else.

But she got up and went into the kitchen, poured herself a juice and walked out onto the deck and sat, reminding him that there would always be parts of her he would never reach, parts only her mother could.

Over breakfast the next morning, she fixed her eyes on him and said, 'I want to go into nursing, Dad.'

His first thought: made for it. And his pride in her peaked again. 'Good idea and it doesn't surprise me in the slightest,' he said. 'Never any doubt about your sense of responsibility and compassion, that you've got your mother's grit, her steely spine. Which reminds me of something Beethoven once said, that character is fate.'

'I know.' She chewed her toast. Also like her mother, she was less than rapturous listening to him repeat quotes from his quote book. Their practical streaks looked to other avenues for inspiration. Still, sometimes he just couldn't help himself.

What was; what is right now. Hello, alcove. Hello, Main Road. Hello, Ahmed across the table.

'You're tough, my friend,' Joe said, intent on showing he was still in the conversation, despite his memory dip. 'You'd survive a nuclear blast if you set your mind to it.'

'Mmm.'

'Sara wore Bali batik scarves, remember?' Joe went on, struggling to sound conversational.

'I do. Still she smile. Still she and Nima cook together, even when she's not feeling so good.'

They settled back into silence and their cards before Joe said, 'Takes a while to get the chemo into you in any one sitting,and you'll have one hand free. Prime time for me to reduce my debt. Reckon you'll want to play a round or two?'

Ahmed nodded before putting down a run of five, eight to four of hearts. 'You might have to sell your house.' He discarded.

What Joe considered saying was 'If I do, it'll be to the loudest, ugliest, arse-scratching tree-climbers this side of the Central Highlands.' He might have before Ahmed's diagnosis. 'Yeah, true,' he said. He took from the pack, put down three twos and discarded.

A cloud shifted, sunlight catching Ahmed. 'Warming up.'

'Mmm.'

Moments later, Joe laid his cards down on the table – aces and kings and a queen-high run in spades. 'This should keep the debt collector off my property,' he said, trying to keep the tone upbeat.

'Warming up,' Ahmed repeated, obligingly.

'Must be an echo in here.'

Ahmed mimed wiping sweat off his brow. 'Any hotter and we could smother. Souvlaki, fish and chips, pizza or dim sims, Joe?'

Typical, after Joe started to gain the ascendancy, Ahmed should call for a break in the day's excitement. It was standard practice for the person who won the last hand to choose the gourmet lunch. But Joe offered Ahmed the choice, thinking this might be the last time he'd be enjoying his food for a while.

A stickler for protocol, even when cancerous, Ahmed aimed a forefinger across the table. 'You to choose.'

'The thought of a seafood pizza, preferably served by the square metre, nearly drowns my mouth.'

'Mine too.'

'And hosting again the two most acclaimed card players in the history of Moonah will bring yet another day of prestige and delight to our lunch providers, no doubt. Important to think of others in this increasingly self-absorbed world – is it not?'

'My thoughts exactly.'

Hands propped on the table, they pushed themselves up. Ahmed donned his sunnies, grabbed his cigarettes and stuck them in his daypack. He took out a doubled-over piece of finely carved cardboard embossed with 'Reserved for the Moonah card playing and discussion club. New members welcomed. Free membership if aged over 60. Back in 15 minutes for application requests' and placed it on the portable table. 'Reckon you can get there without a rest stop?' he asked. 'An old rust bucket like you could break down in this heat.'

Regaining his bite, a good sign, Joe thought. 'The biggest challenge will be managing my brakes so you don't get too far behind me lost in your dementia.'

Together they walked along Main Road in the direction of Top Slice Pizza, or, as Joe often called it, 'The cardiac on a plate parlour,' sometimes tag-lined with 'Where the food never surprises, the coffee's strong, the chatter unending and mostly indecipherable.'

'Heard this one?' he asked Ahmed. 'I'm on a seafood diet. I see food and I eat it.'

'Sometimes I think Sara was the most patient woman in the world.

'On that, my friend, we both agree.'

2

Srinagar, Kashmir

The clamour of outraged voices, guns firing, tear gas canisters being launched had all died away, so Ifra left the house to continue what she had started earlier.

She hauled the skinned goat carcass into shade and sawed away at its breastbone until it split. She reached for the bucket of water and scrubbed and wiped the carcass clean of blood and dirt. As she picked up the carving knife again, the thump of boots coming up the pathway stilled her.

A voice shouted, 'Your brothers – where are they?'

Soldiers.

Still gripping the knife, she bolted for the door.

*

Afternoon.

Big-eyed in shock, Ma stepped out from her men. She placed a hand on Ifra's cheek, bent down and kissed the mess that was her daughter's face. 'We're here,' she said, voice weak and trembling.

Lying on a trolley in the hospital corridor, bandages over her swollen eyes, pellet wounds oozing blood, Ifra replied, 'Soldiers came. I was scared and ran. A soldier was outside the door and he…' Her face crunched. A tear ran red across her cheek. '…shot me.'

3

Ahmed didn't make a year. Chemo affected him in a way he was unprepared for, his pride baulking at spending so much time in the toilet, strange women attending to him. Death was preferable to what the rest of his dwindling life had in store for him. So he refused further medical treatment, but accepted a vault-load of pain and nausea tablets instead. And for a while the tablets allowed him his dignity to go to the mosque, appreciate small portions of food and spend a little more outdoor time with his family and Joe, his winnings increasing to nine dollars and fifteen cents before his body began to shut down and a kindly doctor, Joe suspected, acceded to Ahmed's last wish. Though who would know?

In the Whittle Ward's corridor, minutes after Ahmed's death, Nima handed Joe a note her husband had written, probably weeks earlier, undoubtedly with her help. It read,

> Joe – Nima, our boys and I would be honoured if a teacher of all things 'old and boring' (but never for me) and his daughter Brandy would attend my funeral with my family at the Hobart Mosque and say a few words about whatever you can dig up to fill a short time slot, other than card-playing strategies. And Joe, no candles in the mosque, so no allergy excuse. And maybe you can put the money you owe me in the mosque's collection box. Your thankful neighbour, Ahmed

Hobart Mosque, eh? About the last place Joe thought he'd ever be walking into: on the same probability scale as a shark cage off Port Lincoln, a prison cell anywhere. And decades of classroom experience amounted to little in settling his roiling stomach as the five of them went up the steps, deposited their footwear and passed through the arched entryway into the vestibule. Nima and Brandy veered right towards the women's section, Joe picturing headscarfed Sara rolling her eyes. And he wondered which direction she would have gone. Into the prayer hall to sit behind the men until escorted to the women's section? Probably not the occasion for such temerity. Followed Nima quietly? Doubtful. Grizzling? Good chance, though most likely only to herself.

After dropping twenty dollars in the collection box, Joe followed Ahmed's boys into a large hall, hearing Ahmed: 'Head down – incoming.' Though now he was the 'incoming'. 'Stay calm. You can do this,' he whispered to himself for the umpteenth time, sitting down with Ahmed's boys. And there in that strangest of places, it struck him how endings rarely turned out as you expected or wanted them to.

Maybe sixty or seventy men sitting cross-legged, or with legs pulled up to their chests on the mat-covered floor, women sitting in the alcove off to the right. When his time came, Joe got up – old man design faults never more apparent – and made his way to the lectern beside Ahmed's shrouded body. He took his notes from his coat pocket and scanned the faces looking up at him feeling totally misplaced. First time he'd faced an audience since his teaching days, and that's where the comparison ended. But, he told himself, he had a plan. The imam had invoked Allah; he would invoke Tim Winton.

Drawing a deep breath, eyes locked on his notes, he started. 'Relationships rarely end as you expect or want them to. For example: me up here in the Hobart Mosque, Ahmed, my neighbour and best friend beside me in death as he so often was in life. Ahmed and I were near-inseparable, and in debate I always knew which side he was on – the other side. We talked at length almost every day, often about gardening, but also about travel and ideas and writers, like the West Australian Tim Winton. Very early in his career, Winton wrote a short story called 'Neighbours'. The story is about a young, newly wed couple who move from the outback into a city and a neighbourhood filled with Eastern European migrants: Macedonians on the left of them, a widower from Poland on the right. Barely past dawn each morning the Macedonian family were up watering their garden, washing clothes and shouting from yard to house and back again, while it seemed the Polish widower hammered nails just to add a different scale to the racket. For months, the young couple remained uneasy, wary of their strange neighbours. Then one day, as they were preparing a garden plot for planting, the Macedonian father leaned over the fence and offered advice about spacing, hilling and mulching. Days later, the mother gave the young wife garlic cloves to plant. Over the next few weeks, advice extended to small talk then to an invitation for a meal at the Macedonians' place that included advice about schools and buses, growing asparagus and raising chooks in a small backyard. By the end of Winton's story, the Macedonian migrants and the young couple have become inseparable. Exchange the Macedonians for Ahmed and his family, the Polish widower for an Iraqi one and I could have written that story – at least an amateurish, non-fiction version of it. I could have extended it too, explaining how it was that a once-young husband out of country Tasmania – thirty years later a widower too – came to speak at his mate's Hobart Mosque funeral service.'

He steadied, loosened and tightened his grip on the lectern while encouraging himself with a few silent words, though everyone appeared to be awake and taking in what he had to say.

'Additions to the story would include how Ahmed and his Nima walked a tightrope between Lebanese and Australian customs, of how they got pleasure from the mundane, of how often Ahmed would grin and say to me, "Living the dream here, aren't we?" The story would include examples of his generosity and compassion, and, with a heart bigger than all of Moonah, just what a gem of a man he was.'

He stopped and smiled at a recollection. He didn't need his notes now. 'When I grow up, I'd like to be more like you,' I said to him more than once when he was helping me with some project. If the hose was nearby, he'd use it on me, saying I needed cooling off.' He paused, took a breath. 'In an era of moral and political confusion, of crass self-interest and greed, Ahmed, by his nature and faith and acts of kindness, stood out in making life better for those of us who had the good fortune to know him well. He was a prime example of that most admired man here in Australia – a good bloke. I reckon we've all done a lot right to have been worthy of his friendship. So you, me, our community will carry the best of humanity through our memories of him. At the gates of paradise with a two hundred plus hand, or wherever you're at, Ahmed, know what a great privilege it was to be your neighbour, and how much you're already missed.'

Like some sad aria at the end, wasn't it? Or, by reverting to sentiment, the overwrought drivel of a jittery old man, Joe thought, pleased to get back beside Ahmed's boys. Yet later, the extended hands and compliments he got indicated he was the only one who thought so.

At Ahmed's Cornelian Bay interment, with Brandy back at uni, Joe stood with Nima and the boys as men from the mosque shovelled soil over the grave. That done, he parted company, taking a water bottle from his daypack and walking between wreathed headstones and slabs down the slope towards the entrance.

He stopped at Sara's grave, loosened his tie, slipped out of his sports coat and dowsed the yellow daisies he'd planted years earlier. Bending awkwardly, he placed a hand on the ground, swivelled, sat and drew his knees up. What would it take, he thought yet again, to get a small bench positioned there, attach a brass plate with something like 'FOR THE SEATING COMFORT OF BIBLIOPHILES ONLY' etched on it to make it personal and exclusive; a bench he'd pay for and maintain?

'So find out,' he heard her say.

'You having spent all those years in the local women's association and given so much, they might be interested in providing sponsorship. They'd get priority seating rights as well, a big bonus.' He glanced up at passing visitors then back down at Sara. 'Anyway, Ahmed's close again,' he continued, a little hoarsely, eyeing her name and dates on the brass plaque. 'Don't know if I've ever mentioned Bob Hope to you. He was more my era than yours. Anyway, the story goes that when he reached ninety, his wife asked him where he wanted to be buried. He answered, "Surprise me." Made me laugh.'

How Bob Hope was a logical extension of Ahmed, Joe had no idea:

just another sign of his discombobulated brain adding more question marks than answers to the day. 'Anyway, I won't be telling the joke to Ahmed up there. He's never much appreciated my jokes.' After a pause, he added, 'Though I s'pose you've not been a great fan of them either.'

'You have greater talents.'

Even here, converting her image into conversation. He placed a hand on the slab and spread his fingers recalling the touch of her skin, the shape of her over the years; though slowly, as per her Scottsdale instructions. 'Did I tell you I went to the Lazybones Lounge on Murray Street last week? The world looks a different place under neon lights. Anyway, I saw somewhere that a Lauren someone was singing Eva Cassidy there, so I had a strong coffee, ventured out and found the place courtesy of some helpful pedestrians. Box-like, low-slung brick building, so some fine acoustics; candlelit, small, round tables, single light on the stage. Like those at the Rock Quiz pubs we'd see on TV.'

'You sit next to the entrance?'

'I did, yes. Closer to the ambulance services there.'

'"Songbird"?'

2012 didn't seem so long ago. 'Like the great Cassidy herself was singing it.'

'Get through it unscathed?'

He felt the old sadness again rereading the slab's inscribed details, watching them blur. Nowadays, there were places and situations he was constitutionally incapable of emotional distancing from. And ground zero for that condition was here.

'Never one to ration your tears, are you?'

'I've got a tear duct disorder, as I think I've mentioned before.' Not true, though that's how he'd excuse his spillage. 'Have had since childhood when the dropkick next door threw a bucket of sand in my face.' That part was true. 'Talking of which, there's an old story that when the legendary actor John Barrymore was instructed to cry in a particular movie scene, he asked, "Out of which eye would you like the tears to come?"' Joe smiled. 'I'm good, but not that good.'

Clouds were moving in from the south in keeping with the forecast. Nearby visitors stood as still as the gravestones they were hovering over. He was the only one sitting.

Out of talk, he lowered his head between drawn-up knees feeling the usual emptiness taking charge. Minutes passed before he rolled onto his knees and pushed against the gravestone to stand – Sara still propping him up, providing support – and exited the cemetery. He boarded a bus and got off at the Maypole Hotel a few kilometres away intent on distraction, at least for an hour or two. In the lounge, he spotted the group of retired, surprisingly all-male Belgrove teachers at their biannual luncheon; the first one he'd been to in three years. Since the year he nearly cut his wrists (Sara's words), he'd distanced himself from teaching staff social life.

Working on his Bryan Brown cool pose while rehearsing possible conversation topics – sport and politics surely, drought in the hinterland maybe – he ordered a beer, crumbed scallops and chips and sat in the last seat of the extended table.

'Afternoon, Joe.' Graeme Turner greeted him amiably from two seats down.

The others nodded.

'Nice coat,' Graeme added. 'Looks as though you've come from a funeral.'

'I have.'

Graeme went quiet, but recovered quickly. 'Ah, well, you're at the right place then.'

In Joe's view, that remained to be seen. Across from him a former colleague, the anomaly that was Bosko Pavlich, who managed a minimal smile, which was unexpected: unexpected that he should even be there. Once labelled the Sphinx for exuding all the exuberance of a mortician, he rarely visited the staffroom while at Belgrove and Joe couldn't recall ever seeing him at a staff function.

'How are you going?' the Sphinx asked, almost colloquially, lifting his heavy, jellybean eyes while pawing a glass of orange juice with scarred hand, the nails bitten clean, his strong East European accent still intact.

'Good,' Joe jollied back an answer, though that was debatable. 'Still above ground, still got a pulse, so no complaints.' An apt reply when considering his day, he thought.

'No relief in sight.' That scar on his cheek still pronounced, like a faded red zipper embedded just under the skin.

'Pardon?'

'Rain – no rain.'

'Ah…no.'

The Sphinx coughed, which Joe took to mean he'd reached his conversation limit.

At first, Joe was unfussed by the turned-up talk at the other end – Graeme Turner's latest house renovations and problems with a 'derelict neighbour from over the waters', Derek Webster's Hawaii holiday and investment house purchase, Tim Schneider's Danube and Rhine River cruises, Geoff Sealy's latest financial planner's advice, Mike Adams's new Mazda MX-5, Todd Hampton's neighbour who dressed 'just so last century', and Graeme Turner again on the topic of negative gearing – talk that only paused for the tipping of beer down throats, summoning the waitress for refills and ogling her retreating backside; though, admittedly, it probably warranted the ogling.

As Joe recalled from Belgrove days, the loquacious Graeme Turner – solid science department head with a solid ego – could just as readily talk to a stump as to a human. He reminded Joe of the adage 'Before you speak, ascertain if the person most interested in what you have to say is yourself.' But he was in like company. The others weren't exactly devotees of humble reflection either, bestowing opinions and prices on everything.

Feeling the outsider again, he donned his social smile at all the right moments while waiting for a topic change: Glenorchy's chances of winning the state premiership maybe, or Geelong in the AFL, or who was likely to take out the year's Miles Franklin Literary Award (admittedly, about as likely as discussing floral arrangements at a Fijian wedding); even men's health or the week's weather report would do. Didn't happen. It was like he and the Sphinx were watching the main act from the wings of a stage, or that a curtain had closed across the table – regulars on one side, latecomers on the other. Compared to his input here, the cemetery was a gabfest.

With voices amplifying in proportion to drink intake, their capacity to irritate rising, Joe stopped listening, if not hearing. He ordered another beer and a settling half-measure of Tullamore Dew from the bar and returned and eyed the top of the Sphinx's head; his chin pressed into his chest like he'd discovered two different shoes on his feet, or was recuperating from a recent lobotomy. Nothing more forthcoming from him.

Unkind thoughts an indicator of his fraying patience. Joe reprimanded himself, recalling that someone once suggested 'spectrum disorder' as the reason for the 'Croatian Sphinx' being 'a little odd'. Refreshingly, there was this about the Sphinx: he lacked the others' 'me'-fixations, their talk of neighbourhood apartheid, acquisitions, interest rates and property values, of dinner party wines, world cruises and upgraded business-class travel.

'Doing much in retirement?' Joe asked, once the Sphinx raised his head.

'Nothing of great significance,' answered the man of few words and even fewer facial expressions, while scratching his arm as though after a flea or next drug fix.

'No. Me neither.' Unlike the others at the table, Joe almost said. '"Have more than you show, Speak less than you know,"' someone with a ton of social flair said once. Though, in our cases, that's not to say we know very much.'

Was that the start of a smile? 'True.'

Joe added, 'Though I guess there'll always be those who talk about their personal lives as public lives.'

'Someone said to me once, "In judging others, people will work overtime for no pay."'

Joe gave a hearty laugh that put a three-second pause to the talk at the other end. He suddenly saw the man across the table in a different light. 'I like that.'

The Sphinx cracked a smile – no doubt now that it was – before studying his fingers and withdrawing again into the corners of his mind, or wherever his retreating thoughts took him. Joe had had little to do with him at Belgrove. He taught maths, Joe humanities. Though from some source, he'd learned the Sphinx had migrated from the Balkans, and now he recalled a newspaper headline – 'Romeo and Juliet in Sarajevo' – published sometime during Serbia's brutal four-year siege of Croatian Sarajevo back in the 90s. Fleeing the city together one day, a pacifist boy and a Moslem Croatian girl were running across a bridge hand in hand when they came under sniper fire. Hands parted. The boy was hit and killed. The next shot struck the fleeing girl and she fell, screaming. Over the next few minutes, according to the news source, the girl belly-crawled back to her boyfriend, laid her head on him and died. There was an accompanying photo of their bodies lying together in the so-called Sniper Alley.

Post-World War II, the renowned Holocaust survivor and author, Elie Wiesel, suggested 'Think higher, live deeper' as a basis for displaying one's humanity, that hell may be the people around us, but they're all we've got. And in the storybook part of his brain, Joe constructed an episode in the Sphinx's earlier life: a Croatian trapped in the rubble of the siege, witnessing sniper shootings, rape and executions, over time his family members killed. Perhaps taken prisoner and starved in a concentration camp like over twelve thousand others were. Joe convinced himself such a tragedy happened to this man with chewed nails, scarred cheek and hands sitting head bowed across the table from him.

The meals came; something for the fringe element, the two-man spectator corps to get involved with, so a sense of relief for them both.

With no one meeting his eyes, Joe finished off his beer and stared at his plate of crumbed scallops, chips and salad.

'Crumbed 'roo testicles?' Todd Hampton next to him asked, swinging around and fixing his Chihuahua eyes on Joe's lunch. 'They've a reputation for being more testy than tasty.' He laughed, irritatingly, but stopped short when no one else did.

Joe felt his face warm, his annoyance fester, like he'd discovered something stuck to the sole of his shoe he couldn't remove. He scanned the lounge, giving gravity full play while watching the waitress serve bowls of ice cream with chocolate topping to the old couple at the next table. In their expectant smiles and quickness to get started, they could have been kids again. Still, that did little to assuage him.

To Todd of advanced egotistical traits, Joe strained to say lightly, 'You might want to shield yourself. I can feel my stomach about to respond to your comment.' No ornament to the teaching profession was the trainee Nazi back in the day. Though, in his self-appointed role as teacher consultant and critic, he thought himself so.

'I had a stepfather once,' Joe continued, 'a man of great self-certainty whose mouth was faster than his brain.' He decided against ending the sentence with 'also'. Nodding at Hampton's plate-size steak oozing blood, he twisted his lips into the facsimile of a smile, and with a requisite amount of frost, asked, 'You planning to suppress your roadkill's pulse before savaging into him?'

Hampton's grin turned plastic. With the glare of an aggrieved Heinrich Himmler, he muttered, 'Enjoy.' Probably the hundred-trillionth time that hackneyed bromide of a word had been used when no other sign-off came to mind, the distinction between what is said and what is thought never more apparent. Presenting Joe with his back, Hampton, with the trademark animation of a stonefish, re-entered the echo chamber of odious neighbours, property values and the retirees' own linear lives: born, raised, schooled, employed, married, invested and retired in Greater Hobart – and hadn't Hobart benefited? How well they thought of themselves; how wise their opinions. Prime example of pulsating egos allowed out for a social occasion: the self-veneration bordering on torrential. After scoffing down the chef's Hollywood-mogul dessert, might they pull out cigars, light them up with the flaming end of fifty-dollar notes, order brandy in snifters and, in voices louder than Harvey Norman's, continue their discourses as if occupying the head-quarters of the world, its financial steering wheel set firmly in their hands? No better candidates for Hobart arseholes of the week awards – the month even. And such bog-standard epithets didn't exactly leap off Joe's tongue, not even under these circumstances.

Irritated enough to bite the table, he ordered another beer, backed it with a half measure of what he'd had before, thinking none of those assembled here knew about Sara, had ever asked, and he wouldn't be adding Ahmed to the names of those op-shop-dressed neighbours 'from over the waters' being dissected with such patronising sneers.

He glanced around at the tables. Other than the old couple, every lunch-goer with ears had vacated the place. Feeling estranged, maybe out of practice being a joiner, he decided against waiting for stumps to be called and vacate the place as well. He ate and drank quickly, like he'd suddenly remembered leaving his front door open.

'Dental appointment,' he said to Bosko Pavlich, as he got up still munching his last chip. 'Good to see you. Take care.'

'You too.'

Farewell to the chest-thumpers – their chorusing voices, nodding heads and obsequious necks in full exercise mode – was a waste of breath. He could take out a pistol and fire a round into the ceiling be-fore they deigned to acknowledge him leaving; which effectively knocked into the next century his notion of reconnecting with former school colleagues: the possible exception being Bosko Pavlich. He stalked out, leaving a tip (for sure, the assembled less one, mistaking their chairs for thrones, wouldn't), the pub's elect reminding him of Napoleon and cohorts in Orwell's *Animal Farm* – bloated on privilege, chins and torsos slackening, bellies expanding and filled with so much hot air it was a wonder they didn't float to the ceiling as they continued jawing on. He'd punch himself in the face with brass knuckles if ever he considered attending another retired staff luncheon: the wankers.

Out on the busy footpath slightly tipsy, as anonymous as he was indoors and not exactly harbouring a deep sense of LOL, Joe admonished himself, 'Settle, Broughton. Not worth losing your lunch over. At your age, it's a bit late for the onset of anger management issues, the prospect of yoga and meditation classes for the doddery and irritable added to your busy schedule.' Behind him a sign on the pub wall: 'Happy Hour 5 to 6'. Nothing there to plug their 'Grumpy Hour' that he'd just set the tone for. If Brandy ever had kids, that's who he'd be for them – their grump-pop.

He crossed Main Road, went for the bus stop bench, sat and donned his sunnies. At the other end, yesterday's gentleman, a balding, thin-faced old wreck wearing the no-brand clothes of the self-neglectful: white shirt and blue and red striped tie, a Vinnies' tweed coat, baggy slacks and scuffed, loafer-style shoes. In fact, the bench-sitting antithesis of those – less one – he'd just had the displeasure of sharing a luncheon with.

Bent over, chewing the end of a pencil and looking poor as a bit of stale bread, the old boy was absorbed in a crossword, occasionally muttering to himself as he filled in a set of boxes. He might have come from an RSL luncheon or his own friend's funeral service. Watching him, Joe's faith in humanity recovered some ground. Still old ways, old values hanging on – if precariously; still hope for the world after all, he told himself, while resisting the temptation to ask the old boy how he was getting on with the puzzle. Instead, he folded his arms across his chest and settled back into himself, eyes returning to the traffic, his inner critic getting a recall.

'Cantankerous old sod,' he mumbled. 'Sympathy for the dead in the morning: afternoon ridicule for the living.' Like any septuagenarian, he'd developed a tendency to make a lot out of a little. And when he did, he didn't much care for where his thoughts took him. Over the years, he felt he'd just about mastered relationship theory, like that offered up by Elie Wiesel. It was the application that continued to stymie him. Like the passing window sticker he'd seen recently: 'My people skills are great. It's my tolerance of idiot drivers that needs work.'

So tell me, all-wise keeper of the Book of Virtue, he continued to mind-talk, you whose life could hardly be termed a masterwork, a template for the acquisition of intellectual riches, or riches of any kind, when was the last time you were with someone who shared your erudite views on things? Tough question. He'd need to file it away for later consideration.

A solitary life had its unmediated moods, making some days harder to navigate than others. Still, he remained disappointed with himself. Typical of him to feel great turmoil one moment and soon, in different surroundings, ebb back into peace again. He should have controlled his inner sniper back there, made more of an effort to blend in rather than getting bogged down in fashionable cynicism. A question to Todd Hampton perhaps, irksome as he was: if you wanted to buy some land and relocate to somewhere outside Hobart, where would you go? How hard was that?

Though, admittedly, having scapegoats to kick around on his more difficult days did serve a purpose.

On the back window of a stopped car, a sticker: 'I change the future. I teach.' It pulled his mind fully outside. He continued to monitor the traffic, occasionally glancing around at the footpath's steady flow of people – high brow, low brow and great unwashed – evidence of the browning of the northern 'burbs, all shades and shapes and clothing styles, all with their individual strengths and weaknesses and ways of looking at things: a black tent floating past with a probable woman inside; an assortment of 24/7 screen addicts, their downturned eyes and fingers at work, somehow not running into anyone or anything. Often when watching the smartphoned, it struck him how obsolete he was – the covered wagon in a world of artificial intelligence, drones and stealth fighters – and just how quickly that gap was widening. He glanced over again at the Vinnies' antique (a wonder of the times he was still above ground) studying his puzzle and gnawing his pencil, holding on to what had comforted him the past ninety years or so.

When he was young, no one wanted to be the outsider, a kicking-post for in-crowd entertainment. But the outsider tag suited him now, and he suspected it suited the old boy at the other end as well. Typically, as people passed, he reverted to the solace of history, long ago lyrics getting another replay in his head – 'What we need is a great big melting pot. Big enough, big enough…' Big enough, actually, to accept lifelong Luddites like him. And for very limited benefit, the generous country of Australia had done just that long ago.

There was this about being a part of the great human stew – or 'infestation' if a person sided with the placards at alt-right rallies – from first bicycle age to the present day, with the possible exception of Scottsdale, he'd grown accustomed to differences in backgrounds and beliefs, of looking different, dressing different, talking different, and in reflecting on his more adventurous days, of seeking those differences out. The irony, he supposed, was that by living so long in Moonah, the differences had come to him. Experiencing them nowadays was as easy as peering out his front window, or looking left, looking right from a Main Road alcove or bus stop.

His eyes suddenly filled, for no other reason than his chronic hyper-sentiment affliction. It was a puzzle to him. In happiness too, it could just rear up without warning or good cause. Though, other than when Sara was camped out in his mind, it was almost certain to when a toddler passed in the pampering arms of a parent or grandparent, or some old fossil strove with all their being to take those next few steps. Toddler tenderness and the struggling ancients: his guaranteed eyewash activators. But why now? Ahmed? The cemetery fantasy of Sara's presence? PTSD Bosko Pavlich with former colleagues who ignored him? That old boy in old clothes looking 'just so last century'? How he disliked that phrase, particularly when voiced by the retired luncheon set.

He wiped his eyes, looked around. One positive about being on his own in life, he was his only witness.

Mates4Mates passed on the back of a big, shaved-headed man's T-shirt. It occurred to him that he and Ahmed could have worn such shirts with decks of cards etched under the M4M lettering. He kept his eyes on Mates4Mates, feeling a surge of warmth for his adopted state, a sense of how good it had been to him and how sane it seemed compared to the usual headline-grabbing places.

Another window sticker caught his eye: 'Beer: encouraging the ugly to have sex since 1821.' Where else but Australia such reverence for the national drink? Must have been an important year, 1821. Should organise another Australia Day to commemorate it.

Who needed a book or a newspaper while waiting for transport?

'Women need men as much as fish need bicycles' passed. Half a minute later: 'There are no strangers; just friends we haven't met yet.'

As much of a contrast in window sticker philosophy as people walking the footpath. He particularly liked that last one displayed by one of the northern 'burbs' better angels, obviously. He repeated the words, intent on remembering them until he got home and immortalised them in his quote book.

He lifted his face, the breeze having strengthened, the sky a gathering storm. A pity storms couldn't learn to arrive at night so as not to blight people's days, he thought, almost able to smile again. Soon, a peal of thunder and the metallic smell of approaching rain. The first fat raindrops fell. They felt cleansing. And thanks to the crossword man and passing windscreen and T-shirt philosophy, self-combustion had cooled, his knickers starting to unknot. He glanced in the direction of home, considering whether penance for his poor behaviour was in order, before looking back along the road. A bus was coming. Unusually, he made his decision in seconds. Gripping his knees for push-off, he stood, straightened, shoved his hands in his pockets and walked.

Back on his patch and wet to the ribs, he changed out of his clothes and wrote that one window sticker passage into his quote book. Once the front passed, he went out back in the confidence he could shut his eyes and walk the length and breadth of his yard without misadventure he knew it so well. Though he kept eyes open for pruning Sara's roses, cutting back her yellow-faced daisies, shovelling soil and mixing in compost for another garden bed. Then, knees in dirt, he weeded rows of carrots, lettuces and onions only stopping to stretch his back until darkness drew in. 'Letting go' was the key to discarding angst and sorrow his tattered old Buddhism books said. A process helped along by physical endeavour, of the long walks, plant pruning and weeding kind.

The call to prayer, roosters greeting the dawn and the swish, swish of old style brooms sweeping away dirt and fallen leaves were the sounds he most associated with Asia, especially in the small hotels of rural Bali and foothills of Malaysia. Over the ensuing months, with Brandy at work on the Syrian–Jordanian border now, he started his mornings the same way, grabbing his push broom and sweeping his driveway and the footpath in front of his house clean, then sweeping it again cleaner. Often there was little to sweep up. But it was the ritual, the rhythm and sound, not the collection of leaves and grit that comforted him. Afterwards, he'd often set off on a walk, sometimes stopping in at Nima's first.

'My mother used to say that the best of life was food and family,' Nima said more than once while serving coffee and something she'd baked the previous night. Straightening, she might add, 'Now you need to eat and drink up, Joe, because you're losing weight.' His well-worn third belt hole continued to testify that he most certainly was not. But it felt good to be fussed over, so he followed her instructions like any impressionable young lad of seventy-three would do.

Either alone or with Nima in one of her many short hijabs, he might call in at the florist before visiting Cornelian Bay cemetery. Or he might wander along Main Road, passing the alcove, the hollowness inside him deepening. Sometimes on his own he got so distant from himself, so caught up in his thoughts that when again he took notice of his surroundings he was somewhere as unknowable as Cairo or Irkutsk and would have to ask for directions back to the Moonah he knew. Yet, no matter how far he walked, or how much he read or gardening he did, rarely a day passed that he didn't miss having his say over hands of cards.

As his days formed around his habits, he became more and more equivocating, and decision-making became a chore: muesli or eggs for breakfast, afternoon at the library or State Cinema, a five p.m. one or two-finger dose of the Dew? Plans for the next minute, day or week were debated, decided upon, then changed and re-debated; which served as a reason for rarely doing anything too challenging. Some days he had to think hard to remember what he'd done the previous day, like it had been too mundane and boring to have penetrated his mind.

Then one day he sought incarceration. Believing, perhaps, that touches of his favourite writers had taken root in his skull, he set out to write a novel on his barely used, Brandy-bought laptop (a concession to modernity after stores stopped selling typewriter ribbons), based on his early life in Canada, America and Australia. Four hours a day set aside with daydream breaks for Joe Broughton, literary lion, sharing shelf space with the big name authors, of wooing the reading public with his verve and insights, existing in their thoughts; of celebrity endorsements, newspaper articles ('a book loved by all ages'), book signings, writers' festivals and radio interviews. In going from ordinary to extraordinary in a hundred thousand words, he could easily lose an hour in his writer self and not produce a word or give a single thought to the world away from his new career. But of course, before fame could happen, which bookshop would red carpet him for the much-anticipated launch? And who would launch it? There wasn't anyone he knew well enough to ask, except maybe Brandy, or Nima, and one was half a world away, the other hardly a bookshop regular. But hold on, Broughton, hold on. Step back; get your mind back on the target. First, complete the first draft.

His first day off came after two weeks and thirty-one pages of slow-going. After rereading the last chapter of Winton's *Breath*, he read his own two chapters again and was hardly riveted by their narrative power. Frustratingly, he knew what he wanted to write, but how? He started reading Markus Zusak's *Bridge of Clay* for clues and in the middle of it muttered, 'Broughton, you great pretender. Yours is the scribbling of a schoolboy. Face it, you scribing an acclaimed addition to Oz fiction is about as likely as a chimp writing a sequel to *King Lear*.'

He decided to write a memoir instead, a sort of 'How I got to where I am here in Moonah' account with, perhaps, a few loose-memory flourishes in appropriate places to add some drama. He worked solidly for another fortnight before reading over his work in induced drowsiness. Encouragement through self-kindness was lost on him. Hard facts: it was hardly writing to levitate by; rather more to drown by. If it had heart and energy, it needed a molecular scientist to spot them.

'End it, Broughton,' he muttered. 'Stop punishing yourself. Walk away.' To do that, he summoned procrastination. In truth, writers were in a world of their own, one he'd only ever merit a passing glance into – on his good days. Besides, even if his writing did show promise, what chance a publishing contract when fewer and fewer people were reading the traditionally printed word. Since Gutenberg, over five hundred years of mass-produced wisdom covering every topic on earth had been swamped by the global tidal wave of social media brainlessness. In Oz's big five cities, how many publishers and bookshops had gone bust? Answer: lots.

He opened a bottom drawer. Spotting a few blunt pencils and a Kodak camera he'd forgotten he had, he consigned his work to a USB and dropped the USB into the drawer. Another silly idea abandoned. Even at his age, still pretending to be someone he was not. All in all, he was a septuagenarian widower of thin accomplishments: reader, walker, card player, procrastinator maybe, but certainly not a writer.

Reverting again to on-hour predictability, and once more sensing his life contracting, he sat at the dining table the next day and eyed his two goldfish, room enough in their tank for a couta or two as fishmates. 'What next?' he asked. 'There's got to be something to stimulate the House of Broughton, deliver a much-needed spark to his days.' It struck him at times how much he talked to Max and Mavis, more so than to the walls, the kitchen sink or his tomato plants – though of course not as much as to Sara. 'What about a testing weekly walk to keep the heart rate up, the perspective bigger than in more recent times?'

Over coffee and biscuits at Nima's the next morning, he was quick to tell her about his new initiative. 'Track up Creek Road working towards the Cascade Track. Back down through blue ribbon suburbs to Battery Point and Princes Park for a late lunch. Then onwards to destination Elizabeth Street bus stop for the victory ride back home. Call it the Hobart Geriatric Challenge, years in the planning to allow septuagenarians of the south the platform, the opportunity to experience the great diversity and natural splendour of Hobartian life.'

Nima gazed up at the ceiling as if summoning help before sitting down and giving him a penetrating stare. 'Joe, you are too old.'

In the silence that followed, she sipped her drink while fingering the loose hair off her forehead. That action alone momentarily deflected him from his latest plan. Nothing complimented him more nowadays than her opening the door to him in jeans and T-shirt or jumper, coffee rich in the air, her mid-back, grey-at-the-temples hair uncovered, even unbrushed at times, to the extent that she might just as well have come in from a southerly buster. 'Too old,' she repeated with frowning firmness. In the time it took for his coffee to go tepid, he recalled the first morning she'd greeted him like that, how his eyes slipped from her face to the door frame, wondering if she realised she hadn't finished dressing. 'Come in, Joe, before the imam passes and sees me like this,' she'd said, drawing hair back with a hand and smiling a little at his discomfort.

He sat a little forward on his chair, hands wrapped around his mug and said, 'The Challenge will get me out more. I'll be a regular part of the general population, a familiar face. It'll be my training program for the annual Point-to-Pinnacle Run – the old fossils' division.'

'Old fools' division,' in a mutter escaped her lips.

He stood up taking on a runner's pose, wheeling his arms, lifting each leg – once. 'Summit in sight, arms and legs apumpin' and I'm a-chuggin' at such speed it's a wonder my number doesn't fly off. Watch your backs, runners, I'm coming through! Alongside now! And I've broken through, nothing ahead now but the finish line and glory of gold!' He sat back down like he could use the rest.

She leaned forward. 'Brandy will not like it.'

'What she doesn't know… Besides, she's not due home until Christmas.'

Nima pushed the plate of biscuits his way. 'If you don't have a heart attack before then.'

He was feeling a more prominent part of Hobart just having this conversation. 'As much chance of that happening as Twiggy Forrest applying for unemployment benefits.'

She breathed a sigh strong enough to trigger hiccups, and they laughed. 'You'd best start storing up some energy then.' She reached for the coffee pot and filled his mug.

The next morning, Joe was up and out at dawn and soon tracking across the base of Mount Wellington, its open forest, streams and fern-filled gullies, stopping at viewing points to look out over the city, put names to native flowers in bloom, listen to the magpies and currawongs. Late morning, he found the Cascades Track and descended stick-assisted. Coming into South Hobart, he hid the stick in bush marked by a cairn topped in half a brick. The following week, he'd reverse the route. The climb would start there.

Toughest part conquered, he tramped on through the silky suburbs of Dynnyrne and Sandy Bay, trees canopied over the roads, patches of sunlight penetrating the leaves. Slowing, he inhaled the purple jasmine smothering a day-care centre's wrought-iron fencing and dawdled past its latest equipment and the seagull-like screeching and energetic play of those using it.

Angling back into Battery Point's narrower roads, its heritage homes and old whaler's cottages, feature rosebushes and rhododendrons, a small art gallery and antique shop, he stopped long enough to gaze down on the kayakers and yachts both moored and moving, and the Mona ferry rolling on swells sweeping up the river. Off again, he passed his in-laws' place before her death and his move into a nursing home – halyards below clanging against masts, nearby cafés and outside tables and chairs largely occupied. Mostly thinned-down gym and water-bottle enthusiasts or the fashionably coiffed packing handbag dogs and giving him a look like he'd just escaped his own nursing home. Or, with 'Think higher, live deeper' slow to re-enter his brain, that's how he often interpreted those looks, anyway. Not that he was ever tempted to stop. The pull of coffee sippers chatting away along tree-lined cafés was just one more trend lost on him, as it had been for Ahmed. Clearing the obstacles, gaining free air, he pushed on mumbling, 'One foot ahead of the other, wonder man. Lunch stop just around the corner.'

And just when the street looked to be falling into the river, a sharp turn left brought him to Princes Park. He entered and eased himself down on a bench under the welcoming shade of an old oak tree, sharing its view of the bridge, yachts; a massive cruise ship coming in, a cargo vessel going out. So much movement out there for surprisingly little noise; his tree cover cutting lattices of sunlight and shade on the ground, emitting audible leaf-whisper and occasional magpie song. Once his pulse settled, he grabbed his thermos and salad roll, poured a coffee and ate, drank and thought.

Away in his crowded memories, he recalled how in earlier times he'd daydream about growing old beside his wife, sharing just this sort of bench with her. Sara the resourceful – still blazing with life, bubbling with ideas – retiring and gardening and attending Pilates, Mandarin, possibly kickboxing and skydiving classes; going on decluttering campaigns, assembling their new barbecue, looking at design and renovation magazines and getting tradesmen in. And despite his objections, fitting grab bars beside the toilet and bathtub herself, 'Just as a matter of practicality,' she'd explain, tools at her feet. And him – dreamy and drifty as ever – doing what he always did; that is, when Brandy's kids weren't there on sleepovers, or he and Sara weren't tripping off to Asia, staying at old-folks-friendly hotels: a lift, breakfast buffet, pool with steps and railing, brollies, lounge chairs and side tables for books and drinks; maybe even an air-con, tinted-window bus tour one day to somewhere out of pool and beach range.

At times, Sara must have scanned the enigma that was her husband and asked herself was this antithesis to the modern-age good for nothing else but reading, fretting about Brandy, 'constructive' daydreaming (his term), walking, card playing and travel? Next to useless around the house, older than old-fashioned, and with his stolid resistance to change hardening with the years, he was more than just behind the times; he was terminally divorced from them.

With that thought occupying his mind, he looked left at a couple of grand old dame bench-sitters (Hilda and Wilda?) dressed in their Wednesday finest staring out at the river. What were they seeing? Former husbands or boyfriends, distant children, grandchildren or inseparable pets? Things they'd done earlier in life, or what they'd missed out on? Dreaming backwards he'd heard it called, and there was rarely a day, like today, he didn't do lots of it too.

Soul refreshed, negotiations between resistant body and persistent brain at an end, he pushed himself up as though fused in rust, stiff as the old oak he'd been sitting under. He massaged his lower back and flexed his neck and shoulders. Marginally ready for more, he plodded on, and despite the lure of bookshops and burger outlets, avoided the CBD with its shoppers and suits ranting business into their phones by diverting through the docks and Domain, and from there around to his bus stop. Only one final decision to make at the finish line: whether to self-celebrate with a lubricating coldie at the New Sydney pub just around the corner, or defer and have two the following week?

He went for the one and ended up having the following week's one as well – all the time reliving the highlights of his day.

For a while, he fantasised about a tree change, going at least some way to becoming less conventional, more authentic. Thoreau's small cabin in the woods maybe, or more likely selling his house and investing in one of the eco-villages that were springing up in the eastern states. Not the utopian, free-entry 'from each according to ability, to each according need' commune model of the 60s and 70s. Often little ability and plenty of need. Still the idealism and land ethics, but with differences from earlier times, like solar energy and a one-off, test-of-commitment investment of $200,000.

Yet, gradually, doubts about his suitability stalled his eco-village fantasy. Just another instance of heart trumping head, wasn't it? Not exactly God's gift to the fix-it world, he asked himself how feasible such a place would be for an arthritic old man with a hammering genius for missing the nail but never his thumb. A few gardening tools, shovel, mattock, hoe; and in a child's first tool box a screwdriver, hammer, handsaw, assorted nails and screws rounded out his hardware inventory. About as skill set handy as a one-legged man in a high jumping competition, he told himself. Moreover, he'd spent more than half his life in his 'renovator's dream house' that had yet to approach its 'dream house' potential, and Sara's clothes were still in their closet, her toiletries and painkillers in the bathroom cabinet, hairbrush on the bedroom dressing table. And there wasn't an hour that went by that he didn't feel her there, or Ahmed close by. True, by modern standards his place might reasonably be described as daggy horse and buggy, but it was part of his chemistry, the sense his DNA had melded into its weatherboards and plaster walls. And familiarity had a big role to play for old dogs grown wary of social intercourse, and with a preference for living in the past. Besides, he took comfort from his caffeinated mornings at Nima's. He'd miss them and her.

At night, in his old horsehair armchair, wearing his high-end Big W tracksuit and flannel shirt (scarecrow clothes his mother called them, that along with the 60s surf fashion craze of Levis and boardies never dated or disappointed him), something eaten regardless of use-by date, the latest Trump tweet, or priest sex abuse prosecution, or climate expert pilloried, or bank and corporation practices that when done by individuals guaranteed imprisonment, or bombs, bullets or vehicles used as weapons to mow down innocents all reported for the night, his opinion of the human race flirting with new lows again, he turned off the ABC news and poured a pacifying Tullamore Dew. Back in his armchair he sipped, read and listened to the fridge purr, the 'tock' of the clock on the mantelpiece between his shoebox of photos and four silver framed ones of Brandy: eight months, four, seven and sixteen years old.

Often, with a little help from his Dew, they softened the evening's news, the race to the bottom that 'strong man' politics had become in places like the Philippines, Hungary, Cambodia, Brazil, China and Bill of Rights' land.

That first photo in Scottsdale, Sara on her back on the bed, Brandy perched on her belly like a bloated slug. Second one at the entrance to her room, backdrop of Disney characters and Attenborough elephants on the wall, animal mobiles hanging from the ceiling. Brandy standing as if at military attention in her first-day-at-kindergarten uniform, Pooh Bear bag strapped between her shoulders. Big, unflinching eyes on the camera, tight-lipped grin like she was about to pop. And just hours earlier she'd cried out in the night.

'Your turn or mine?' he asked Sara.

'Yours.'

'Right.' He shook himself awake like a dog. 'Keep the bed warm.'

'Your side, your issue.'

He stumbled out to Brandy's room, turned on the night light and sat on her bed stroking her forehead.

'I'm having bad thoughts, Daddy.'

In his most aggressive voice, he growled, 'Go away, bad thoughts; far, far away and never come back or…' He punched the palm of his hand. '…pow! You'll have me to deal with, the number one bad thoughts' exterminator in all of Australia.'

'That's what you said last time and they've come back.'

'Mmm – must be different ones.'

She grabbed her rabbit and shuffled over, making room for him. 'Stay with me, okay?'

She slept soundlessly, he barely at all.

Into every corner of the house, her things everywhere, half her meal spilled on the dining table and her having another go at spooning it off and into her mouth; an hour later on their bed being read to.

A quick year or two later outside on her first training-wheels bicycle and pedalling hard, helmet on, chin over the handlebars in mini-BMX racing pose. Mornings pulling on his hand, anxious to get to school; weekends digging in the Cremorne or Clifton Beach sand (her choice), or on his shoulders using his eye sockets as finger-holds as he high-stepped them into the surf. And though she lagged at naming the stars and tying shoelaces, she earned a kindergarten reading award at her end-of-year school assembly, to be framed a day later and hung in the hallway. With that, she'd already exceeded his school prize haul.

In that third photo, Brandy playing dress-up adult, the phone in her hand seconds after she'd answered a call from her Battery Point gran: 'Good evening. This is the Broughton residence, Brandy speaking. Sara and Joe are in the kitchen and can't come to the phone right now. How may I help you?'

Fourth one, taken after they'd both hugged her for as long as she let them. Animated smile, flushed with excitement in her new sky blue, off-the-shoulder dress, gold loop earrings, eyeshadow, crimson lipstick, new blonde tips in her hair, all primed and pumped up to attend her Leavers' Dinner. No photos taken the next morning, though, as a life-hard lesson learned, she knelt, hung her head in the toilet and deposited the remnants of her dinner and backroom vodka. That day 'the worst of my life', she exclaimed – slit-eyed, loose-jawed – until it was sup-planted later by the death of her mother.

She went to concerts. If as a fan girl, she was quiet about it. Two boyfriends as far as they knew. After the first break-up, she kept herself apart for days inside her room. They ached to help, but knew they could only wait until she was ready to invest in life again, however traumatic and unfair it could be. And she did, gradually, and though visibly hurt-ing, got on with things.

Those 'why' years between her 'bad thoughts' and start of university: why to bed, can't have a second story, have to eat 'yukky' broccoli, can't be on her phone after nine o'clock, have to be picked up instead of tak-ing a bus home from the Saturday night party, and the most challenged twelve o'clock boyfriend curfew augmented with her version of a death stare as she sniped, 'I'm not five, Dad.'

And yes, there were differences too over what constituted 'loud', 'late', 'music' and 'clean', but thankfully no anxiety disorder, anorexia, depression, self-harm; no tattoo sleeves or rings anywhere but on her fingers.

Hairstyles by electricity for a year or so to keep mother and father guessing, followed by the close-cropped Buddhist nun look, followed by a no-fuss bob or ponytail, loose strands of hair habitually tucked behind her ears. As for teen fashion, a selection of strange, colourful garments better suited as picnic blankets, as he could remember; though admittedly she looked a rainbow when beside him. So it seemed to him, muggins high school teacher with his years of exposure to the topic, a teen revolt amounting to little more than a whimper.

'Raise your children like a gardener, not a carpenter,' Sara read to him once from the cover of a library book. They shared such book title convictions, as well as the knowledge that their daughter occupied a space inside them that nothing else could touch. But they were also quick to admit that luck played a big part in her upbringing. She had her parents' genes, so experimentation and small acts of rebellion were a given. Though, for the most part, she stayed as docile as the stuffed toys she slept with well into her teens and with rarely more than two different moods: people around her – happy; on her own less so, but okay. Importantly, her love of reading blended nicely with her homework, Facebook and phone, listening to hip hop, or whatever that noise was called, and chanting slower versions of it into her bedroom mirror. Genetic engineering would be stretched to design a better daughter. From post-colic babyhood through her animal poster years, supplemented later by those of all-boy, all-girl bands and their voices blaring from behind her bedroom door, to adulthood and her equanimity, compassion for animals and people, including her parents. Like those cereal packet endorsements, 'an abundance of natural goodness'. And like her mother, the full package: determined, unpretentious, empathetic and always oblivious to the fact that she was. In her last email from the Syria–Jordan border, this:

Not the easiest of gigs currently at the Rukban Camp. I could write a book about the waste of life here, and I might one day. Every day the stories are so excruciatingly raw and tragic. And the fact that kids can't be kids but have to turn adult at such an early age. Yesterday a family arrived in the back of a ute. The father was holding his eight-year-old son, whose right leg below the knee had been blown off in an air attack. The mother carried the severed part and pleaded for it to be sewn back on. What I had to tell her was that infection had set in, so it wasn't a question of the leg being sewn back together, but whether the boy would live, and if so how much more of his leg would have to be amputated.

There are so many challenges, not least trying to maintain, or fake, an upbeat attitude and smile for the sake of the children.

He had, admittedly, a habit of making saints of his girls.

And now with her room as she'd left it, her experiences in dealing with turmoil and tragedy already exceeding his own, he thought constantly of Brandy's return at Christmas, of sitting her down and drawing out her thoughts and experiences, of sharing them a second time over drinks and biscuits next door. He often recalled the morning, days after she'd graduated, dropping an empty milk carton in the bin and retrieving a Save the Children application form from it and placing it on the table.

'It surprised me seeing that in the rubbish,' he said to her, pointing, as she came in. 'I thought such things were filled out online these days.'

'Yeah, mostly.' She grabbed a spoon, a bowl, the muesli and fresh milk carton and poured.

'So that's what you've done, onlined it?'

'Not exactly.' She sat.

'Right… So…can you tell your old man what exactly? You see, he's developed this interest in you over the past couple of decades that he just can't seem to shake off.'

'Royal Hobart Hospital has openings for nurses. I've sent an employment application to them.'

'Walking distance.'

'If you're fit.'

'Remember shortly after your mother's funeral, coming in here and saying to me there's a place called Aleppo?'

She nodded, not looking up.

The fact she remembered and was prepared to admit she did said a lot. 'So what's happened?'

'Convenience I s'pose.'

He put the kettle on, spooned a measure of coffee into his mug and turned around. 'I'm going to say something. Then if what I've said is complete rubbish, tell me... Here goes – I experienced a lot of solitude time before I met your mother, both overseas and here, and I learned back then how best to deal with it and for the most part turn it to my advantage. You know my walking shoes are about the only item of apparel I don't buy from Big W, Kmart or Best&Less. And what's overflowing from the bookshelf in there points to what I'm doing if not walking in my name-brand shoes, or gardening or yakking away to Nima. So lots of choices, lots to do. You're my world, but I'm perfectly capable of living solitary, especially when I know you're somewhere you should be, doing what you should be doing – making a difference. Okay, sermon over. I'm done. Open up on me if what I've said hasn't anything to do with your Royal Hobart application.'

She spooned away at her muesli.

'Right. Well, I might run the iron over Save the Children today,; get the wrinkles out, ensure it's in a pristine state for you to use tonight. I'll have a reference ready for you as well. It won't have to be from me. Sign it with any name that suits.'

His evenings: the mantelpiece clock doing its work in time with his pulse, indicating where in the house he should be, what he should be doing. At nine o'clock, if he hadn't nodded off beforehand, he'd lift himself out of his armchair, the jarrah floor creaking, arthritic in its joints too, it seemed. 'Me or the house?' he'd sometimes ask himself, before passing the ceiling-to-floor oak bookcase (thank you, Ahmed) that Sara dubbed 'the Broughton wall of fame', with their mini-disk player – bought during the fourteen months they were still relevant – at mid-point, the rest packed tight with their 'face-books' (books faces had been in), the older ones yellowing, rag-eared and full of annotations. Books, too, measured the years since her death in the overflow either side of the shelves; an overflow that, like Sara's toiletries and clothes, still waited a culling he could never seem to follow through with.

Tossing away books amounted to tossing away parts of his life, the books' abilities to create meaning and purpose in the memories of the stories they told. And there were the down times when he relied on story to sustain him, knew exactly which book to return to for the solace he needed. To hold and cherish till death do us part – yes, he would. Hence, despite visions of Kindle-reading Brandy having to box up the collection after his death and drop them off at Vinnies on her way to the tip, amassing went on and the overflow spread, and with it the boundary of his silverfish holiday park.

On he'd go past indoor plants struggling for the right light, the pine tabletop clutter of bills, newspapers and bank statements interspersed with a cling-wrapped plate of something from Nima, near-redundant laptop, honey jar of paper clips and mostly inkless biros, fish tank, stray socks, sunnies and brimmed hat. More a flinger than a folder or a filer of things, he'd long accepted that the drifty and dreamy were born un-tidy, that their neatness skills would never approach expert, or even ad-equate.

Entering the kitchen, he followed his habit of taking the ice cream carton from the freezer, his smallest unwashed teaspoon from the sink and initially scooping out small amounts for his tongue, nursing the lie that after five, then ten teaspoonfuls he'd put the carton away. He right-fully blamed Sara for this, his only addiction outside of daydreaming, reading and berating the modern age, and he often told her so.

Finally he'd check his daughter-bought senior's phone for messages, though they'd only ever come from Telstra, or occasionally from Brandy or Nima. He had never, nor would he ever, own a smartphone. Why would he? Social media and its made-to-fit news would send him apoplectic. He hadn't taken a photo since Sara was alive, and he was perfectly comfortable reading a newspaper in the time-proven way, dealing with bank staff from in front of a counter; perfectly adept too at using a street directory, a ticking alarm clock, a TV remote while watching free to air. What electronics he had were more than adequate, and should have been for the rest of the world too.

Washing up and adding to the dishes stacked on the draining board, he might watch a line of ants as they worked on the last remnants of his Turkish bread, or consider again a coat of fresh paint for the walls or a blind to replace the frayed Van Gogh-flowered curtains. There was also the matter of a new microwave to replace the temperamental original next to the toaster, for he was of the belief that if he used the stove for anything more than frying eggs or meat, heating soup or vegetables, he might go absent-minded and set the house alight. So, yes, the pleasures of the table were limited, due to uninterest mostly. Fussing about in there, he'd eventually turn on the kettle and peep out the window (a peeping Joe in his mind) at the rows of cars and street lights and houses he'd never entered while trying to work out where the mother he'd seen in the billowing niqab that day, and a few times since, might live; finally settling on one of the red-brick blocks of flats, with all the allure of military barracks, further up the road.

In a city of half a million, with the exception of Nima and Ahmed, he'd pretty much grown old surrounded by strangers. Periodically, a For Sale sign went up, and yes, sometime later disappeared, but the new faces stayed the same: strangers.

Occasionally a door slammed, an engine roared, a no-name neighbour's car flashed past, his eyes straining to follow it. And it struck him again how he was more familiar with the neighbourhood's cars than those who drove them.

Then, after a mug of lemon and ginger tea in his armchair, he'd undress, often mumbling to himself the next day's possibilities. He'd lay his clothes over the arm for re-dressing in the morning and grab whatever he was reading. And with knees once acrobatic, now fully tested just getting him out of chairs, he'd push himself up and plot a course around the clutter and clothes to bed. Anything of rare interest on the box after nine he'd record, if he could recall how to. Falling asleep, he'd wake between one and three with his book perched on his chest, at exactly what page to be worked out in the morning. After using the loo, he'd turn off his reading light and lie awake, that Robert Frost line 'I have been one acquainted with the night' getting a thorough workout in his head. Usually sometime before dawn, he drifted off again.

He allowed his beard to grow however it wished, his hair to grow longer than that of the great majority of septuagenarians with more face to wash, less hair to comb. Soon, a near-clone of Moses-on-the-Mount, hair above and below thick, wavy and white as laundry powder, he imagined Ahmed looking up from his cards, smiling, and calling him 'imam' instead of 'teacher'.

Still, he wasn't exactly lighting up the septuagenarian world with inspiring oratory and stunning exploits, was he? Sitting in his armchair eyeing the walls, mindful of the seasons passing – one, two, three, four and back to one. Favouring the cool of autumn before it moved into winter, the warming of spring before it moved into summer, he grew increasingly conscious of his decreasing time on earth. In such a frame of mind, he felt a need for something – anything – to counter his introspection: of viewing life as essentially over, of going soft-headed and sour-hearted waiting for death in his Moonah holding pen. Too much time maybe listening to the fridge reboot, fashioning its sound into a message that stirred up his old vagabond yearnings. Older than he ever thought he would be, but still dreamy and drifty, a longing for a new horizon chewed away at him: and this despite having seen so much of the earth, of studying and having a family and a house to come back to each day. Like the story he used to read to Brandy about the hundred-year-old man who climbed out the window one night, grasped a tree, and descended back into the world.

'One is always looking,' said cancer-struck novelist Jennifer Lash after attempting the Santiago de Compostela pilgrimage walk in 1993. 'Perhaps finding is simply looking further.' A statement seared into his brain. Gutsy woman, wonderful writer.

'I've had a couple of busy days,' Nima said one morning, looking at him over her coffee cup. 'The fruit shop has increased my hours to as many as I want to work. It seems the youth of Moonah have bigger ambitions than stacking and selling fruit. Also, I've decided to enrol in university next term.'

That she'd been chosen as an astronaut for a Mars launch would not have surprised him more. 'Really? That's terrific! Studying what?'

Her cooling breath blew steam off her coffee his way. 'Comparative Religions and Sociology One: Issues concerned with Speed-dating a Groovy Muslim.'

He stared. 'With what?'

She laughed. 'Well, the first subject anyway, then we'll see what happens. Do people still say "groovy"? I'm just asking…for a friend.'

'And it's me you're asking?'

'I should know better, shouldn't I? It's just that…' She stared at her drink. 'You know the story of my marriage, don't you?'

'Arranged through parents after Ahmed returned to Tripoli looking for someone exactly like you. That was his version anyway.'

She looked up at him, smiling a little. 'Then that's the version we'll stick to. I'm reminded, Joe, how much your company agrees with me sometimes. Anyway, the truth was either of my sisters would have happily accepted his offer, such a fine man that he was. But it was me he asked for, me he wanted to take back to Australia. And being the youngest of three daughters, my parents weren't troubled to see me go to such a good country, or at least my father wasn't. The answer to my prayers, he said, while my mother kept silent. Yet I always wanted to go to university, and that was not easy for a Muslim girl to do back then, especially when their parents believed that looking after a husband and children was the most important part of a girl's religion. So maybe I wasn't as excited as my sisters would have been going with a new husband to a strange place halfway around the world. But I went, and in forty years I've never been back, and I've never lived anywhere else in Australia but here. It was easy to say next year I will go back for a visit, and the next year would come and I would say next year again. But Ahmed's parents were killed in the civil war and he never wanted to return and I couldn't imagine being separated from him and my boys by a big ocean and so many strange countries, not even for a short time.'

Yet, from such a stunted upbringing, the obligation to stifle her youth-driven dreams and with the grief of Ahmed's death to deal with, there was still in grandmother Nima a sense of playfulness, a quiet optimism and determination, a Sara-like ease with people.

'So now's your chance to study. I could say the obvious – that you've long-earned it.'

'Yes, I believe I have. It's taken me this long to be satisfied enough with my English.' As always, she spoke precisely, every syllable distinct. She brightened. 'And when you're our age, Joe,' (though she was no older than Sara) 'and find yourself in our situation, suffering from… rele–, what do you call it?'

'Relevance deprivation?'

'Yes, that. I think it's good to try and open up more to the world, not just sit at home thinking only about what was.' An 'Are-you-getting-my-drift?' smile started in her eyes and spread to her lips. 'What do you think?'

At their ages and still seeking reassurance. It struck him at times how the wife of his deceased best friend had in some ways assumed her husband's role. His time at Nima's certainly never approached the gabfests that she and Sara had had, but it was important to him nonetheless: a maintained connection with a long-established friend. The fact that Nima, like Sara, had more to talk about in fifteen minutes than he would have in a month never bothered him because it never bothered her.

'Still coffee available here…as a continuing opportunity for me to open up more to the world?' he asked.

'Of course. And as a teacher, Joe, maybe you can help me a little with essays. Maybe just look them over before I pass them in. Yes?'

He nodded. 'Nice to feel needed.' He swigged his coffee. There were times, as with Ahmed, when he felt he'd known Nima all his life. 'Difficult for some people, it seems, not to continue recycling parts of their past.'

Back home, ABC news started to depress him more and more: the great divider's latest tweet, the mass shootings and chemical and terrorist attacks – victims cradled in strangers' arms, another candlelight vigil, flowers heaped at the killing site, as many balloons as fatalities rising into the air. There was also his growing issue fatigue – feeling a little number after the latest debacle, his soul a little deader – that added impetus to Joe's desire to get away – right away.

He took to alternating between SBS and ABC news, tossing a soft slipper at the screen and turning the volume down during the toxic cheetah's noise bites – just his custard hair, showman's pout and bright, crotch-length ties – before turning the sound up again for the sport and weather forecasts in foreign capitals.

Tim Winton's *Island Home* helped: passages that tweaked a yearning for distant places, some far-flung corner of the planet, or the outback maybe – at least somewhere vast, horizon-dominated, steeped in tradition, unfettered by Apple or Google.

As it was, the steady drumbeat of routine kept messaging that tomorrow would be the same as yesterday; that getting old was no better than dying young; that the good life existed only in his memories. In his timidity, he compared himself to a stock animal finding the paddock gate open and ignoring it for the familiarity of what he knew. Then he'd hear Sara say, 'Man up.'

One day he answered her, 'A prolonged case of the doldrums, true. But no longer for the born-again dreamy and drifty needing something soul-stirring to point to.'

Synapses connected, neurons fired. For him, it became a question of man of action versus incurious dullard. And, like Nima and Jennifer Lash, why shouldn't he go on looking? He wasn't shackled to the house, a hostage to his age (yet anyway), reading nursing home brochures, keying in myagedcare.gov.au: an old man cliché turning witless and will-less waiting around for incontinence, stroke, cancer, another dementia-addled day too many. Apples into the freezer, ice cube tray into the microwave; a card around his neck with his name, address and Nima's mobile number on it weren't his only options left in life. Like that RV sticker that said, 'Adventure before Dementia'. Importantly, since settling Brandy's HECS debt, he had the money to go wherever – different day, hemisphere, culture – before his final countdown, the final stop.

'Where will you go?' Nima asked, after he'd mentioned again his interest in a trip.

'Not sure. Maybe I'll just climb a mountain somewhere to run the risk of being alive.'

'No, you won't. I don't want to lose the longest, best neighbour I've ever had.'

He felt himself warm, liking that comment. 'Okay, nothing I can't climb in two minutes then, meaning nothing more challenging than an anthill.' He sipped his coffee. 'There's an old adage that time and tide wait for no one, including me. So I'd better decide soon.'

'Canada?'

'No.' Though he had fond memories of western Canada's scenic beauty and good people, of wolfing down its oversized roast beef, club and turkey sandwiches heaped in mayonnaise and buried in fries, the country was just too close to the Disunited States – home to the hateful and heavily armed, to manic hyper-capitalism; its arse-out-of-trousers public squalor bordering splendiferous private wealth. Besides, he'd spent half his youth on its west coast. 'No,' he repeated. 'Rather, a trip to some corporate powerbroker no-go zone: quiet, Luddite-friendly, far removed from humanity gone Twitter-mad, where 'digital' still referred to fingers and toes – the polar opposite of big city Australia and the rest of big-end Earth.'

Back home, as the idea took hold, a moment of the Dew inspiration prompted this question: had he enough left in heart and mind; in street talk, crude as it was, had he the balls to pack a bag one last time and, coffin-dodging resurrected, head off to a place he'd only recently redis-covered on a map?

Riding high on the idea, he looked over at the goldfish tank and pumped his fist, reciting –

> Do not go gentle into that good night,
> Old age should burn and rave at close of day;
> Rage, rage against the dying of the light.*

In his mind's eye, Max and Mavis ogled him through the glass, nod-ding and raising their pectoral fins in agreement.

Done then. Fifty years on, the old embers of vagabondage stoking up again, it was once more into the unknown. Call it his geriatric gypsy rite of passage: oiling his wheels, lubricating his joints (a traveller's flask of the Dew would do that nicely), expanding the still-working parts of his brain big-time by breaking out of his bunker in search of… Well, he'd recognise it when he found it, and when he did, no grandiose no-tions: ten-star hotels, business class, cruises for wrinklies with fat wallets. But neither would he be occupying a tent, hostel bunk, long-haul truck or bus seat as in times long past. For this, his absolute last trip, something in between: selected social intercourse, okay, but otherwise slow and quiet, Winton's 'endless horizon', falling asleep in the open air under a big, clear sky, rooms with a view, partial to analogue so no app-ing, sep-tuagenarian sexting (though he hadn't a clue about those things anyway). Six to eight weeks – no more. Back in spring to check on Nima and the goldfish, his freesias, daisies and agapanthus; to weed and hoe the soil, plant, throw netting over the fruit trees, have a beer with his young let-tuces and beans. Sara and his good neighbour would expect nothing less.

Simple, except for the complications.

* From *Dylan Thomas: Collected Poems 1934–1953*, Everyman

4

Srinagar

Like the whole district was under attack again, or defended if you happened to live there; the tumult of laneway conflict reverberating over the city: stones and Molotov cocktails hurled at soldiers, pellet guns responding, tear gas canisters landing, spinning and hissing, mists of gas rising and spreading. Youths – faces wrapped in damp cloth – shouting and chanting, 'Tyrants, killers, occupiers! Indian dogs go home! Freedom, freedom, freedom!'

Shops were shuttered.

Roller doors banged down.

Tyres burned, black smoke billowing up.

People disappeared; though not the Pandith brothers, Parvais and Sameer.

'Kashmir is ours! Freedom, freedom, freedom!'

Pellet guns cracked, demonstrators screamed fury back. Then came two thunderous shotgun blasts: a final warning?

Cameramen appeared behind the rioters. They ducked down and dashed forward over the cobblestones, filming quickly and retreating before turning and waiting for their next opportunity.

More youths arrived, bent to pick up stones and rushed to join the fray. More banners and Pakistani flags rose in the air.

'Tyrants, killers, occupiers! Indian dogs go home!'

Parvais turned, tied his scarf around his face, black eyes fixed on his brother. 'For Ifra?' he asked, taking a lighter from his trouser pocket.

Sameer nodded, tying off his scarf. They donned goggles and caps.

Parvais scooped up their Molotov cocktail and they sprinted into battle, avoiding the canisters piercing the air and rolling on the ground. Parvais stopped, lit the cocktail's rag wick and hurled the cocktail at the line of soldiers just as a shotgun blast echoed overhead. His head snapped back, bits of scarf, blood and flesh flying.

*

It seemed all of Sopore district had defied the curfew as they filled the road moving over the Gaw Kadal bridge and veering right towards the martyrs' cemetery. Angry voices shouted, boys beat sheets of tin with sticks as Parvais's and two other white-shrouded bodies on wooden biers, showered in rose petals, rode high on friends' shoulders.

Military helicopters appeared and hovered, providing an aerial escort to abuse and shake fists at; though not for Sameer and what remained of his family, who mutely followed the bodies allowing others to scream their vengeance. Parvais, university-bound and the centre of Baba's and Ma's dreams, now dead. Ifra blind in one eye, partially so in the other. If Baba complained to the police, he'd likely be arrested for an offence concocted on the spot like being a Hizbul Mujahideen facilitator. And then how would his family survive?

That's what Baba brooded on after the funeral during the forty days of mourning, before he returned to his tile masonry work and Ma, on her own, continued to care for Ifra. Staying 'strong' and feigning calm – though often in tears under his blankets at night – Sameer asked for more after-school hours at his uncle's fruit shop and got them.

His family shattered, Sameer fixated on seeking justice through revenge, the only way open to him. And one night he formulated a plan.

Each day before school, he went to the mosque, prayed, watched different men and listened to conversations. When the opportunity came, he chanced asking casually about Hizbul Mujahideen, mentioning nothing about his craving to be a freedom fighter. Sometime later, knowing there'd be no going back, he approached his mosque confidant again and said he wanted to join Hizb and was told to be patient, to continue his studies, especially languages, and one day he might be contacted.

As instructed, Sameer waited and continued to smile at the bidi-smoking Indian soldiers he passed on the road, though he wanted to kill them, and thought of ways he could. As Parvais had reached for his Molotov cocktail that horrible day, he pictured himself reaching for a Kalashnikov, taking aim and pulling the trigger until not a soldier in sight remained standing to go about their duties of beating down doors, taking away men and boys, lording themselves over Kashmir and its people. He lay awake at night picturing powerful Indians making Kashmiri policy in their rich Delhi offices, and how he might steal into one and do to them what was done to his brother. Weeks turned into months. Was he being watched, judged? Or was he simply placing too much importance on himself and what he could personally do to harm the Indian occupation? After all, there were so many others, older and probably more capable than him, wanting to go *sarhad paar*: to cross the Line of Control into Pakistan and train and fight until free or martyred.

One morning in the mosque, his confidant approached, slowed and, avoiding eye contact, said quietly, 'Hizbul Mujahideen. Are you still interested?'

He felt his pulse quicken. 'Yes.' It was happening; it actually was – Sameer Pandith, freedom fighter, Ifra and Parvais Pandith avenged, and more.

'Then be here tomorrow morning, this spot, this time.'

The fifteen-minute walk from mosque to school seemed to pass in a blink and a heartbeat.

5

While locals on his side of the bus just glanced, if that, Joe stared out at the crumpled motor scooter ten metres away and closing, its once bare-headed rider sprawled lifeless in a pool of petrol and blood. On the edge of that pool, a policeman in fluoro feebly directed the gridlock while flick-glancing at an emaciated white cow about to cross the road. How inconsequential that dead man looked (no sheet over him, the cow getting more attention) as Delhi's vast industry of roadside life ground on indifferently around him. The place looked more like the perimeter of a refugee camp than the centre of a capital city: tarpaulin and sack tents, roadside vendors, women road workers sweeping or carrying pots of tar on their heads, skin-stretched old women and gaunt children – stick legs, bared collarbones – going from vehicle to vehicle banging on windows, begging or selling trinkets, while under billboards promoting hair products and mobile phones, footpath families lounged on cardboard cooking over charcoal-fuelled braziers, aromas of spices and petrol fumes wafting through the bus, the cooking smoke adding just that little bit more to the muggy, haze-filled air. Life out there as transient as a cloud; poverty and death so openly displayed, so casually accepted.

A train rumbled overhead, four storeys up.

About the long-haul bus seat, Joe had been forced to drop his vow and change his plans the previous day after seeing the newspaper headline, '17 soldiers killed in militant attack on Srinagar army base.'

Sitting down in the hotel lobby, he'd scoured the first few pages of the paper filled with the attack and appeals for counter-attacks. 'All flights in and out of Srinagar cancelled,' he read on page three.

His hopes, which had been inching upwards, plummeted again. The last thing he wanted was to stay in Delhi. He consulted Lonely Planet, reread information about his alternative destination. He went into the travel office, sat, and spoke slowly so as not to betray his nervousness about whether or not Ladakh was doable.

'Leh no problem,' came the response, the consultant's smile bright as a meteor. He chortled and fussed about checking on flights, as if Joe's mere presence had completed his happiness for the day. Then his smile dimmed. 'Soreee – there is small problem. No seats available for another three days; but cheap, cheap to go by bus to beautiful Manali and spend time there resting and seeing beautiful Kulu Valley before going on to beautiful Leh.'

It was 'the only way to see the beautiful landscape', he was told; observe at close hand the great variety of people; the gradual climb the only sensible way for an 'older person especially' to adjust to the rising altitude and thinning air. It was a message he'd heard before from his GP, the ever-candid David Ridgeway, who'd warned,: 'It is the old and the young who are most prone to dying of altitude sickness.' Words supported by *Everest* – the movie he'd watched on the flight coming over – a graphic portrayal of how oxygen deprivation could and did kill climbers.

Moreover, 'gradual' appealed. Back home, he'd imagined getting to Delhi all energised and excited, and shortly after, heading off to somewhere on the local tourist map; perhaps a tour of the city's Red Fort or Agra's Taj Mahal three hours' drive away. But, in keeping with someone's law of unintended consequences, the flight proved taxing: outsized escapism meets airport security crackdown, a part of the conveyor belt herd questioned, barked at, ordered back through the metal detectors, the beep-beep alerts and flashing lights, bags opened, contents yanked out.

Then into the first toilet he went, where upon leaving to be confronted by rate-the-experience emoji faces, from full marks clownish smile to accident-happened grimace. Little doubt which one he went for. His crankiness cranking up, old man eyes, ears and patience didn't adjust well to the melee involved in getting from departure lounge onto plane (in Sydney not finding his seat belt until a flight attendant mentioned he was sitting on it) or to the long flights themselves. Seven hours of a baby screaming behind him on the Singapore leg, to the mother's lament, 'Ah, it's his ears again, his ears – and being so cooped up.' And the next leg, groggy and leaden, his seat a kicking post for a young Indian boy, and when he asked if the boy could please stop, the mother instructed him to and he did, for all of a minute and a half. Later, bone-stiff and giddy with fatigue, disgorged at Delhi airport, the long queues just to wait in more long queues, while every minute checking his multi-zippered travelling trousers to ensure his passport, customs form and wallet hadn't disappeared.

Finally in his layover hotel room and feeling an embodiment of the *Antiques Roadshow*, so tired he barely knew where he was, anxiety fed into regret. Forgetting where he'd put things had become more habit than novelty, and he soon discovered he'd lost the key to his bag lock, couldn't find it anywhere, and had to request a hacksaw from reception to get into his things. Dusk, and unable to turn on the lights, he searched for his missing room key card (Was there a worldwide metal shortage? What had become of locksmith-cut keys?), his panicky gaze jerking around the room until finally, from behind his book on the bedside table, it just appeared. Moments later, he realised his passport and wallet weren't in the side pocket of his travelling trousers. Where did he last have them out? When? Wallowing in self-doubt, mental phantoms taking control, he scurried about, criss-crossing the room, moving in and out of the bathroom, hands trembling, heart hammering, before finally spotting them in the near corner of the floor. How they got there he had no idea. He bent in stages and retrieved them.

Old age a long way from comedy and contentment day one in Delhi as he sat on the edge of the bed and stared down at the floor. Full-on dementia rehearsal, had to be: born to run like Springsteen back in the day, slowed now to a gibbering plod. What better example of his obsolescence could there be? Broughton unhinged. Like the hits he'd taken to his youthful skull had metastasised, grown teeth and were feeding on his brain.

'Why am I here?' he asked, his sense of inadequacy rocketing as he straightened and tried unsuccessfully to set the digital clock on the bedside table (Sara or Brandy would have had it working in seconds), which propelled him on to more punishing thoughts. Expecting the worst, he was getting it. If he could make time run backwards, he'd be back home now swallowed up in his armchair watching the ABC news. 'A step too far. Half a world too far,' he mumbled, picturing himself clawing away at the imagined gates of Moonah, desperate to be let back in. It was like he'd been caught up in a vortex. He couldn't settle; heart racing, hands shaking like he was suffering his first full day of Parkinson's. He felt vulnerable, trapped, scared even; had done since Sydney airport when his beard-trimming scissors had been confiscated from his daypack. For which he'd received a look like he was the greatest moron on earth, followed by a reprimand issued in the same manner he'd once issued them in his teaching days.

He-who-once-hitchhiked great distances on pocket change and the generosity of strangers stayed muddled in small-room gloom and indecision, weighing up his sanity, feeling the tug of home and his good neighbour's sheltering friendship (even another retired Belgrove High staff luncheon was preferable to this) and thinking of everything that had gone and could still go wrong, rather than in his ability to make things go right.

Why had escaping Moonah been such hard work? Long-haul flights were something he looked forward to and did with consummate ease in earlier days. And something else loomed large: an acute sense of loneliness he'd not felt for ages. All in all delusion cracks heads with hardcore reality.

His head sunk further; much lower and it could suffer floor abrasions. He listened to the traffic noise below; Main Road Moonah a meditation zone in comparison. Finally, he lay back on the bed, arms over his head, rolled onto his side and curled into himself. 'Lunacy, these stupid doubts and fears,' he mumbled, wrestling with his turmoil. He was safe. There was no danger beyond a tired mind, slow to adjust, playing tricks on him. If being here is your biggest problem in life, he told himself, look out the window and see what real problems are. Everyone has their trials, their own brain-born, shifty-eyed clawed monsters intent on knocking them off their perch.

From Sara: 'Whatever – we'll deal with it.'

Stephen Hawking: 'Look up at the stars, not down at your feet.'

Samuel Beckett's Vladimir, while waiting for Godot: 'I can't go on. I'll go on.'

So find some spine, you goose, you of mouse-hearted breeding stock. Rally, right the ship; uphold the Broughton name.

He sat up, reminding himself that according to old Bill there were seven ages of life; so why couldn't there be seven ages of old age? And he was still in age one, the youth of his old age. So think juvenile, he told himself. To help himself do that, he went for his duty-free Dew. Tipping a two-finger measure into a glass, he studied the depth for its anticipated effect, sipping it slowly, feeling it warm his belly, mellow his mind.

Ordering himself downstairs, he left his room, located the computer room, read the time-faded instructions on the wall then sat down to write to his family of one, as she had instructed him to do. He hesitated, though, recalling reading somewhere that Russian intelligence services had reverted to hack-proof box typewriters to write out their top secret reports. Must have the world's sole supply of typewriter ribbons in that country, he thought. Gives the Luddites of this world some hope the digital age's days are numbered. He smiled, liking that idea.

He waited for words to form before logging in and forefingering away at communication:

My Brandy –

In a Delhi hotel close to the airport after a long, uneventful flight via Singapore. Worked out the in-flight entertainment after two hours in the air and a neighbour's help. Slow bones and brain cells are adjusting. Change of plans, though. Conflict in Srinagar, so am off to Leh, Ladakh tomorrow via the scenic route, at least according to the travel gurus downstairs from whom I purchased my bus ticket. Got my altitude tablets [Or did he? He couldn't recall getting them from the pharmacy. He'd need to check.], Tullamore anti-freeze, Geelong puffer jacket, beanie and socks at the top of my pack.

This email seems to be going all right, and the chances that it'll get to you must be good. So will do it again next from Leh if it stays this easy.

Love you, Dad

Brandy started googling about the time she started walking, thanks to Sara. Been instructing him on the delights of the digital age ever since, though never with much hope he'd turn devotee.

To Nima's same email he added, 'Looking forward to reading the first essay. I'm missing your good biscuits, coffee and conversation.' He signed off with 'Neighbour Joe'.

The contact helped.

He searched for his altitude tablets without success and made a mental note to find a pharmacy and get some before departure.

Hungry, he descended to the café and read on the menu 'Python stew has a different taste. You must be very open-minded with your mouth.' He liked that, although he had no intention of ordering it. Mental equilibrium at least partially restored, he lectured himself on staying slow and steady and in control aboard the bus to Leh by way of Manali.

Now, still in Delhi – a city with more people than all of Australia – the trip already seemed interminable; that he had scored a perfect ten on the Boofhead Tourist Madness Test. So what had possessed him to take a bus over the Himalayas just to acclimatise, view the 'beautiful' scenery and great 'variety of people'? He could name fifty places he'd rather be, and most were in Tasmania, including at Nima's table.

Out there still, Dalit women in saris carrying bone-thin babies, begging at driver-side windows in the stopped traffic, a tent city squeezed between the roadside and a mass of corrugated iron, canvas and scrap wood housing: backdrop of construction cranes, street noise of pile drivers and jackhammers mangling rock and concrete, of half the city being torn down, the other half steel and dark glass high-rises for the high-born rearing up like Gotham City against the smog-dimmed sky. Close by, a broken-down lorry was on the verge, other trucks trying to bully their way past it; carts and bicycles pulling loads, two-, three-, four-wheel vehicles converging at all angles and jockeying for position, horns beeping, drivers gesticulating. There were concerns inside the bus too: his lower back stiffening up, his bladder filling. Feeling besieged, he was ready to bail out, risk lung cancer in catching a ride back to the hotel and a plane to Leh in three days' time. Bus company shareholders, in the guise of travel agents, had to have provided the recommendation, surely.

And supposedly he'd been long-retired from stress.

He reached in his daypack for the Dew, his defence against the chaos of Delhi, when Schopenhauer's comment about apes came to mind: 'There is one aspect where apes, with little expectation, show real wisdom when compared to humans – their quiet, placid enjoyment of the present moment.' His apes had obviously not experienced the cramped buses and dodgem-car traffic heading north out of the world's most polluted capital city, through its people-littered landscape, passing a dead body and hordes of the poor resembling street bandits in their cloth smog masks, just their reddened, watery eyes bared to the world.

Yet he left the Dew where it was, and not for the first time scolded himself. He wasn't about to be murdered in his sleep, was he? And it was hardly severed head-on-a-stake territory he was going to. And the people out there, how many could afford a hotel room with private facilities, had been on an airplane, took holidays, carried a Visa card, cash thick in their wallets, owned a house and a restored Vee-dub Beetle? How hard was it for them to scrape out a living while he fretted over the comfort level of an air-conditioned bus? He closed his eyes as if to refocus, breathed evenly, listened to Sara telling him to 'man up'.

Eventually they passed through a toll station and entered expressway nirvana, the sounds and sprawl of Delhi shrinking into the distance, the northern flatland opening up ahead. As they moved along unimpeded, picking up speed, the sky grew cleaner, landscape greener, the passengers sleepier. The morning wore on, the vast agricultural plain paling under a blazing sun. Fewer men, women and children worked the fields. Slow-moving ox carts and their half-naked riders bumped along narrow tracks back towards villages with tree shade and spiralling Hindu temples. While up ahead the road unravelled black and smooth and straight, like the roads of his 'elsewhere' past.

With little but near-deserted farming land to compete for his attention, the road drew him back, testing the length and breadth of his memory.

About the time he started to doubt the Easter Bunny and Santa Claus, the first of his setbacks hit him like a ten-ton truck. His mother married an American luxury car salesman working as a consultant in Calgary, and early on he took them 'elsewhere' (his oft-used word that so aptly described him) on roads long, windy through the Sierra Nevadas, and straight again to destination Sacramento.

Two years later, elsewhere was further south down Interstate 5 to home in Ventura. Two years after that, US citizenship finalised, elsewhere was home ownership in soulless North Long Beach, splat in the middle of a massive residential tract; street after straight flat street of near-identical houses.

And in ensuing years there were hints of heading elsewhere again in the many phone calls from stepfather (aka 'Dad' plying his persuasive powers in places other than car yards, he later learned) saying he'd be home late from work, in his mother's preoccupation and gloom, in the tension in the house, and weeks later the slammed doors and shouting later at night, and once the sound of something shattering.

He'd spent more time with his cat than with elsewhere Dad, until Amos died. Still, in a recurring nightmare, elsewhere Dad glowered down at him with the look of a Patagonian toothfish, saying, as if in expectation, 'Scream softly, Joey, so you don't disturb the neighbours.'

Dinners turned brief and quiet; any talk, strangely, directed at him. In bed shortly afterwards, shadows on the walls turned ominous as he lay there gathering up fears for his next nightmare.

Insecurities peaked, pushing him out of the house early and not returning until dusk, stepping lightly over the fault lines back to his room and turned-up record player. After weeks of sleeping with a knife under his bed, in keeping with his tendency to overdramatise, he arrived home from school one Friday to see his mother's rust-eaten Plymouth packed, his halves – stunned sister and booster-seated brother – squeezed between suitcases and boxes in the back, and in the front seat a place arranged for him.

'Get in,' his stressed mother exhorted. 'I'll explain later.'

Order, as tenuous as it had been, dissolved in another elsewhere upending; this time a welcomed one, at least for him. He and his mother jumped in and shut their doors. For so long wanting to go and finally he was, if… His mother inserted the key, turned the ignition. Yes! Moody beast fired up first attempt, as anxious to be off as its driver and front-seat passenger.

'Broken homes are often an improvement,' his mother's aunt-provider said to him days later in Santa Cruz.

He didn't need convincing. As it happened, a divorce and life in limbo until the great-aunt connection got them into a small house; got his mother full-time secretarial work, got him a second-hand surfboard and wetsuit. Bottom-of-the-ladder dishwashing work too, rivalling Orwell's in *Down and Out in Paris and London*. Never destined to be the brightest star in the highest of all worlds, but still thought he had more potential than his surfing mates – scholars of the breaking wave, all – gave him credit for, voting him the one least likely to ever own a Corvette, or indeed anything sold outside the perimeters of a wrecker's yard. Maybe because promotion, like for Orwell, not part of his life plan; only needed money for burgers, fries, strawberry shakes wolfed down under the Golden Arches; for surfboard repairs and wax, records, six-packs, Ripple wine, two dollars unsyphoned petrol, drive-in movies and later his share of the rent. Until, at the behest of a judge hearing the case of underage drinking of alcohol and contributing to the delinquency of a minor – a runaway girl who wandered solo and unknown into his party and, like him, didn't escape the neighbour-summoned police – court-ordered military enlistment beckoned.

A partial adult in the eyes of the law, with barely two coins to rub together and knowing next to nothing beyond the shape of waves and a few sporting skills, he chose the navy to avoid Vietnam. No shortage of ocean. Aircraft carrier across the Pacific. Three-month induction to shipboard life cleaning floors, metal sinks and toilets, then an office job sending ship's company to naval schools. Suited him; other than his teaching years later on, it was the only job he ever respected. Got his only promotion, ever, to third-class petty officer. Sought refuge in books too – though rarely in the ubiquitous porn dreadfuls or Wild West shoot-em-ups – to fill in the spare time, keep his brain cranking over. Felt less alone with a book in his hands; that he was linking up to something beyond his insignificant self: though most likely the 'something' was just escape. First taste of Asia too, at least the port towns and bars, Tiger Beer and bikini-clad ladies serving it up, along with awkward proposals – at least for him who barely shaved – of a more private, horizontal kind. ('How 'bout it, cowboy?' Texan Tommy Smith yelped at the table. 'Double your pleasure: poke the carrot while advancing the Philippine economy. If you won't, I will.' And he did – a week later reporting to sick bay and the start of three months' shipboard confinement.)

A year later, last day crossed off his calendar, handed his honourable discharge to contrast his reason for enlisting.

Intent on becoming less stupid, enrolled for probationary study (at least average marks to stay, low marks to go). Worked in restaurants, a teriyaki beef stall, an insulating glass factory, a toy store: summers in

Canada unloading boxcars in Vancouver, or rerouting them off 'the hump' as a late-summoned, beer-mellowed midnight shift brakeman in Calgary before the days of railway workplace health and safety. Five colleges and universities while trolling the highways of western America searching for the key to belonging: Santa Cruz, Santa Barbara, Idaho, Fullerton, Hawaii and back to Santa Cruz again like a tongue to a broken tooth. Surfing, basketball and free-ride scholarship football until third concussion: surfing, handball and road biking after that. And in contrast to high school disconnect, attended all classes, sat up alert and eager, read assigned texts and more; took words seriously, felt the power in them.

Still, moving on, a travel bag with legs came at a cost. Friends lost in going elsewhere; eventually first-time long-time girlfriend too; parent-sent to a faraway university, second-time boyfriend, first-time husband.

'Never get attached to anyone you can't instantly separate from,' Boomer counselled on the water one morning as though he'd lived the experience, done an advanced degree on the topic. 'Spoils your surfing for ages if you do.'

Too late. He carried the torch as if moulded to him, wallowing in his 'shoot me now' martyrdom for months, probably years, and later asked himself, Would it have been better not to have had the experience than feel what he did afterwards? He'd never so much as held a girl's hand before she reached for his. And most everything he learned about touch, from fumbling to patient, he learned with her.

Odd what closely sticks. He stared out the window and considered again 'the experience', the one carved into his memory that had shaped and coloured everything he did for far too long back then. And he followed that with a question. Why was it that the things he preferred to forget always seemed to hang around the longest? One lesson learned, though it took a while to learn it: there's no surer way not to forget someone than tell yourself to forget them.

A smile crept onto his face as he slipped back to elsewhere:

'Prepare for more youthful disappointments,' great-aunt said one day, after asking after him and getting an answer. 'The evidence is in. People don't grow old enough to be immune from such heartache until they reach their sixties. But take solace, Joey, things like that remembered are often far better than they ever were at the time.'

Maybe, but he didn't have the years on earth to gauge that, so stayed raw and empty, like his heart had been ripped out and tossed to the birds. Relationship deficit disorder (RDD for the acronym-minded) after that – his Neanderthal-minus-the-club approach leading to awkwardness and embarrassment in trying to find her again in someone else.

'Be sure to wear some flowers in your hair…'

That last eighteen months a lonely time in supposedly cruisy Santa Cruz: work, classes, yet still the pull of Saturday nights, hormones and loud music. Polished his choppers in preparation, coated his armpits, lathered his face in Old Spice while practising his lines and 'Hi, I'm Joe' smile in the mirror until the smile earned a Pass. Out alone, often to the huge, ear-ringing Oarhouse, like a people-packed hangar bay for 707s on full throttle. A jug of beer half drunk for the confidence to approach a girl of his imaginings and shout-to-be-heard something rehearsed – both in 'cool' language and Steve McQueen pose. After two or three hours of auditioning for the deadpan uninterested, and rehearsed out, the pull faded for another week in the uncool drive past former girlfriend's former front door and back to his room thinking how stupid his bumbling pitch for female attention had been – again.

Not the most edifying time of his life – no. Hard to believe that who he was then and who he was now shared the same brain. Not unprecedented, though, was it? From Yeats' 'A Dialogue of Self and Soul' discovered around that time.

> The ignominy of boyhood, the distress
> Of boyhood changing into man,

The unfinished man and his pain
Brought face to face with his own clumsiness.*

Years later, whenever the old humiliations began to pulse back through him again, he'd recite those four lines, thankful to Yeats for pointing out there'd been other youths as inept as him down through the ages. Still, memory punished. As a reminder of his dopey naivety, he should have had that poem printed, framed and forever hung on his many different walls and doors.

He often wondered nowadays, did all old men think like he did about their past selves? Were they all imbued with melancholy, nostalgia, regret? Did they continue to feel embarrassment over their failures no matter the circumstances or how many decades had passed by? A pity time wasn't like a passage of music you could keep returning to until you got it right.

He glanced around the bus. All was as he'd left it.

Dear Brain, it's your boy-turned-fossil's nostalgia hour again. Shreds of the past unspooling like an old home movie. He looked out the window and drifted back.

Six years of itinerant study and minimum wage work before redemption. A Governor Reagan movie-star-signed History degree to augment his honourable discharge, though academic awards and offers of graduate study avoided him. Still, he felt like doing handstands when he held his BA up to his mother's eyes. She'd not seen one before.

Accepting it as genuine, she said, 'First one of those ever in the family awarded to you who comes from nothing.'

A strange sort of compliment, he thought. Maybe 'next to nothing' would have been more precise. After all, a roof over his head, food and clothing, handball and gloves, fishing pole, five-speed bike, a scrapheap car and battered surfboard amounted to something.

Still, despite the comment, she smiled, looking genuinely proud.

* From *Poems of W.B. Yeats*, Macmillan

'Congratulations, Joseph. You worked hard for it,' she said, kissing his cheek and rubbing his arm.

So while the uni-enrolled, Vietnam War-deferred marched and attended rallies and the non-deferred escaped to Canada or went to war, he studied maps, empowered by dreams of new places and like-minded people where everything fitted just right – loneliness the initial trade-off for a life that favoured the naturally curious, as great-aunt provider put it to him one day. Though another person asked, 'Having a problem with self-acceptance are ya, Joey boy? What're ya runnin' from – yarself?' And days later came two less cutting comments: 'What do you think you're missing out on that you can find somewhere else?' And, 'You're like a dog looking for a spot in the sun, but the sun keeps moving.' All made him think at the time and at intervals later on. To one inquirer, he mentioned something about following his instincts rather than the expectations of others, as though his forbearers had been full-blooded gypsies. Sounded so learned at the time, so lone-wolf-like. In his twenties and still trying to impress others, it seemed.

With elsewhere surge running white hot, all that unlived life in him bursting to get on the road, start the summer of '69 with a new plan. Loading up his backpack, he talked in excited bursts to his mother, 'Taking a lash at the University of Highway Sciences, from sea to shining sea. Who knows, might find a graduate programme somewhere on "'vagabondage – observations of life from the road as seen through the eyes of Kerouac, Cohen and Broughton".'

She gave him a look, nothing more.

Told himself that vagabond living meant taking risks, overcoming fears, living on the cheap – five dollars a day, sleeping rough, loaf of bread and something to spread over each slice. It could be scary, for sure. But, beyond that, intriguing too, his luck changing daily, having no idea what the next hour would bring or who he would be sharing it with. In his mind, once-cloistered student Joe Broughton revamps hopes and confidence and launches himself into transcontinental highwayman.

Decide again for ocean destination, for action man indifference to discomfort and safety in the quest for unique experiences. Man of Steel attitude to stranger danger and travelling light (change of clothes, map, small-print books, torch, backpack, one-man tent and sleeping bag) à la the T-shirt and wall poster icons of the time – Gandhi, Che Guevara, Ho Chi Minh – while hitchhiking to New Orleans to join the Merchant Marine, Janis Joplin occupying his head space: 'Bobby thumbed a diesel down just before it rained...'

From known into the unknown: freeway traffic, factories, suburbia sprawl, oak, sycamore and palm trees, almond groves and orange orchards all give way to scrub and scrub to desert. Longest ride in and out of the Mojave most of the afternoon and night and over high mesa country towards the panhandle of Texas, later sharing a six-pack of squirrel piss optimistically labelled Lucky Lager (lucky if you survived it) – though hailed by its donor as his 'long-haul survival kit' – before the car stopped off road and he was asked to drive. At two a.m., having kept his head out the window much of the last hour to keep awake, finally arrive at his junction drop-off spot. He pulled over, said thanks, good luck and goodbye, and headed off into the high weeds for a hard-ground sleep.

Waking with his shoes still on, sun on his face, rumble of trucks, he packed up, returned to the road and pointed south-east.

Surprised three days later in New Orleans when told to return in six weeks to pick up his Merchant Mariner papers. Thought it was same day service; that he'd be on a ship within the week. Probably all dreamy and drifty types thought that way. Still, anything felt good that was some sort of departure. So out on the highway again, his destination further on, feet back-pedalling east, thumb leading the way.

Somewhere in the back blocks of Biloxi, Mississippi, shared the cost of a flophouse room with a Jesus-clone muso thumbing his way back to Mexico City from the Woodstock Music Festival. 'So here we are back in the time-warped south, man –where the noose and rifles rule, where the road signs are bullet-holed and if your skin is pale, your neck is red. And man, I'm tellin' ya this for free. Survive the night and I'm outta here. Everything good is somewhere out of the south.' Dressed in tie-dye clothing headband to ankle, head propped on a pillow, guitar propped on him, his great horse teeth on display while sucking the skunk weed and, still in full voice from the four-day concert, he sang – 'Get yar' motor runnin', head out on the highway…'

'Hey man, you heard of Augustine – the saint, not the town?' he asked minutes later.

'Not in the past few days.'

'He had some ideas, man. He spouted some smart stuff. Like, waddabout this for you, me and the rest of the thumb-travelling community? "The world is a book and those who don't thumb rides to new places never get past the first page." May not be word perfect, but you get the saint's drift, don'tcha? Gotta' keep yar motor runnin'…' He sang the entire song again, before babbling on in his whiskey and marijuana mellowness for however long.

Fortunately, he could have slept on the median strip of the nearby highway that night, or competitively for Team Canada or America if the request came in.

Two days later in a shambolic boarding house in Daytona Beach, Florida – hallway whiffs of armpits, old food and socks, the same lonesome lilt of a country and western song coming across the airwaves from three different kennel rooms – he picked up a *Playboy* from the common room table and read the magazine's feature on Australia. That afternoon, in a near-empty cinema, sat through Mike Nichols's *The Graduate* ('Hello darkness my old friend…') thrice in succession, mind drawing up images of red earth horizons and kangaroos, surf beaches and matchbox bikinis. Movement obsession kicked in again – though in reverse mode.

Next day, back-pedalling along Highway A1A, thumb westward pointed signalling Australia as his new final destination. Five days later, Santa Cruz, his mother's stunned look then relieved smile and long hug; a fish fingers, peas and spaghetti loops evening meal to celebrate his return.

There were evenings again, usually after a glass of sherry, when his mother voiced her feelings about issues through a staunch Republican lens. More often adversaries than allies when she did, her comments and his retorts did little to draw them closer, the climax often coming with an outburst. 'There are things you'll come to understand one day, Joseph, when you settle down and learn to pay attention long enough!'

Yet, when things calmed again, he saw her as a good mother, doing the best she could with her patched-up life and the very little she had. One night, a thought came to close down the distance between them, to wrap an arm around her and tell her he loved her. Instead, he stayed put and told her he was going to Australia for a couple of years, no more.

She stared. 'What do you want to go there for?' she asked eventually, as though Australia was the world epicentre for pestilence and bad behaviour.

Like before, taking a leap – admittedly a much bigger one this time – to somewhere better, but she didn't need to hear that. He shrugged and turned away, cognisant of the blind spot he had for her needs. Again the choice: serve family or serve self. He'd only ever shown form with the latter. 'Two years there, Mom, then overland to Europe, then take a merchant ship back here.' Spoken like the world was waiting to embrace him with open arms and golden opportunities.

'I see,' muttered his mother of thwarted dreams, being left again to keep family afloat, mend mended clothes, deal with her domestic demons – dust, dirt, credit card debt – cloth, scrub brush, iron in hand, washing machine whirring, vacuum cleaner droning away her weekend regimen for distancing feelings and thought, the fear of her future matching her past. The Javanese proverb that had her name all over it – 'Like water from the moon, wanting something you'll never have.'

Application for Australia sent off. Find toy shop employment conducive for constructive daydreaming of action man future in the land down under, until Qantas departure for Sydney a week before Christmas – his three hundred dollars and vagabond optimism propelling him onwards.

'Adventures in the art of being alone', someone once wrote, having gone past the borders of birth-based belonging as well. Exciting for a few days exploring Sydney, taking in the surf breaks and bikinied, the eateries and pubs, adjusting to the new language – mate, bloke, sheilas and differences between 'midis', 'schooners' and 'pots'.

Then, with novelty wearing off, he sought connection, and reality ambushed him, baring its teeth: Australia is nowhere near as impressed with his presence as in his fantasies. It's been getting along quite well without him.

New Year's Eve, no job, money halved, occupying a ten-dollar-a-week bedsitter, newspaper propping up the bedsprings; small fridge, two-burner stove, mouldy shower and toilet down the hall. Walk to Kings Cross. Join other solitaries sitting mutely around a bar eyeing their beers, James Taylor's 'I've Seen Fire and I've Seen Rain' playing over and over in the background, setting the tone. Eventually, the New Year arrives and celebrations ring out, but not at the bar. Minutes later, someone raises a glass, others follow, small talk begins and vagabond optimism gets its long-awaited reward. The 'bloke' beside him asks questions, answers his. There's a teacher shortage: such a shortage that untrained graduates – even North American ones – are being employed. From this chance meeting, his future is launched. Later, this thought: where would he have ended up had he not been at that bar, on that stool, next to that 'bloke' at precisely that time?

Spend the next year and four months adopting native habits (end-of-week drinks, a lash at the nearby RSL's pokies the most damaging), dress standards (towelling caps, short trousers and knee-high socks), picking up more local lingo (wog, bludger, budgie smugglers) and trying to adjust to Oz understatement and emotional minimalism as a PE teacher at Ibrox Park under-100 IQ Boys' High School, Leichhardt, made up of seventy per cent second-generation Greek, Yugoslav and Italians and a daily lunchtime line outside the office of the Special Master and his cane.

Two buildings, L-shaped like two red-brick shoeboxes right-angled together, constructed during an obvious economy drive; the only grass that which filled the cracks in the bitumen quadrangle. As living quarters, a sixteen-dollar-a-week terraced Paddington room crawling distance to three pubs and a bus stop for the CBD and Leichhardt.

Fifteen months pass before a same-staffroom English teacher breaks with her boyfriend, the Ed Department three days later, vowing to go west and get as far away from Sydney as her Mini-Minor billycart with windows will take her.

Fresh idea, fresh destination. His ears perked, his mind painting an Indian Ocean sunset. A realisation too that wanderlust and limited ambitions were still a prominent part of his DNA. Over the short course, assimilated, unassimilated still felt pretty much the same to him. So he offered to split the petrol and driving. Though he didn't have a driver's licence and had never driven on the left-hand side of the road, offer accepted.

Not so lonesome roads this time; endless scrub and red earth topped in the clearest blue sky he'd seen since the Mojave, tin roofs of tiny settlements flashing in the sun, longest straight stretch of road in the world, flatness of a sort he'd not experienced before. Little traffic, shortage of constabulary or modernity of any description crossing the corrugated Nullar-boring (for her, not him) – its bull-dust and windscreen glare, racing the sunset to find a camp spot in the salt bush, star-surfing the night sky, occasional road trains rumbling by. Then the sunrise, like witnessing the dawn of humanity caught up in the long ribbons of first light, the early morning road kill providing gourmet breakfasts for the wedge-tailed eagles and crows. And him thinking if they should hit one of those whopper 'roos, they'd be breakfast for the scavengers too.

Shortage of teachers out west as well. His companion and sponsor – whip-smart and resolute – given a prime position at City Beach High School in coastal Perth; he a temporary one replacing a teacher who had had enough of the far north at Derby, its mud flats and king tides, majority Aboriginal population, two pubs, Tuesday night darts and Wednesday night basketball competitions.

Back in Perth the following year, offered bonded assistance to do education courses leading to a teaching qualification. Choice: accept offer or head elsewhere into Asia and Europe and finish up where he started with nothing more than he'd set out with, other than the experience. Decide to settle for the easily reachable. Get a driver's licence, a V-dub Beetle and the needed teaching qualification. Meant staying in the country; meant continuing to turn his back on home; meant the halves would have to continue looking after their mother unassisted. Work off the two-year bond south of Perth at industrial Kwinana. Having completed the contracted time, and still in the grip of unsettledness, head elsewhere back over the Nullar-boring towards the Bass Strait ferry and Scottsdale, Tasmania: family, citizenship and Moonah to come with the next turn of the wheel.

It would happen – eventually it was bound to happen, his war with memory; but not today.

So in what thrice-concussed cavity of his brain had such memories continued to flourish? A legacy from those early boyhood years of eating so many fish fingers – had to be. What were the chances then that unlike his mother and great-aunt he'd be spared dementia? According to Canadian kin, he was a clone of his father – a pike and Arctic char eater, also a pipe smoker – who reputedly died from lung disease soon after conversing clear-headedly with his family. There was a degree of comfort in being told that.

'Every person has their story,' he'd read somewhere, 'but they are seldom important ones.' There were times, like with Kerouac and Cohen, when he thought of his wanderings as story, probably in an attempt to give them significance. And in so doing, he asked himself how many residences – shared houses and couches, flats, on-site caravans, bolt-hole bedsitters, tents – in an average inconsequential lifetime? Nearly twenty-five years of packing up and moving on, living the life of a marginal, a drifter to himself and briefly in the lives of others until the day Sara pointed the way down that dirt road.

Back to window-watching, the bus veering off the expressway and joining a secondary road bordered by more farming land, thin farmers, women in saris and a donkey cart moving between plots.

Eventually they re-entered urban mayhem, or at least he thought so at first, but Chandigarh, with its wide, modern streets and parks lined in banyan trees, was street-beggar-free and so much cleaner, smaller and roomier than Delhi. After a short stop at the modern terminal, they were off again along a straight track of good road, flanked by the meandering Beas River. Gradually they climbed, passing over a series of short bridges before entering a curvy, long tunnel and avoiding by a short arm's length two oncoming trucks, their horns working to deafen all of northern India, their headlights in need of immediate repair.

Out of the tunnel, the road narrowed and deteriorated. Wind came up blowing grit in the air. In between brief stops, he squinted out at hills casting shadows on neighbouring hills, or watched passengers talking or sleeping in contorted positions that his old bones couldn't mimic to win a new car.

No one next to him after the last stop. Across the aisle, an older woman with high cheekbones and a long jaw, her berry-brown skin wrinkled as an old purse, plaited hair like mating snakes falling down her back. She wore a red beanie, flannel shirt, knitted red and blue patterned cardigan, ankle-length heavy blue dress with an apron and tie-up boots. A profile carved in stone, it seemed, until he noticed a necklace of Buddha beads passing through the forefinger and thumb of her right hand, one bead at a time. He couldn't recall seeing the woman after Chandigarh, so she must have got on at the last hill town.

On the side of the road, a battered green and white sign, the colours of the Lebanese flag. On it, 'Over-speed is a knife that will cut life.'

Between the seats in front of him he could make out a young Western couple, earphones threaded through long, blond locks, eyes fixed on their phones, ignoring the trees for their screens. Ah dear, he'd done it again: a pre-television museum piece sitting in judgement of the modern-agers. Still, could there be a greater contrast to that Tibetan-looking woman on his left staring into the air as though listening to the Buddha?

The road angled up into switchbacks, the low gears of the bus grinding out a low whine.

Another road sign: 'I am curvaceous. Be slow.' Something Sara might have said.

Too windy to read, so in keeping with his fetish for word comfort, he tried to recall a favourite poem, quote, or mouth the lyrics of a favourite song until brakes screeched suddenly and the bus shuddered to an abrupt stop. A man with a dog and small herd of goats wandered across the road like he owned it. Took him a while, like he had a point to make, before the road cleared and the bus went on.

Above the Indian plain's pollution blanket now, in the low, raking light, terraced fields, orchards, stone houses and pine trees all dimmed as sunlight glimmered out and departed the long, green slopes, the sky turning soft and pink before merging into night.

6

Outside Srinagar

It felt strange, edgy even being on the Indian side of the Line without his Kalashnikov, combat jacket, six grenades, five hundred rounds of ammunition and black balaclava over his face. Though his jeans, woollen socks, sweater, *pheran*,* boots and rucksack were both combat and non-combat-proven. Strange too being there at midday and able to see over villages and trees and into mountains a day's walk away.

As the bus picked up speed, Sameer took out a packet of Tiger biscuits and opened it up. He stuck one in his mouth and peered out the window at the people and roadside shops that eventually merged into a long whitewashed wall riddled with green graffiti – both faded and recent – much of it exhortations to the highest of all godly duties: martyrdom. He wondered how likely it was that those responsible for the graffiti would ever take part in what they were so passionately advocating. Full of furious words and emotions, prepared to protest and paint slogans, yes. But would they commit to the drawn-out process of being accepted, going *sarhad paar* and trekking into the Hizbul Mujahideen training camp, where boys went to become freedom fighters, to master the Quran, weaponry and explosives, remote area communications and survival techniques? Could they endure the primitive mountain living, winter frostbite and bad food, the Indian ambushes and shelling? Could they dismiss fear, weakened family ties and sense of self and adhere to the rigid discipline? Unless of course those family ties provided further motivation, as Ifra and Parvais certainly did – occupying a permanent

* *Pheran*: traditional male/female outfit composed of two gowns, one worn over the other

100

place in Sameer's thoughts. Her the pretty one in her colourful *pherans, poots** and hijabs, once perfect skin, big dark eyes and gold studs in her ears and nose; Parvais, the talented one, the charmer, who turned girls' heads and would have been the first in the family to attend the University of Kashmir, his expenses paid for by prideful family members.

Being a freedom fighter demanded such undiluted motivation, as well as patience and, sometimes, subterfuge, like the letters with money attached sent monthly to Baba and Ma from his supposed place of employment, Leh's Gomang Hotel – a place he'd not ever been within five hundred kilometres of. That last letter to his family, though, already written and only to be posted if he died, was a very different one, long and so very challenging to write, much of it suggested to him by his former schoolteacher turned Hizb instructor, Salman. Yet, no matter how much he wrote, how important Hizbul Mujahideen deemed his actions to be, Sameer knew that mere words of his martyrdom would never soften his parents' shock and pain, regardless of their most honoured position in the community. And so he was torn. Given his family's circumstances, where did his primary duty lie? It was a question that stayed with him. And when he eventually asked it, his instructor said only that family and country were one, which, in his mind, did little to settle the issue.

Still young, still learning about himself, he discovered that if offered the choice by his one-eyed commander, he preferred to work alone. His next mission – after being praised for night-guiding four martyred cadres to the Indian army base outside Srinagar for their devastating attack – would be the culmination of everything he'd been trained for and perfectly suited to his preference for solo work, or so he was told. The why and how it did would be explained to him in Kargil, eight hours' bus ride to the east. Though, with what he'd learned from writing his last letter, only the mission's details needed clarification.

Another graffiti wall ended as the bus started to climb out of the valley, his eyes scanning the lush farming plots and tree-covered moun-

* *Poot*: essentially the same as a *pheran*, but lighter and worn underneath a *pheran*

tains with their cloudy peaks. Second time he'd been on this bus: the first time six months earlier when he'd been given bags of sticky rice, sweets and nuts and buffalo cheese cookies and seen off by his sad-faced Baba and Ma – once so full of smiles and talk: childhood stories, their courting and marriage, plans for this and plans for that – but still touching, touching, kissing his forehead, embracing and clinging to him, thinking he was travelling the eighteen hours to family-supporting employment in Leh.

Half an hour later, his mind still full of his parents, he got off atop a rise, rendezvoused with Ashfaq, another approved trainee, and descended into the valley. No sky, only night and the sounds of crickets and distant howling of dogs as they wended their way behind weak torchlight through mist and apple orchards, over a mountain pass and finally the Line of Control, staying off the track used by bullock carts, army jeeps, Indian ambushes too, but allowing it to guide them. There were times that night, as he stared into the blackness and listened as he never had before, when Sameer imagined his first firefight, discharging volleys of bullets, dashing from tree to tree, red flashes of mortar shells exploding around him, shouts from his cadre comrades – like in the movies. At dawn, though, any hint of play-acting ended. Tired and dirty, but riding a wave of excitement and expectation, he and Ashfaq arrived at a second rendezvous point and from there were escorted into the Hizbul Mujahideen camp already abuzz with activity.

Other than travelling those few kilometres outside the city and living and training across the Line in Pakistan's Azad Kashmir, Sameer had never been beyond Srinagar; though in his daydreams he regularly had. As a child, he knew the times planes took off and landed at the airport. And whenever he could, from an opening between screening fences, he watched passengers board and disembark from their planes, wondering what it would be like inside one flying to somewhere huge and strange, like Delhi or Mumbai. Though, after he learned to hate Indians, his fence line destinations changed to Islamabad, Lahore and Karachi.

The bus swerved around some obstacle, beeping its horn. Ahead, he'd been told, was a much harsher, drier land: grey of stone, beige of plateau, just a few bits of green in the scattered villages. So he absorbed the sun-brightened valley, its village and great variety of crops – possibly for the last time. And as his gaze lingered, fear of the unknown ahead rose up in his belly and tightened in his throat.

Moments later, shame flushed his face. He pursed his lips and asked himself, 'Freedom fighter or still a schoolboy?'

It was a question he would ask himself many times in the coming days.

7

Touts, only moments earlier milling around the small depot chatting together, were competitors now, pushing past each other holding up hotel cards, their urgent voices calling out.

'You want good hotel, warm room, warm bed? I have, I have.'

'Cheap, cheap. Breakfast too.'

'You come to my hotel. Discount just for you.'

Joe was the last one to exit the bus into the pine-fragrant air; the late night sky a starry, shining black, the half-moon rimmed in golden light. His spirits rocketed. Hard to credit he was in the same country as twelve hours earlier. Manali felt exactly like the place he'd been told it was and, after Delhi, didn't dare believe it could be.

Without a destination now and suddenly surrounded by haranguing touts, he claimed his bag and sought escape. Paths led up and down in different directions, darkening as they went. To his left he spotted the Tibetan woman, small backpack strapped on, hobbling off where no one else was going. In his mind, he tossed a coin. It came up 'follow'. So he did as she started to climb past double-storey hotel buildings, their nightlights illuminating the pathway now. Feeling every bit a stalker, he quickened his pace, drew alongside, and, unsure if he would be understood, asked, 'I'm looking for a quiet guest house or hotel. Do you know where I might find one?'

She stopped, breathing hard, and scrutinised him as though considering his threat level. Non-existent, apparently, as she nodded her head at somewhere further along, but without speaking. Instead, she pointed to her watch, stuck an index finger in the air and mimed walking on.

Not certain he understood, Joe asked, 'So a minute up this road is a guest house?'

The woman nodded.

'Does it have a name?' he asked, slow to realise a vocal response was unlikely.

'Appleview,' she said, surprising him. She turned and hobbled onwards, swaying side to side like the ground was a see-saw. A minute later, she pointed again and he thanked her.

The Appleview Guest House had an open entryway, a small counter with a bell to one side, a blanketed attendant asleep on the divan in the foyer and a staircase leading into darkness upstairs. Other than light snoring from the divan, it was quiet. For Joe – guest house gold. He rang the bell; the attendant woke, got up groggily and dealt with his request.

Upstairs, his was the last room, furthest from the pathway. He went in, turned on the single roof light: the room musty and cold as a tomb, with canary yellow walls, a chair, triple bar heater, bed and bedside table. Folded at the foot of the bed was the thickest quilt he had ever seen. Somewhere a stream was running. He sat and listened a while then took out his travellers' flask. He found a glass and with a single-finger measure of the Dew to chase away the chill and commemorate a completed stage, he toasted himself – 'Brilliant work, Broughton,' he said. 'This will do nicely.' So nicely that he would sleep in, request the room for an extra night, wander Manali, drink Indian tea at outside tables and take in the views: a septuagenarian regimen that, like his dreamy and drifty ways, was a prominent part of his DNA.

*

Birds were awake, little doubt of that. Otherwise the street was quiet.

The cold nagging at his bones, he sat on a bench close to the Leh bus ready to go, ready to stay. Little to see but narrow beams of light boring through the morning mist before a few ghostly passengers arrived and boarded. Two nights in Manali and the temptation to go no further was strong. But after hours of sleepless debate in his hotel room and a final exchange of words with himself there on the bench, he got up, walked and tossed his pack in the hold and boarded the bus. Ten minutes later, it departed, chugging higher and higher through steep terrain criss-crossed in walking tracks above the lush Kulu Valley – villages clinging to hillsides, scarves of mist stretching, parting, re-forming.

Mid-morning they stopped off-road beside a row of food stalls that sold tea, canned drinks, eggs, roti bread and plastic containers of yellow dhal and white rice. Food was eaten on rickety benches, or on the ground with the cold bark of pine trees as backrests; the nearby 'gentlemen's and 'gentlewomen's' corrugated-iron squat toilets monitored by a woman in a chair collecting five rupees per entrant. Smells of old clothes, dhal, diesel and sewage rode the air. Villagers with trekking sticks and packs on their backs came and went, their faces showing not a hint of exertion or discomfort.

With his container of dhal and rice, a plastic spoon and a canned drink, Joe found a tree trunk and sat down awkwardly, leaning back, bark pressing into his back. Propped against a nearby tree were two locals, smoking and spitting. Crows picked over the ground. Gangs of raucous monkeys leapt and swung overhead watchful for food-theft opportunities. A stray cat yowled and a tethered goat bleated for handouts. Bus passengers surrounding him included three young Western trekker types and warmly dressed Indians: three women in saris, a big, black-bearded Sikh – head wrapped in a green turban, hair sprouting from his ears and nostrils – two red-robed monks and further away assorted passengers of Tibetan extraction wearing brimmed hats or beanies, their hair tied back, earrings prominent.

From behind him a bony, bobtailed cat yowled and slunk into view, nose to the ground, coat matted, skin stretched. Joe dropped kernels of rice an arm's length away, coaxing softly, 'Come on, you can have it.' The cat's yellow eyes locked on the rice, locked on him measuring its chances, then with one slow, measured step at a time, closed in. A motorbike ascended the road, seconds later a truck. Joe fingered more rice and stretched his arm out, slow to turn his head…

'Yowww!' the cat screamed, its paw lashing out and swatting the back of his hand, before dashing off.

Startled, Joe found a rag and alternated dabbing droplets of blood while finishing off his dhal and sweet tea.

They reboarded. The engine took a few moments to catch before they were off and the climb continued up and up, the road turning rough and gravelly, light thinning, windows misting as they pushed up through clouds and above them, the driver working the gears hard and at each bend sounding the horn.

Joe yawned and swallowed and watched.

Here and there, clouds parted to reveal glacier-carved rock, ridges and crags crumbling into scree, and up ahead a rising, plunging strip of gravel road.

Road sign: 'After whiskey, driving risky.'

'Rohtang Pass ahead,' he overheard the young male Westerner in front of him say. 'In Tibetan, Rohtang means pile of corpses.'

'Thanks for that,' the girl next to him replied.

'Popular tourist spot as well in the summer, though you should have your life insurance policies up to date. Last month, eighteen people were killed on this road.'

'Terrific. That's even more encouraging. With you chirping away, on a one-to-ten enjoy-your-trip survey, I've just ticked the half box.'

'Not impressed with the commentary, eh?'

Silence – and Joe visualised the look she might have given him: those touring barely-adults, sparring away, models of who he was and what he was doing, saying and thinking more than half a century earlier.

Someone up front barked a cough that refused to go away.

Cloud thinned and rose, the road leading steeply upwards again, the bus struggling in low to second gear and back down to low again.

His thoughts turned to his Arctic father, how he would have loved the mountains and remoteness. Then he grew nauseous; a thumping headache coming on. He tried to concentrate on what passed by outside. But as they neared the summit, nausea and headache deepened, only easing when the bus descended the middle of the road, pitching and diving, down, down, down, edging towards the roadside on hairpin turns, passengers gripping the seats in front of them, occasional lorries, tankers and Enfield motorbikes heading the opposite way. Little sign of habitation from then on, the once-treed landscape giving way to barren plain and chains of mountains folding back on one another, the highest peaks capped in glaciers and snow.

Levelling out, the bus accelerated past a ragged little village, lines of prayer flags – embodiment of air, earth, water, sky and fire – atop every structure; skeins of smoke rising from rock chimneys into the still air. Onwards past snowmelt streams, the bus bumping and banging along with all the aerodynamic marvel of an orange crate; the screech of brakes, squeaky suspension, shriek of the horn when stray goats wandered onto the road or a colourful, flat-fronted truck, smoke blowing out its side exhaust pipe, squeezed past – engine roaring, horn bellowing.

Road sign: 'Love thy neighbour, but not while driving.'

The day wore on, the trip reverting to an exercise in discomfort and nausea durability. He took to leaning his forehead against the seat in front of him, trying to stretch his neck and lower back, aware of every stiffening joint and muscle in his body and giving thought to the unlikely chance of finding a chiropractor in Leh. Out the window a half-dozen flat-roofed stone houses appeared, rickety ladders leaning against them, attached stone animal enclosures and little cultivated plots, but peopleless, as though the place had been abandoned.

From valley, they lifted back into high mountains again. Nothing to do but continue to endure, the daggering sunlight and increasing altitude going from irritant to torturous again. Biggest mistake of the trip was forgetting his altitude tablets.

Then the rush of air, rattle of metal and glass again, as though the bus was about to disintegrate spiralling around bends and undercut cliff faces, the jolt of potholes, suspension bottoming out, past the shell of a rusted-out truck, then endlessly looping across slopes before finally flattening out again. But not before a young Tibetan man two rows up puked softly into a cellophane bag, while his friend by the window stretched his head out and hurled, windows behind catching the spray.

Queasy, Joe tracked the far horizon of rock, glacier and snow.

Road sign: 'Three enemies of the road: liquor, speed and overload.'

The bus shuttered across a bridge above a grey stream and laboured up another rise, engine low-geared and revving to full capacity.

The young female head in front of him leant sideways, finding a shoulder, stirring in him distant memory:

'You having it off with someone else?' she asked in an even tone.

He'd read the same paragraph three times. It may as well have been written in Farsi. 'As much chance of that happening as cycling to the moon,' he answered, surprised that, even as forthright as she always was, she should ask such a question.

'Well, in that case, next question: your toolbox fully operational?'

'No reason to think it's not.'

'No?'

He bookmarked his page and looked over as she wiggled and pried her singlet and jeans off, her panties next, tossing them into the air, then her bra. On went her black 'Are you getting my message?' negligee.

She lifted the covers, got in and scooted close. 'Okay. Well, then, I'm available, if you're not otherwise engaged: I have been for a while now.' She placed her head on his chest, a hand on his stomach and waited. 'So talk to me,' she said some moments later.

He spoke again of the bad year he was having, how it had taken up permanent residence inside his head, 'Dog's work. A biped theatre of the absurd. Ashton's Circus could throw a tent over my classroom and sell tickets,' he said, going on to describe the Manic Five's feature acts, finishing with 'Like sharks: one makes a splash, the others join in. Can rob your will to live sometimes.'

'A few sandwiches short of a picnic, you used to say.'

'Yeah, I did, when I was younger and didn't feel out-energised by them.' He was reconciled to losing some skin each year teaching on the lower decks of Belgrove High, but not being skinned to the edge of a breakdown. It was like he'd lost his management key. His classroom turned brain-dead by five budding sociopaths, progeny of dysfunctional families, fomenting trouble in his grade ten English and social science classes, so leaving him feeling diminished and stressed to fixation point: fixation he couldn't put to rest. How distant everything else in his life had become; like the 'everything else' had fled to the deepest recesses of his brain, never to return. How tired the problems made him. Yet he slept only two, three hours at night, wandered the house like a shadow, sat in different places trying unsuccessfully to read, divert his mind. And even when he did briefly get back to sleep, the Five inhabited his dreams, their voices like flies plaguing his ears, the exultant looks on their faces saying, 'This is what makes us feel alive, so get used to it, dickhead.'

Cut the anchor before it drags you down, someone said once. But the anchor was chained to their livelihood, his sense of purpose and self-respect, built in the past on overcoming such problem students.

'Put signs up on your school's front and back gates,' she said. 'Due to its fucked-upness, this school is being donated to the RSPCA.'

A smile of sorts stretched his face. 'Publicly attacking the school's image, that would get the admin out of their chairs. It would need to be forensics-proof, though, with maybe a slight softening of the language. But okay, then what?'

'Up to the bureaucracy gods, isn't it? But whatever, we'll deal with it.'

The weight of those three words. 'I'm trying to do that now…not all that well.'

Outside on grounds duty, walking, walking, past the giggling and gossiping, boys shoving and shouting and kicking balls as he edged past them towards the sanctity of empty space, while daydreaming of making a living by some other means than his mouth. It was a reprieve of sorts being out there, the mountain as backdrop, before the resumption of four-walled attrition, his classroom armour cracking; the minutes crawling to the end of class, the days of the week to the temporary sanctuary of three p.m. Friday afternoons, the weeks until the holidays.

First time ever students had challenged him for control and succeeded; overcoming their inventory of antics and idiocy beyond him; beyond the school too, it seemed, with its simple solutions to complex problems. First time his teaching trinity – intuition, principles never abandoned, drawing a permanent curtain over a bad day – had failed him. His small contribution to human betterment, everything he'd done to establish himself, take professional and personal pride in, unravelling before his eyes. First time he hated his job: skin flushed, blood pressure keeping it that way, the sense of gloom when entering his classroom like it had turned into enemy territory, of being slow to respond to another thrown biro, another ruler pressed into someone's back, a book banging a desk ('Fuck! Oh, sorry, Mr Broughton – accident.'), loud cackle or play-act scream, and him uselessly trying to eye-dagger silence or point his .44 Magnum finger to coerce.

Little sense pouring forth a volley of full-throated venom, they'd only deem it another win. 'If you feel inclined on vacating this classroom on time, then realise we complete this exercise before we go.'

'Geez, give us a dictionary.'

More sycophantic sniggers, grins from the provocateurs at the back; watching, watching, wanting more, planning for it; the cogs in their heads working only to disrupt, to get inside his head, fasten their sticky claws on his soul.

Had they access to mini smoke bombs, party poppers or paint pistols what would they do next to ensure chaos reigned supreme in his once learning-engaged classroom? Time spent reprimanding, coercing, exiting (though not 'a creative strategy', so highly discouraged by the pillars of authority – including Todd Hampton – quick to criticise, mute in suggesting realistic remedies). Probably the worst of it, seeing his serious students' resigned faces, of him being the subject of the take-down gossip that just had to be going on, of other staff members passing in the hallways averting their eyes or smiling token sympathy, thankful his problems weren't theirs: and throughout his growing sense of isolation in being left to 'deal with it'.

'Okay, Dylan,' he said, withdrawing the stick and offering up a carrot, 'no dictionary, but something else for you.' He picked up a manila folder from his desk. 'I'll read you a quote that's inscribed on the grave of James Scullin, prime minister of Australia from 1929 to 1932. If you can give me an accurate, everyday example of the quote, I'll give the class an early minute. And it's okay to get help, quiet help, from anyone in the class (obvious who they would be). This is the quote: "Justice and humanity demand interference whenever the weak are crushed by the strong." He wrote it up on the board.

Blessed peace and quiet as the Five huddled like trough-feeders around Dylan's desk. But with their capacity for quiet measured in seconds, it didn't take long for them to come up with a response, Dylan standing, bowing and delivering.

'You know, Mr Broughton, the Knights have been getting their arses…sorry, their backsides whipped the past few weeks by most every fucking…sorry, useless club in the state league?'

'Yes. A good friend of mine backs the Knights and he's suffering.'

'Well, justice and humanity would be if the Knights' players could each snort a line of coke before they took to the pitch…'

More sniggering, accompanied by Dylan's grand bow and Jacob Dillman mining the contents of his nose and storing the forefingered finds under his desk.

'Nothing better, Mr Broughton,' Dylan continued, 'to quick fix your energy and talent levels than a white powder nostril injection. You should try it sometime.'

Privately, he gave Dylan credit for his accurate, descriptive use of language. He was far from dim-witted. Of that there was no doubt. Yet the answer was typically distasteful and in reply he couldn't bring himself to muster anything more than a tired 'Off you go.' Turned out an early three seconds, as the bell sounded ending class; no one more thankful than he was.

In shock and awe Walter Mitty moments, Joe daydreamed tasering the Manic Five, of them being stretchered out of his classroom to the applause of the other students and returning the next day meek and quiet as space dust. In his clearest, most satisfying vision, Joe asks the class, 'Could former Prime Minister James Scullin have been considered a man of the people? Who would like to answer that in more than a single sentence?'

Dylan's hand shoots up. Joe points to him.

Dylan sits erect, hands folded on his desk. 'Yes at first, no later on, Mr Broughton. As prime minister, Scullin was caught between a rock and a hard place. He was the son of poor Irish immigrants and he was a labourer and grocer before becoming a politician. So yeah, he knew what hard work was like then and was a man of the people. But when he became PM in 1929, the Depression started and the country went bankrupt, so he was forced to drastically cut government spending, including pensions. So, like can happen in life, Mr Broughton, circumstances that he wasn't responsible for forced him to do what he didn't want to do but was for the greater public good. And riots broke out and had any of the workers got hold of Scullin, they probably would have done some serious alterations on him and he would have had to be taken to Emergency for a new face.'

'Fine analysis, Dylan. Ten out of ten.'

At the start of second term, he began to disengage from the staff. Often he felt an urge to simply disappear.

Then one three a.m. moonlit night as he paced the lounge room floor, there came this thought: he was blowing the situation out of all proportion (that propensity to overdramatise again); that something in his chemistry was breaking down and dissolving. That the only person whose sanity was in doubt was his own. That the Five, while animalistic, foul-mouthed and deft at pushing his buttons, had got to grade ten, hadn't they? Others had had to deal with them, survive them. The problem was to do with him, how he was reading and reacting to the disorder.

Truth, however, provided poor company, as more and more he doubted himself. And no matter how long and hard he obsessed, there were only ever two options: battle on exhausted until year's end (seemingly a decade away), or go down trying. Either way, early retirement was calling – no, it was shouting.

'People break, and that's the greatest shock of all to them,' he said to her.

'When's the last time we had a proper restaurant meal?' she asked after turning on her reading light, propping herself on an elbow, head in hand.

Puzzled: 'A while.'

'Mmm. Something else gone missing… Verb form of incentive, know what it is?'

His mystified look came first. 'Incentivise.'

'Good. You need incentivising in at least two important categories of life, at least until the year Joe Broughton almost cut his wrists ends and is forever stored away in Education Department archives.' She kissed and stroked him. 'You got any small bills in your wallet?'

'I don't know – probably. Why?'

'I want to go to the MAC 1 with you and split a dozen oysters, a fisherman's platter for two and a bottle of their priciest Chardonnay.'

'Right. When?'

'Soon. Prime food and prime wine there, say the prime eating experts.'

'Prime prices too.'

'Indeed. So how do you feel about prostituting yourself…?'

'What?'

'…and regaining your celebrity status, at least with me? I'm for it.' She stroked and kissed. 'Because I intend to make a booking at the MAC 1 within the next month and because the food there is reputedly worth fucking for, this is…'

'Perhaps better,' Joe interrupted, 'to express that worth in slightly less winceable words, do you think?'

'Sorry. Delicate ears, I know. Anyway, this is how I propose we pay for it. Each time we practise coitus in this bed, we both throw five dollars into our soon-to-be-labelled Fine Dining Jar. When Brandy's out, should we do it somewhere else in the house, ten dollars. Backyard, twenty. The car, thirty. Clifton or Cremorne beaches after midnight, unwitnessed, fifty. If witnessed, a hundred. I think we should go out to a top restaurant once a month to celebrate our lives, at least until the end of the year: take taxis, get our blood alcohol levels up. I'll make the bookings and you watch the calendar, and the jar. If our funds are running low and restaurant time is close, your ingenuity will be called on, and hopefully not too severely challenged. Agreed?'

A line from Old Bill: 'Nor custom stole her infinite variety.' And he thought how she was always willing to move the boundaries. What else could he say other than 'Agreed.'

She stroked, locking him in with puppy eyes and a held-in smile. 'It appears we'll be starting tonight.'

'Uh huh.'

'So class dismissed?'

'I think so.'

Mostly, up to the start of that year, he'd been the teacher he wanted to be; but not since. From teacher, he'd turned penitential time-server crossing off the days until the end of the year. It was 'by the distance of light years', he told Sara during the last week of school, 'his hardest, most demanding year ever. Never to be repeated.' He'd taken his full allotment of sick leave, and with those breaks managed to reach the end – albeit totally drained, retirement-date fixed and never the same in front of a class again – while having eaten at more pricey restaurants in eight months than he had during the rest of his lifetime: eight more to be exact.

'Like riding a time machine, I feel I've aged tenfold this year,' he added that last week.

'Yet it's had its compensations, wouldn't you say?' Her gaze level and cool, she waited.

'I would – yes.'

The following year – his last – despite their depleted savings and a marked improvement in his classes, incentivising continued, though on a quarterly rather than monthly basis; so the need to take his sensitive knees and back outdoors if the jar got low, largely and thankfully negated. Whatever it took to deal with a problem; to that, Sara was always prepared to contribute.

Road sign: 'Life is a journey – complete it.'

Nowadays, sex had gone the way of teaching – never again at the end of a dirt road, on sand, amongst the eucalypts or anywhere. Indeed, he couldn't remember the last time he'd intimately touched or been touched by anyone. Still, he was lucky enough to have found intimacy and connection in Sara and could smile, even now, at her counselling techniques, while wondering how other couples dealt with upheaval and depression.

Back to his window study of geology and topology – river, valley, gorge, the serried gaps, scarps and high-up glacial moraines – the sounds of the bus a part of his flesh and bones now. Out there Ladakh, surely, in the Himalayan rain shadow, its high, dry, rock plateau; clouds banked up to the south. 'Mountains stop clouds like they do extended sunsets,' someone wrote, or should have written anyway. Annual precipitation in Ladakh about enough to fill a teapot, though glacier-melt rivers, streams and irrigation channels kept crops and fruit, willow, juniper and poplar trees growing – or so his Lonely Planet service informed him.

More climbing and plummeting, here and there small rockslides, sections of guard rail missing on bends, two-metre mani stones chiselled in prayers to mark the headachy summits. Then, like a high mountain version of a Luna Park thrill ride, the careering, shuddering, brake-screeching descents – imagining the road's crumbled edges, of missing a turn and plunging down, down – before the breathe-easier valley basins welcomed them again. After a while, the valleys narrowed and the direction went skyward again.

There came the storied TaglungLa Pass, highest point of the trip at 5,350 metres and said to be 'the second highest motorable road in the world' during the three months it was open. And once again his life moved in a way unintended. At high altitude his head began throbbing like a second heart. Higher, and with each turn of the bus, a blade pushed deeper into his brain: his limbs twitching, chest tight as if bound in plaster. He hunched over and groaned, putting a hand against the pain in his forehead.

Quickly, someone was over him; a Western voice at the edge of his ear. 'Not flash, eh?'

'No.' He removed his glasses, turned his head just enough to take in a young Westerner's concerned face.

'You got altitude tablets?'

Spasms cut through his temples. 'No.' His limbs shook; headache turning cyclonic.

'Stretch out.'

Someone shouted.

The bus shuttered to a stop in gravel.

In seconds, the bus driver was beside him holding a cylindrical canister.

'Oxygen,' the Westerner said. Tubes were inserted in Joe's nostrils. 'Just breathe normally. We'll be going down in the next few minutes. Just breathe, that's all, just breathe normally.'

The bus took off and soon descended. Gradually his body stilled, though his head continued to throb. He held on to his seat, listening hard to the rattling and screeching tyres in an effort to distract the pain.

They levelled out finally and stopped outside a wide metal gate. Minutes passed, Joe slumped over, before the Westerner approached again.

'We're at a military base,' he said. 'You're booked into their infirmary. Good treatment, I've been told.'

The shock of it all diminished Joe's voice. 'If I have an option, I don't know what it is.'

'Infirmary or cremation: it's too rocky out there to dig a grave.'

'Right option then. Thanks.'

'Not to worry, sir,' a man in camouflage uniform interjected. 'Many times this happen. You stay and get better. Tomorrow we find you another bus or truck.'

Or a vehicle to the local funeral parlour, Joe almost said, head absorbing more punishment.

Westerner: 'See you in Leh.'

'That is my foremost hope.'

Oxygen tubes were removed, the canister taken away and Joe helped wobbly to his feet, the Westerner on one side of him, the soldier on the other. He staggered down the aisle, down the steps; maintaining a level of dignity all but impossible. Metres away a jeep, his daypack and suitcase already pressed into the back.

He sat gripping the seat, and they were off, past a guard post, elevated spotlights, satellite dishes and howitzers, armed personnel carriers and concrete barracks, the cold air whistling through before stopping outside a ribbed-metal Quonset hut, a large red cross above the entrance. Head wrapped in black silk and wearing tiger stripe fatigues as though a military encounter was imminent, a burly, black-bearded Sikh came out and introduced himself as Doctor Travindra Singh. He helped the soldier get Joe into the infirmary's sudden darkness before a light came on illuminating the stark walls and five metal-framed beds; oxygen tanks on wheels like midget orderlies at each bedside.

Into the far bed he went and propped into a semi-upright position, blankets spread over him. The soldier left and returned with a hammer and an end wrench. He banged and yanked the oxygen valve open, as though it had long ago frozen over. The doctor hooked the mask over Joe's face and turned on the oxygen.

'To get the fluid off your brain, we use oxygen followed by an injection, tablets and black tea, for you'll need to stay awake a while. Once you stabilise, you'll get a little food and drink and a supply of Diomex tablets to get you into Leh tomorrow in whatever transport we can wave down. Let me guess – New Zealand?'

'Australia.'

'Not a country of great heights, is it?' He took Joe's pulse then left and returned with a loaded syringe the size of an ice pick and injected Joe intravenously.

Within minutes, he was painless and feeling replenished. The doctor took off the mask and switched off the oxygen.

'Leh's looking a distinct possibility now,' Joe said. 'I couldn't have said that earlier.'

The soldier re-entered with a tray of food and mug of tea and placed it on the bedside stand and left.

'McDonalds has yet to open a franchise up here,' the good doctor noted.

'So no Happy Meals?'

The doctor shook his head, smiling. 'You're not a Catholic, are you?'

'I've long been defrocked and out of confessional range.'

'Then you'll not mind eating dhal with chicken and rice on a Friday. Up here, fish are about as common as elephants are in Australia.' He cranked up the metal bed, putting Joe in a better eating position. 'Mountain sickness strikes some and not others, and no one knows why, though the young and old seem most susceptible, a category you would fall into.' He poured Joe a glass of water. 'The battalion stationed here is called the Mountain Tamers. They're mostly in their twenties, but some of them have been struck down hard as well when they've gone too high, and know what it's like to spend time in this ward.'

'Like brain surgery without anaesthetic before the oxygen arrives.'

'Yes. You might want to think about returning to Manali tomorrow. It could be the safer option.'

'Still passes to get over.'

'True… Your plan then is to fly back to Delhi from Leh?'

'After this experience, I'll take a seat on the fuselage if I have to.'

'If you wait a couple of weeks and adjust, you should be able to get an inside seat of your choice. Not much passenger demand the next six months or so. Anyway, I'll leave you to all the excitement in here. Toilet is there in the far corner. There's an alarm buzzer on the side of the bedstand. The button next to the light button is for room service.'

'Room service?'

'Press it and the soldier on duty will come in.' The doctor couldn't hold back a smile. 'We're conscious of our Trip Advisor rating.' He wished Joe a goodnight, turned and left.

Save for the hum of the weak fluorescent lighting, silence was absolute, like the building was buried under snow. Third strange bed in the last four nights, he thought, after more than a decade of not spending a night away from home. Alone in the Mountain Tamer medical ward, four thousand metres up in the Himalayas after starting the trip on the Indian plain in one of the biggest cities in the world, he had indeed gone some way towards responding to the humdrum predictability of his life in Moonah. And he considered again the age-old fantasy of things ever going according to plan.

His eyes went heavy. He turned off the light. Clothes remaining on, blankets drawn up, he slept heavily until the doctor and a soldier with a tray of tea, scrambled eggs and roti bread appeared beside him like morning apparitions.

'For our Western guests only,' the doctor joked as the soldier cleared a spot on the bedstand and set his breakfast down. 'How're you feeling?'

'Like I'm twenty again and on testosterone overload.'

'Then we'll have to find you an empty seat and an understanding driver.'

Joe reached for his wallet on the stand. 'I better fix you up. Forgot to inquire about the room rate last night. It wasn't high on my priority list. What do I owe?'

The doctor watched him a moment. 'Your accent? Were you born in Australia?'

'Canada. I moved to America then migrated from there to Australia after I'd grown too ugly to walk down the fashion thoroughfares of Hollywood and Beverly Hills any more. Like my mother had mated with a camel, someone said to me once, and that I'd blend in better in Australia where camels wander the outback.'

The doctor laughed. He glanced around the back of Joe. 'Can't see any humps, though you do stand out. Probably more for hair than camel features. Tell me, do you follow cricket in the land down under?'

'Suni "Sunny" Gavaskar, the greatest opening batsman the world has ever known. Sachin Tendulkar, the little magician. Virat Kohli, captain of the first-ever India cricket team to beat Australia in Australia.'

'Ahh. Such knowledge deserves reward. No charge for the meals. And in return, maybe next time the Indian test team visits Australia, you might offer them some support.'

'If I meet them at the airport with garlands of flowers, how would that be?'

'Good enough to qualify for free medical treatment here.'

'Done then.'

'But remember to take your Diomex and that old bones need lots of rest in high mountains.' He stepped back. 'I'll go and check on the transport services to Leh.'

In the quiet, Joe nodded off again.

Mid-morning the doctor returned. 'I've got you a seat. Not first class, but the driver looks as rested as any that pass by here and the bus roadworthy enough. And it comes at the morning price.'

'Difficult to access an ATM up here, I suppose.'

'Seven hundred rupees. What's that in Australian dollars?'

'About fourteen dollars.'

'Need a loan?'

How friendly the high mountains were now. In his head, Dinah Washington's best-ever song:

> What a difference a day made,
> Twenty-four little hours
> Brought the sun and the flowers...

Well, the sun anyway, if not the flowers.

'No, no loan required.' He mentioned again how good he was feeling, how thankful he was to the Indian army's medical services.

Outside in the crisp air and sharp light, the doctor – flanked by two soldiers – took on a more formal pose. He extended his hand, saying, 'Happy we could be of service.'

'No more than I am.' There was nothing formal about the way Joe shook the doctor's hand with both of his.

He climbed aboard the jeep, careful not to bump his convalescing brain, and was driven to the open gate where a bus waited, engine running, the luggage and passenger doors open for business.

He paid the driver, took a seat towards the back and the bus departed and in minutes began to climb, winding around the usual hairpin turns. He leant his head against the window; the bus soon moving in and out of cloud that rose like steam; the road behind disappearing quickly, a sense that civilisation with its welcoming military outposts and congenial doctors was disappearing as well. Soon, with the grumble of the engine growing distant in his ears, he slept.

'BAM!' The bus swerved to avoid an oncoming truck, hitting a pothole instead, gravel machine-gunning the undercarriage. Startled awake, Joe looked out.

Road sign: 'Always alert, accident avert.'

Undaunted, on they went topping another pass, sunlight cutting through cloud and spreading quickly as though intent on providing viewing opportunities over all Ladakh. The bus veered, exhaust popping, and they came to a stop on an extended shoulder of road. The driver killed the engine. The door opened and everyone scrambled out of confinement into the cold, their breath steaming, Winton's unbounded space there for all to see. Avoiding the sleeves of ice, Joe walked to the edge of a deep drop and looked down into the abyss, imagining a sudden wind gust pushing him over and plunging horror-struck through the frozen air, his body breaking up on the rocky crags below. Gone slightly queasy, he backed off, his need for what could double as a toilet such that despite the onlookers and tricky breeze, a spot further along the edge looked a possibility.

The driver stepped down from the bus and, as though reading Joe's mind, pointed across the road, saying in both Hindi and English, 'Toilet over there.'

Shivering a little, Joe followed others past a two-metre white plaster Buddha sitting cross-legged, right hand held up, left palm held out, and further on a rock-targeted 'SHAUCHAALAY/TOILIT' sign blistered in rust and flanked by grey humps of boulders. Beyond, no attendant, no fee for using the sheet-metal-enclosed drop toilets, red-paint-labelled 'gentleman' and 'gentlewoman' that looked more suitable for punishment than relief; though those in line to use them probably didn't think so. To his left, a gap between boulders led steeply upwards. From a rocky knoll thirty metres or so up, a vulture the size of a hang-glider tensed before springing into flight.

That space looked too good to ignore. So, armed with Diomex tablets, Joe climbed: legs struggling in the loose scree, heart quick, breath misty and short, the icy air biting into his nostrils and throat. But where he got to, under a line of frayed prayer flags soundproofed from passengers by monoliths of rock, and with a view Winton would have turned cartwheels for, made his discomfort seem a mere itch. Gimpy and grumpy maybe, but up there he was King Mountain Goat in sunnies scanning his vast domain.

And what a domain it was; like entering a world of his boyhood dreams. On the long, long horizon, under all that infinite sky, a land so high that fell so far in the thin, unadulterated air: the jagged, glaciered peaks, sprawling plateau and an astral silence so still the landscape seemed to be listening as well.

Tilting his head back and wolfing in a lungful of air, his spirits soared: from on-high altitude sickness one day to on-high elation the next. Like being incarcerated in a cell and suddenly escaping to the emptiest spot on earth, where he might have been the last person on the planet. Where were the developers, the 24/7 construction zones, the commercial world of spin and appearances, talkback radio, blaring horns, sirens and alarms, or even a goatherd and his dog, or signs of any life at all? Had he ever felt so detached from modernity, of occupying a place so perfect for a dreamy old man to ponder the state of the world below – its rage-fuelled aggression, civilisation at war with itself, nature in retreat, the rising oceans and expanding deserts? He'd forgotten there was such emptiness and silence in the world. Forgivable, he supposed, when considering how close he lived to Main Road, Moonah. That thought made him smile, and as he looked into the vastness a tingling sense of pleasure spread into every one of his nerve endings.

In response, having travelled eight minutes and twenty seconds to get to this spot, sunlight flooded a vast section of plateau to his left, while on his right light dimmed as though starved of power. Over him, flags ruffled in a nudge of breeze, dispersing their prayers, before going limp again. Part of something metaphysical going on, working its wonders just for him, that, like the third rock from the sun called Earth, the universe with its black holes and time spans merging into infinity, defied his understanding as well.

The only thing missing was a bench, though a low, rounded boulder would probably do just as well. Having located one, how good to be thickly bundled up like Mawson of the Antarctic, passing afternoon into evening, watching the shifting light and cloud shadow, a flaring sun touch the mountains, the gradual fade-out of sunlight, shadows deepening, night spreading as a dark tablecloth across the plateau and up the summits, before a full moon rose above the glaciered peaks to his right.

Someone whose name avoided his memory wrote about remote places and the beautiful loneliness that so often broods in them. Out there, an oasis for the worn, weary and reflective, had to be right up there with them, and he wondered how many other seventy-three-year-olds had sat where he was sitting. It had been a long time since he'd felt so good, so invigorated, solid and eternal. Without a doubt, getting here was worth even the altitude sickness and closeted night at the army base, and that was saying a lot.

Ah, right; he was being watched over after all, like his death was imminent. A vulture – probably the one he'd disturbed earlier – wheeled over him in the thermals, wing tips curved upwards like the fingers of Balinese dancers. He watched it as it was surely watching him.

Had to give the earth credit for preserving such places, didn't you? A Wordsworth epiphany, he'd heard it called; that great poet's 'spots of time', experiences so intense they informed a person's life forever after. He couldn't remember when he last felt such a positive 'spot'; maybe the day of his marriage, or when Brandy emerged from Sara's belly, eyelids batting. Or maybe all that perfect emptiness out there was just a form of thin air trickery, the altitude reverse of mirages in the desert: which, of course, as a member of the closing-in-on-death set, he'd be most susceptible to experiencing.

Still – there was something far more mundane to attend to before the fullness of that epiphany or trickery could be realised. Standing and following his bladder out from under the flags, he unzipped and presented himself. 'Look, Tim, unassisted,' he crooned to his writing hero in the pleasure of the moment, blowing his foggy breath into cold, cupped hands while glancing up at the neighbourly vulture continuing to circle, sunlight angling in, woolly clouds scaling the peaks.

In a million years or so, the slight rise of the mountains, advance and retreat of glaciers, the construction of that windy thread of road occupying the time frame's last millisecond; everything else the same.

In the next few years, if ever he felt the need to desert the world again, this was the place to return to, though it would be easier to parachute out of a plane than take a bus. How could the earth, spinning forever forward, be speeding around the sun at thirty kilometres a second, around the two billion stars in the Milky Way at two hundred kilometres a second and this spot remain so peaceful and still? Incredible. But whatever the reason, it was for this he'd left home. If he dropped dead there and then, it didn't matter. Toss some rocks on him, let him harden, an eternal smile ossified on his frozen face. Though an afterthought told him the chances of becoming vulture meat were probably greater.

In need of his hands again, Joe praised his prostate for forcing such a memorable interlude. Wiggling his bean and storing it away, he laughed out loud for the first time since leaving Moonah – and it felt good: he'd forgotten just how good. Why he laughed he wasn't sure: the unravelling of brain tissue maybe as a delayed response to altitude sickness; or maybe just the relief from having got this far into Ladakh and liking it and feeling rewarded. No, more than rewarded – feeling privileged, realising there was still room for astonishment in an old, muddled septuagenarian's life. Spotting two perfectly symmetrical stones, he stooped and picked them up. Not for targeting toilet or road signs with, but one for adding to a cairn below as a thank you, the other a 'spot of time' souvenir for the mantelpiece back home.

He scanned the landscape a final time, painting it into his memory, each minute brushstroke. Such a fine place for surrendering yourself to expansive thoughts, and it didn't get any more expansive than life, earth and the stilled universe. But with the cold seeping into his bones, like cracks were opening up in his skin, it was time for Mahatma of the Himalayas to confront whatever cosmic fate had in store for him further along the road.

Sun on his back, he descended like the stone-jointed old fossil he was, arms flung out at full wingspan, slaloming the shifting scree and once nearly toppling over before the scree gave way a second time and his legs shot out from under him as if jerked by an invisible string. He hit the ground hard, left elbow taking the brunt, and lay there stunned, moving fingers, lifting arm, checking for damage. Bruising for sure, but nothing broken as far as he could tell: just something else to be thankful for. He got up slowly, took a couple of deep, settling breaths while reclaiming his stones and side-shuffled down the few remaining metres to the bottom.

He was the last one to reboard, the engine rolling over sluggishly, the heated air beard-thawing. He found his seat and sat down, quickly stowing his stones in his daypack. And despite his fall, he remained giddy, full of exhilaration for the Himalayas and Ladakh, the experience running and whooping back through the corridors of his mind. He wanted to talk to someone. Post-Sara, post-Ahmed, had he not slipped into his own social Siberia, he might have hopped up and sat next to the first likely listener and told them all about what he'd just done, seen and felt, although nothing had happened up there but silence and time. He might even have supplemented the account with a few lines from Louis Armstrong's 'What a Wonderful World'. As it was, he sang a few lines anyway.

From the seat in front of him, a local's 'she'll be right' thumb lifted in the air, under it a male voice: 'Happy, happy?'

'Yes, happy, happy. Wonderful place, wonderful world.'

'Me too happy, happy.'

The bus coughed into start-up mode. Cold as well, it took to the road, turn indicator not required. Down, down they went past cairns and shrines, around sharp corners, under rock overhangs, a sense that the smallest tremor in the earth could instantly bury them. His hands again warm and workable, Joe gripped the seat in front of him, swaying side to side with the bus and holding on through all the winding and bouncing and braking and turning, like those who constructed the road had no concept of smooth or straight.

Road sign: 'Leprosy is curable.'

Late afternoon; and from out of the rock and dust emerged a valley of poplar and juniper trees interspersed with dun-brown fields running to the bank of a glittery stream. With gravel popping and rattling in the undercarriage again, the bus ground to a stop next to two white, three-metre-high stupas, like giant chess pawns guarding either side of the village entrance. The door opened, though the engine remained idling tentatively, like it was about to stall but didn't.

On a small rise a hundred metres or so away, maybe a dozen small, double-storeyed, whitewashed houses. Their honey-coloured, wooden-framed windows were the shape of half open eyes. Tiny balconies protruded between them, while prayer flags ran in X-patterns corner to corner atop flat, straw-covered rooftops. The stream, bordered in parts by poplar and willow trees, wound around the back of the village then coursed parallel with the road. A network of canals veered off it towards fields divided by shoulder-high stone walls protecting apricot trees, vegetable plots and what looked to be late-season hibiscus and potted marigolds. Though you could be forgiven for thinking the main crop was rocks. Atop the walls, mounds of prayer stones were interspersed with drying clothes and cakes of dung. Two zigzag tracks led away from the village; one up to the brow of a hill and the faded white walls of a small building, the other towards a distant mountain range before disappearing.

And there they were in the wandering light, Ladakhis grooming the mounded earth: stoical men, obviously, taking on the harsh conditions, the short, hot summers and brutally long, frozen winters. In an outer field, a shaggy dzo – half cow, half yak – pulled an ancient-looking plough guided by a bow-legged man in a wide-brim hat. Was it the eighteenth, nineteenth or the twenty-first century? Without the bus, passengers and bitumen road, it would have been hard to tell.

Bundled up against the cold, three villagers appeared from between the stupas: two men and, incredibly, someone Joe recognised: a bent, broad-faced older woman swaying pendulum-like as she tried to keep up with the men. She wore a grey beanie over a thick strand of silvery plaited hair, daypack, ankle-length heavy dress with aprons front and back, leggings, boots and dangly earrings – and that's how he remembered her. The three pulled themselves up into the bus, the men finding seats quickly and the woman left to totter onwards towards the back. He picked his daypack up from the seat next to him and waved, putting on his brightest 'Look it's me' smile.

When she spotted him, she scowled, her eyes registering puzzlement. That had been her response in Manali too, like she was trying to decide whether he was harmless or an axe murderer.

He pointed to the seat and waited. Would she or wouldn't she?

She picked him for harmless, continuing on and dropping down beside him, blowing air between her lips.

The bus pushed on.

Joe turned. 'Remember me? In Manali, you led me to a guest house.'

Her mouth lifted at the edges, but she stayed quiet.

Either a faulty voice box – although it was operating reluctantly in Manali – or she chose to stay quiet. Joe's look reverted to the window and the last of the barley fields, before a tap on his hand turned his head.

'Yes, Manali. I not know you go to Leh.' She poked her chest, offering a smile. 'Ten-zin Dho-lup.'

'Your name?' he checked.

Her dark eyes glimmered, the whites tinged yellow. She nodded and pointed to him.

'Joe: last name Broughton.

She said the first name and that was enough for her.

'Good,' he said anyway, the teacher in him never far away, even here, after so many years.

Again she poked her chest. 'Sixty-six.'

Whenever people asked his age, or when he was about to volunteer it, it always took him a few seconds to catch up with where he was at. 'Seventy-three.'

'Oh. Too old to dance,' she said, challenged to get her tongue around the words. She gave him a snaggle-toothed grin that reminded Joe of Scottsdale's Zac sitting at the bar beside him so long ago.

'But not too old to ride a long-haul bus,' he said.

Her English seemed to improve as she adjusted to it. 'Many times I am on dis bus and not see person more old than me. But now I do.'

'Joe Broughton, oldest man ever to ride a Ladakhi bus, eh?'

She grinned and her eyes lingered on him an extra moment. 'Now I second most old.' She giggled like a six-year-old and pointed to his head and face. 'White hair.'

'Yes.'

'So much. You paint it?'

'No. It just grows that way. Has for the last forty years or so.'

'Nice – like snowman: snowman England.'

'Australia.'

'Ah, kangaroo.' She lifted her arms in front of her chest, let her hands go limp and bounced up and down without assistance from the bus. 'Jump, jump.' Pantomime over, she rummaged through her bag and took out a bead necklace. Transitioning from marsupial to devout Buddhist, she started running the beads through the thumb and forefinger of her right hand, one bead at a time.

Interest aroused, questions formed in his mind, like where did she learn her English? Did she live in the village they'd just left, or was she just visiting? Which, if she was just visiting, would lead to what she did in Leh and whether she knew of a quiet, comfortable hotel to stay in? Her recommendation had been spot-on in Manali. But it was as though they'd reverted to strangers again; her beads and whatever was passing through her mind occupying her completely.

Road sign: 'Be Mister Late, not the late Mister.'

Joe sank back in his seat, rested his head against the window, continuing to look out at the stark *Mad Max* country with its Buddhist overlay and accessories. His mind blurred, the hum of the bus growing faint.

He slept, Tensin alternating between watching him and the terrain, her thoughts wandering.

8

Close mountains, steep passes, glaciers, snow and scree, constant reminders of how she survived the crossing to live in Ladakh. Always on these trips – sitting on a padded seat, warm air circulating, passengers sleeping like the Westerner next to her, their possessions stowed away dry and safe – frightening images of her distant past loomed up in her mind, followed by screams and slogans, the turmoil and suffering of those horror-filled times. So clear still, that in elapsed time it could all have happened just days earlier rather than almost sixty years earlier when she was a child.

As the men were going into the fields, children to school, from down the road they came. Maybe two hundred or more strung out, both Chinese and Tibetans in khaki clothes with red armbands and Mao hats, cymbals clashing, drums beating, red flags stretching in the breeze. Few of them looked old enough to head a household, shave or be mothers or fathers, until men appeared with placards hanging from strands of rope around their bowed necks, hands bound, cone-like hats strapped on their heads.

Scattering the ducks and pigs and dogs, they entered the village chanting, 'May Mao live for a hundred years!' Other chants followed, but were made up of words no one appeared to understand, some shaking their heads and looking dumbfounded at those around them.

'Abandon the four olds: culture, customs, habits and thought!'

'Purge the revisionists!'

'Eliminate enemies of the Revolution!'

The mob stopped, lowered their flags, slapped and spat on their captives. From metal beams, planks and steps a platform was assembled, loudspeakers hung either side. Two men mounted it: one Chinese, the other Tibetan. As the Chinese man spoke, the Tibetan translated.

'Today you do not work. Today you are to go into your houses and bring out old clothing and books, especially those about religion.' He pointed. 'Take them into the field and pile them there, then step back and sit. Today your village will turn warm, cleansing itself of the past and beginning its new future. And as it does, you are to listen to me very carefully. Now go and do as instructed.'

Everything changed after that day. Chinese ruled like angry bosses, close and loud. By day, villagers worked. At night, they gathered. She lay awake sometimes listening to young voices urging resistance, elders urging patience, though the talking always went on longer than she could stay awake for. Then one night she was woken and told to get up. Her mother dressed her warmly and quickly, and like her brothers, given a small pack to carry.

'What's happening?' she asked.

'We must leave and go to a new place.'

A truck came. They piled in, squeezing between other families wrapped in thick *chuba*s* and gripping large packs.

At dawn, they were deposited atop a steep, windy road amongst rock and ice with strangers from another truck. Soon everyone started walking.

'Where?' she asked her mother after a while, tired and distraught.

'India.'

The birthplace of the Buddha; though for her it seemed like the moon.

Guided by a big man with long plaited hair (how had he avoided the Chinese who forbade such hair?) and a small turquoise in his ear, they didn't arrive that first day, or the next, and all she could remember after that was hanging on to her mother's hand, tired and scared and trying to keep up; or being strapped to her father's chest after her feet started to bleed and looking up and seeing vultures circling and mountains disappearing into clouds then reappearing again. At night under

* Traditional Tibetan coats

rock overhangs or in caves spiked with ice, they shared tea and noodles with so many others then slept cold on the hard rock.

The next morning, waking up in the freezing, grey air to more tea and noodles, and continuing along the narrow path flanked by man-size boulders: wind blowing sleet in their faces; plastic sheets being pulled out to cover the children first then the old. Going over their first snowbound pass, she saw a frozen body just metres away.

And then there was Lobsang the young monk, who one day, after her mother got sick, took her hand, though monks were not supposed to, and day after cold, slow-passing day watched over her, encouraging her on. And how, after her mother improved, he remained close, helping with those who needed it most. Lobsang, a close friend still and now the Rinpoche* at Stakna, a place they would soon be passing.

Tenzin let her beads rest and glanced over at the hairy, rosy-skin man, looking as though he'd just lifted his head out of a bucket of snow. She watched as he slept, head against the window, nasty scratch on the back of his hand, his mouth opening like a baby's about to nipple-feed.

She couldn't remember the last time she'd sat so close to a Westerner; not in the past two years anyway, since the time she last visited her second daughter, year-old grandson and son-in-law in Mandi, then her husband's bird burial site on the outcrop above their former village.

Her mind went back to earlier in the day. Up there with the vultures circling, their shadows passing over her as though measuring her nutrient value as she sat and talked to them and later prayed. Thirty-year life spans, so most were probably the same ones that had devoured Nawang's remains, transporting his soul to heaven to await reincarnation. Little doubt in her mind the vultures would be transporting hers also before too much longer, though in the changing times, as traditions loosened, the vultures could run out of corpses after they did.

Born and raised in Tibet's Larung Valley, where bird burial was widely practised, Tenzin, like her husband, clung to tradition while rejoicing in their freedom after fleeing Western Tibet at separate times

* An honorific for an abbot of a Tibetan Buddhist monastery

for Ladakh: religious freedoms certainly, but everyday ones too. Like growing her hair and arranging her plait, every night unravelling it, combing it out and in the morning braiding it again. In Tibet, the Chinese cut plaits off while threatening to do more to the 'offenders' if they were caught wearing them again. Certainly a familiarity with fear was instilled in Tibetans from a young age under Chinese rule; fear many devout Tibetans tried to overcome by continuing to live and worship as they always had. And when prevented, they either capitulated, or set themselves alight, or were imprisoned or fled south, as she, Nawang, Lobsang and so many others had done.

Born in Ladakh, her children thought and did things differently, like not insisting their mother live with one or the other of them, though she eventually did; like attending nearby school for adults to learn Hindi and English (and help their mother with those languages, as it turned out); like writing on keyboards instead of by hand, like disregarding so many centuries-old customs. For example, Dorje, her son-in-law, chose cremation for his father, which most Tibetans seemed to be doing now, instead of bird burial. And 'now' was a significant word for the young, as fixated as they were with it. Still, importantly, both her son and daughter maintained their core Buddhist beliefs, with large pictures of the Dalai Lama on their walls, as well as on what was called desktop on their computer screens. And that was the greater comfort, even though she knew nothing about computers.

However, she'd not be admiring those pictures, nor lighting incense sticks or filling monks' begging bowls at dawn with her family again, unless in Leh. Next time she left Leh, she'd informed her second daughter, it would be as a corpse. She was getting too old for bus travel, although Seventy-three next to her seemed comfortable enough with such travel. Still, if her daughter or village relatives wanted to see her again, they would have to come to her: though no more than two at a time, please; three being the maximum capacity of her Leh room.

The warmth was having an effect on her too; weariness setting in. Had

Seventy-three been Nawang, she'd have leaned into him, placed her head on his shoulder and dozed off. And certainly Seventy-three had enough shoulder space for that to happen; enough for one and a half of her heads in fact.

Instead, Tenzin clasped her beads and moved them again between forefinger and thumb, her thoughts continuing to travel between Mandi and Leh.

*

Joe woke to the bus thumping over another bridge lined in prayer flags, his head pressed against the window, his left ear against a woolly head riding his shoulder, a hand – cool and dry – covering his own. For a few disoriented seconds, they were Sara's, before a careful sidelong glance took in the bead necklace on the old woman's lap as she breathed slow and deep in sleep. He smiled, thinking, so it's come to this, unconscious intimacy with a total stranger. Yet, for a moment, it served to remind him of what he didn't have back home.

Staying as still as possible, he looked out the window at the glacier-melt river and an old monk in a maroon robe and orange undershirt, his shaved head jutting vulture-like from his shoulders. He was standing on the stony riverbank staring at the aqua water, and as the bus passed above him, the monk rotated his walking stick and twisted around to get a better view. Had Joe been closer to him he might have used his free hand to wave.

Beyond the river, angled sunlight struck more stone walls and a squat stone house, the slightly sloping roof covered in thatch. Bordered by rows of poplars starting to lose their leaves, the fields ran almost to the river, with just the last of a few cabbages showing above ground. Joe looked back at the monk, who was still turned towards the bus, before he disappeared as they veered and climbed, the fading sun flaring off a whitewashed monastery high up on a craggy knoll.

Road sign: 'Live for your today. Drive for your tomorrow.'

Darkness set in, stars emerging and brightening, Leh's lights spot-

135

ting on and edging closer. He kept his eyes on them, his mind urging the bus onwards, until diverted by a full moon rising out of the mountains and casting pale lemony light over the land.

Tenzin's head shifted, fell off Joe's shoulder and rebounded up like a basketball. She turned and looked at him with dazed eyes that widened in alarm. 'Oh – sorry,' she exclaimed, before realising where her hand was. She jerked it away, unfolding herself in an instant and scooting towards the aisle, rubbing her face and shaking her head to more fully wake up. 'Sorry,' she repeated.

Joe held his smile back. 'Don't be. I haven't had a head on my shoulder for longer than I can remember. Forgotten what it felt like.' A case of acute touch starvation, he almost added, but didn't.

As she pressed her offending hand between her knees as though punishing it, Joe allowed himself a small grin, taking note again of just how good he felt. It had been his best day by far since leaving Moonah, his spirits riding as high as the moonlit peaks that surrounded them.

9

Kargil, Ladakh

His thin, angular face frowning in response, eyebrows meeting across his beaky nose yet again, Waqas Commando fixed Sameer with a crow's glare, as though deciding whether the question was worth his time answering. 'It's called Stinger,' he said sharply, like Sameer was proving a burden to him. He lifted up what appeared to be a massive rifle with a wide barrel, large trigger and tubular sight mechanism and propped it on his right shoulder. Leaning back, right eye hard in behind the sight, he took aim at an imaginary target on the ceiling and squeezed the trigger, blurting, 'Whooosh. Watch it. Watch it tracking until KABOOM.' His voice softened. 'And the plane and all its infidel soldiers fall in burning pieces to the ground. *Maashallah.* As Allah wills.'

He lowered the launcher to the floor with a clunk and eyed Sameer as a hardened instructor would a slow learner, with frustration and intimidation. 'Now comes the part where you use your brain, see if it's up to the task.' He pointed to two large hessian bags on the floor. 'I will teach you to disassemble the Stinger and stow its parts in the bags there, then we'll reassemble. Watch closely, for before we leave here, separately, you will be required to disassemble and reassemble the launcher in no more time than you do your Kalashnikov. *Alhamdulilah.* Praise be to God.'

'*Alhamdulilah.*' Sameer repeated, glancing around the room that contained just faded, threadbare blankets and a few scarred furnishings. Like room, like his sombre mood, as he met his self-appointed overseer's concentrated stare again.

'Not that long from playing at your mother's feet from the look of you. I'm assuming you can disassemble and assemble a Kalashnikov.'

'I can.'

'Quickly?'

'Yes.' He'd never seen the black-bearded, rough-looking Waqas Commando before today, so assumed he was from Jaish-e Muhammad, or maybe some other group operating from deep inside Pakistan, like the most honoured Lashkar-e-Toiba.

'Then keep your eyes on me and listen closely while I take this God-pampered weapon apart and...'

The muezzin in the nearby mosque interrupted with his last call to prayer for the day.

Turning in the direction they thought Mecca to be, they unfurled their prayer mats together as supposed equals, stood with faces stilled in concentration, bowed, prostrated themselves faces to the floor and leant back on their knees and prayed.

10

There in the Stakna valley, Tibetan monks owned no watches because the only ones cheap enough for them to buy were made in China. And even if given such watches, they'd serve as reminders of spiritual repression and genocide and the monks would not wear them. Instead, they relied on the clock of the sun and shadows to steer their days, and only the change of seasons marked the passing of calendar time.

So, as Lobsang squinted up at the Leh bus passing overhead and disappearing, engine noise lingering, he calculated about three more weeks left before the high mountain road closed and traffic dwindled to nothing. He thought too that his great friend Tenzin might have been on that bus, as she was due back about now, give or take a week or two. If she were on it, she'd most likely visit him soon with gifts of spices and dried fruit and a lively and lengthy account of how her trip went. She was like a sister and added much to his life: had done ever since they first met as young monk and child fleeing Tibet a long time ago.

Except for the gurgling river in front of him, everything had gone still again before two black-billed magpies called from rock to rock – 'deet, deet', like muffled bells. Lobsang listened and thought how, in the process of becoming monks, novices learned to value their ears here as much as their eyes. At least he had. After all, a tenet of Buddhism was accommodating oneself with what the natural world had to offer, and the essence of that was communion through thought, meditation and ritual, and, importantly, mastery of the inner self. No foot in each world for him. Even away from the monastery, he doted on solitude and silence as much as anyone he'd ever known; and that the more he used his ears, the more solitary he became and the more affection he felt for the valley's wonderfully cloistered surroundings. Of course, he was imperfectly human. Chinese tourists, in particular, could still grate on his nerves as well as his ears. But that weakness he would only ever admit to himself before taking measures to deal with it.

He looked around. Rarely did he feel more grateful for being alive than when he was standing by this river, the only person, and, other than the birds and river, the only source of movement in sight. Yet, when a vehicle did pass on the road, an occasional military plane or helicopter overhead, the spot served also as a brief window on the outside world, reminding him of just how important solitude and silence and being a Stakna monk were to him. He simply could not imagine what living inside or outside the Buddha anywhere else in the world would be like. Was a monk ever more suited to being what he was, where he was? He smiled. While indulgently dwelling on himself again, he took pleasure in answering that.

The birds flew off and he shifted his eyes to the suspension bridge's prayer flags, there to keep the river from getting angry. Many were in a bad state and would have to be replaced. As he considered the steps in doing that, memory intervened and he dropped his gaze to where the river narrowed beside a long mosaic of exposed stones. For almost forty years, that was where he'd forded the river, even during the spring thaw when the river was at its deepest and fastest; the same years he carried a small ladder and scaled the bridge when flags needed replacing. Nowadays, as abbot, he just reported what needed to be done; arranged delivery and watched younger monks or volunteer villagers do the work. One of the benefits of nearing the end of a life was doing less with body and more with tongue – a thought that brought a smile.

A convoy of army trucks rumbled over the bridge. The Mountain Tamers, he assumed, on their way to Leh for their last remaining parachute drops for the year. The whole operation was clearly visible from the monastery, perched atop a hillock, and Lobsang rarely missed a drop, sometimes watching from there, sometimes from the river bank.

The trucks went the way of the bus, soothing silence enforcing its right to be heard again.

He tended to stay longer by the river – eastern boundary of his warm season existence – when the days started to shorten and the chill of winter approached. In the seven months of deep cold, he'd rarely venture away from the monastery grounds, staying close to the burning coals in his cubicle room or bundled up with monks in the courtyard and the shrine rooms doing what he'd done for so long there: meditating, chanting prayers and sacred texts, turning prayer wheels and completing chores; and, for an hour each night, studying and conversing in Hindi and English with two monks young enough to be his grandsons had he not turned his back on the secular world as a youth. Much as he relished solitude and silence, there was a part of him that had always been interested in the outside world; at least those places not dominated by despotism and aggression. And, alert to the monastery's summer visitors and the opportunities to eavesdrop and try to understand and speak with them in simple sentences, language study maintained that interest. Nowadays, other than listening to Tenzin's latest news, no other person-to-person activity provided him with more enjoyment.

Though summers had changed a lot in the past decade or so, as more and more walkers and climbers, and, surprisingly for him at first, monastery visitors came from so many different places. When he was young, every family would send a son away to be a monk. Now it seemed every family wanted their sons to be tourist guides.

For an old abbot who had only visited two towns in his lifetime – Shiquanhe in western Tibet and Leh, thirty kilometres to the northeast – Lobsang found it difficult to curtail his interest in visitors. 'Tourist season', he'd heard people say in English, and that's how he'd come to think of the Ladakhi summer. And with each passing year, he looked forward to it more than ever. Though, as a dampener, during the past few seasons, more and more groups of Chinese tourists, speaking loudly and continually, were coming to Stakna. Though no fault of theirs, hearing them carried him back to those nightmare years over half a century earlier.

All of it, the cold, forbidding cell and torture room, concrete floor and walls, the large pulley with rope and hook hanging down from a ceiling beam had been replaced by open sky and a small courtyard packed with soldiers and prisoners, many of them lamas and monks. The Chinese officer and his interpreter sat behind a long table. When the officer shouted, so too did the interpreter.

'Bow your head!'

From behind he was pushed and nearly fell off the stool.

'Why have you been arrested?'

Second day of imprisonment, interrogation and the same questions, the same script: 'A poster.'

'A poster you stuck to the side of a shop while taking part in a re-bellion.'

Rebellion? It will be written and spoken as such in the Chinese-made history of controlling ignorance and violence in demented Tibet.

'Who was on the poster?'

'We are six million Tibetans. Our leader is His Holiness the Dalai Lama.'

'I thought my kindness yesterday and a night spent in your cell thinking and learning would improve your effort, but no.' The officer nodded and he was baton-struck from behind – shoulder, neck and shoulder again – then prodded, electric shocks streaking through his back. He fell to the ground screaming, guards immediately lifting him back onto the stool.

'The wolf in monk's robes is what you meant to say, isn't it? Let's see if the baton has improved your memory. Who masterminded the protest?'

He stayed quiet.

The officer mimed drinking out of a cup. A guard brought over a steaming pot and a drinking cup and poured tea for the officer then went behind Lobsang and poured the rest of the pot's contents over his bare arms and hands. Again he screamed.

'I thought you'd lost your voice. But no, you haven't. So tell me, what is religion?'

Tears ran down his face. 'May the sun of the Buddha's teachings rise again.'

The officer pointed to the concrete room and he was hoisted from the stool and marched inside. In the middle of the room, a rope with a hook on the end was lowered to waist level. He was punched in the belly and, as he doubled over, the hook was attached to the handcuffs that bound his wrists behind him. He knew from stories told what was coming next and that the pain of the last few minutes would be as nothing compared to being hoisted off the ground, hanging in the air, shoulders wrenched from their sockets.

A guard pulled. The rope tightened and lifted, and from his feet he went to his toes in horror. The guard stopped, tied off the rope and left the room with the others.

'How long?' he shouted to the guard, but there was no one there to interpret. He chanted scripture, sweating, striving for detachment.

From the courtyard, vaguely, he heard another interrogation starting; one that conformed to Chinese script.

'Why have you been arrested?'

'For protesting.'

'Who planned the protest?'

'The Dalai Lama.'

'Who?'

'The wolf in monk's clothes.'

'What type of life did he lead when he was here in China?'

'He was a pleasure-loving lama who loved women, jewels and money.'

'What is religion?'

'A poison used by capitalists to oppress people.'

'And monks, lamas and monasteries, what are they?'

'Tools for exploitation.'

'Why should the Communist Party be thanked and honoured by all Tibetan Chinese?'

'It liberated us and gave us food, clothes, houses and land. It is

kinder to us than our own mother and father. May it live for the next
ten thousand years.'

'Good. An extra allowance of food for this prisoner.'

And just where would that come from? Lobsang thought. Food was
brought in by family or friends. Otherwise there was just watery broth
and the grass of summer.

Soon another interrogation, followed by another. The worsening
pain in his legs and feet challenged his ability to concentrate, until, incredibly, in answer to 'Who planned the protest?' he heard the start of
the Tibetan Underground song being sung

> Do not mourn people of Tibet.
> Independence will surely be ours.
> Remember our sun people of Tibet.
> Remember His Holiness and…

Cut short, there came the screams of a man in sudden agony, as the
Chinese, terrified of Tibetan dreams of liberation, brutalised anyone
who dared speak, much less sang, of it.

Guards entered the room and lowered and unhooked him. In his
place went the bleeding, semi-conscious monk, Gyen Yongzin, from a
monastery near his own. Though he would never see Gyen Yongzin
again, he would never forget his screams as he was lifted a metre off the
ground, and spent the rest of the afternoon hanging by his wrists bound
behind his back, shoulders dislocated, everything else silenced by the
horror of his suffering.

'Guilty of opposing the Communist Party and the Motherland,'
came the verdict the next day, after he'd passed the morning's interrogation session.

He would take his punishment, bide his time.

The officer-judge glared invincibility at him then continued. 'Sentence cut in half by you finally learning what needs to be learned and
said.'

Three years spent in a tiny, cold cell: damp dirt floor, rough brick walls, straw sleeping mat on a raised platform, toilet bucket in the corner, always the smell of fresh mud and sewage. The only relief came from family or friends bringing in tsampa, butter and fried biscuits. The pattern established from day one: labouring in ankle irons – during winter like rings of ice glued to his skin – attending meetings and being ordered to recite assigned thoughts of Chairman Mao. Afterwards, back in his cell, he placed his blistered, work-swollen hands on the cold concrete, meditated, prayed and chanted in whispers, before scratching at lice and sleeping sporadically.

At struggle meetings, prisoners were told of Tibetan refugees living as beggars in India and that the Dalai Lama would soon be returned to China. And that under the huge blue sky there was no escape from the Party.

At thamzing sessions, forced denunciations of anyone non-Chinese in positions of authority took place. As leg-ironed prisoners watched, victims – often lamas – were brought before Chinese officers accused of being counter-revolutionaries: 'You are criminals, oppressors, enemies of the people. You have sucked the blood of the poor.' They were beaten, prodded, spat and urinated on; sometimes pulled into the small room and strung up by their wrists for half an hour, just their toes touching the ground.

Released, finally; his parents dead, his sister reported to be living close to His Holiness in Dharamsala, India, he returned for a few days and nights to his destroyed monastery: a maze of shattered hallways and rooms, the inner courtyard surrounded by crumpled walls. Still, there was enough left to provide him with a semblance of warm season shelter. After his prison experience, the ruins bordered on comfort.

Tibetan proverb: 'When you have known the scorpion, you look on the frog as divine.'

He returned to his village and eventually was ready to attempt a March crossing into India, with others from his village joining a neighbouring group that included young Tenzin. Just one thing remained for him to do. Locating a Tibetan flag or a poster of His Holiness had proved impossible, but an uncle unearthed a magazine with a photo of His Holiness in it.

On a moonless night, he cut the photo out and, with paint can and thin brush in hand, walked cautiously along the outskirts of town. Arriving at the Chinese-owned shop where he'd once stuck a poster, he glued the photo to the back wall, and in black paint wrote, 'Do not succumb to the wolves of China. Continue to dream this, Tibetans. Under the blue skies of India, living in freedom close to the Dalai Lama, the brightest sun of our hearts. And read this, Chinese occupiers. For ten thousand years may you, Mao Tse Tung and Communist Party dogs grovel in Hell.' Hardly monk-appropriate words and actions, he knew that. By prayer and penance – prostrating himself daily and doing one more than the day before – he would try to make amends for his spiteful act: though probably not until he was safe across the border.

Returning birds whistled, warbled and trilled, ending Lobsang's reverie. He took off his sandals and stepped a little unsteadily into the water, stones shifting underfoot. When up to his knees, he stopped and braced himself against the current, propping his chin above his hands on the end of his stick. A thinking monk's pose, he thought of it, smiling. And he did think and listen and watch the water swirl around his legs like the turning of the wheel: snow to river to sea to snow again. No better example of impermanence than a flowing river. The moment you looked at it, that moment had passed. He recalled asking himself in earlier years, 'Can you fall in love with a river?' Not a question he'd have admitted to asking. Not that he needed to, though; he'd long known the answer.

When he could no longer feel his feet and legs, he stepped carefully back onto dry land feeling cleaner, refreshed again in the passing of things.

Recently, a group of Chinese chased after him in the parking space below the monastery. In his haste and awkwardness, he tripped over his walking stick and landed in a pod of dzo dung. The Chinese, laughing like they'd never witnessed anything funnier, helped him back up and clustered around, pointing cameras fastened to the end of sticks. As they went shoulder-to-shoulder with him and took photo after photo, it was all he could do to stand there dung-soiled, grazed and bleeding and pretend not to understand them; all the while counting the seconds until they finished their frantic posing and left him alone.

Afterwards, in complete silence, he washed himself and his robe and hung it up in the courtyard to dry. He worked a prayer wheel. He went inside and lit candles. He prayed, prostrated, chanted scripture and let time pass – as it would with or without him. Later, he walked to the river, disrobed and waded in waist deep, his peace restored.

Lobsang first saw a person killed when he was just a boy, and the person shot was his neighbour and the shooter was a Han Chinese soldier from a contingent of green-uniformed soldiers who swept into their village one morning like the wind. Three of the soldiers peeled off and went into the fields. They dug a trench while the others searched and found his neighbour among the animals below his house. Through an interpreter, they accused him of destroying property at Shiquanhe and being an 'enemy of the people', whatever that meant. Leaning into his mother, her arm tightly around him, Lobsang struggled to grasp what was happening as the soldiers tied the neighbour's hands behind his back, blindfolded him and marched him into the fields. He was forced to kneel beside the trench and a soldier stepped up and shot him with a pistol. Those soldiers, he soon realised, knew nothing of Tibetan customs. After the Chinese left, men recovered the corpse, filled in the trench and carried the corpse to the top of the nearby hill where vultures were congregating.

From that morning on, Lobsang refused to enter the fields.

After completing village school, boys had a choice: work the family plot or enter a monastery. At ten, he became a novice monk.

Negativity had no place in monastery life. But for him – or at least for his rebellious pulse and blood pressure – encountering Chinese on monastery grounds was like being targeted by a lightning strike or an avalanche. He had long ago escaped them, but lately they had reappeared. In his youth, when his legs were strong, he would have quickly distanced himself from them. Nowadays, he could but plant his walking stick on the ground, swing his useless left leg – broken in a fall – around in a small semicircle and hobble away like the semi-cripple he was.

He did so now, moving towards the embrace of his monastery, thinking that one good thing about the onset of the frozen cold was that he would not have to listen to Chinese again for at least another seven months. After a few steps, he stopped, disappointed with himself. A lifetime as a monk and abbot committed to study, meditation and prayer and still there were times – arguably too many times – when self-mastery failed him.

He squinted at the mountains, river and intense blue sky – stillness of stone, flowing water, descending sun. There were innumerable ways of being alive. Only one was right for him: the way of the Buddha – a Buddha who would not in the slightest have concerned himself with avoiding Chinese, or anyone else who visited him.

Reprimand over, gratitude fortified him again. He started the slow ascent back home.

11

Moonlight fell like liquid on Leh. Yes, but in the bedlam outside who was noticing? And it did nothing to ease Joe's discomfort as he looked out on Leh's main road snarled in smoke-belching trucks and battered Suzuki minivans, brakes screeching, horns blaring. Stiff-bodied and suddenly aware of how tired he was, he followed Tenzin down the aisle and out amongst other passengers on the side of the road waiting for their bags.

Collection took a while. At one point, Tensin squeezed his arm as if testing it for quality. 'Are you married, Seventy-three?' she asked, giving him a look like he topped her evening's interest list.

'I was. My wife died.'

'So does my husband.' Rolling onto her toes now for extra height, she asked, 'Where you stay in Leh?'

Another reason for his discomfort. He looked around for hotel signs. 'I don't know. Can you recommend somewhere? Your last recommendation was perfect.'

'Soon winter come. Many hotels close end of month.'

'Two weeks here will be enough.'

'Good time for cheap room. Almost no tourist.' She spotted her bag and went for it and for a moment Joe thought he might be seeing the last of her. But she returned, opened her bag and took out a biro and small pad of paper and, as though running an accommodation agency, asked how much he wanted to spend for a room. She waited, staring up at him as he calculated.

'No more than three thousand rupees a night.' He saw his bag, excused himself and retrieved it.

When he was beside her again, she stopped writing and said, 'My nephew, Dorje, work at Gomang Hotel. I think now he is dair. Good place. Tourist time costs five thousand a night for room, but now not so much.' She tore the paper from the pad. 'For Dorje, or person at counter. Also name of store where I work.' She lifted the paper up to his eyes and pointed. 'See, I write it at bottom. Read and say to me, "Singay General Store".'

In the dappled moon-shadow, without his glasses, he struggled, but managed to say it, at least to her nodding satisfaction.

'Good.' She handed him the paper. 'Store in main square. Big sign. Easy to find. And you can buy all what you want. I give you special price.'

He thanked her.

'You welcome, snowman.'

'Joe.'

She said his name, rewarded him with a smile and pointed to her head. 'From far away, I always see you – daytime, night-time, all time. Stay here.' She stepped out onto the road. 'You need taxi.' She walked, raising her right arm and emitting a series of high-pitched whistles capable of ringing the ears of anyone next to her.

A minivan from an ensemble of them pulled up next to her.

She had a quick word to the driver then waved Joe over. 'Taxi take you. Driver name Ahchook. He is my friend and I tell him where to go. Say to me one time more, "Singay General Store".'

He did, laughing, and got in next to the driver.

'And snowman, you good to be on bus with.'

He pointed to himself. 'Joe. Say to me "Joe".'

'To me Joe.' She gave him a finger wave and a grin as the van shot back into the traffic.

*

While she was in Mandi, Geshe told her about huge buildings in Delhi that had... She'd forgotten the name, but they were like huge containers that could carry many people up from one level to another with just the push of a button.

From the narrow, night-quiet laneway, she trudged up the concrete stairwell clinging to that thought as well as the railing, head drooping, her steps slow; each one counted. How she wished a whatever-they-were-called could be installed here, quickly, before the approaching winter when freezing wind blew half the year and the steps turned slippery with ice.

On the third landing, she fumbled with the loose door handle, finally getting it to work, and entered a dim corridor, shoes and boots lined up on both sides. She added her boots and went through the red hessian entryway to her room, the dim bulb light on casting shadows. She dropped her pack and sat wearily on her bed, refamiliarising herself with home. That same hessian material covered her small window that leaked in sunlight only during the warm months. Between her bed and the window were her cushioned chair under a shelf with polished stones from a creek, a clock, an old radio and a framed picture of His Holiness the Dalai Lama – his smiling face and bowed shoulders the features. Beside the chair was a table with a two-burner gas cooker on top and underneath it a big wooden box containing a gas canister, bucket, a few cans of food and kitchen items – porcelain bowls, mugs, a ladle and utensils included. She'd brought them from the village after Nawang's bird burial. They were to help provide her with a modicum of independence, but with the exception of heating water for tea, she couldn't remember when last she used them. Her place during meals, her daughter-in-law insisted, was with them helping in the kitchen and at the table in the main room. She'd always thought well of Norba's judgement in a wife.

To the right of her window were a broom, dirt pan and five shelves assembled with concrete bricks and lengths of scrap wood that Norba had collected from a friend's building site. On the top shelf sat her small granite Buddha – the focus for her prayers – a small mirror, hairbrush and framed photo of her, Nawang and Norba sitting on an inner courtyard step of the Stakna Gompa* five years earlier. Nawang had just told a joke, so they were still laughing when Lobsang took the photo on

* Gompa: monastery

Norba's phone. She recalled Lobsang laughing too, which he spent considerable time doing, at least around them. Under Norba's instruction, it was the first time he'd used a photo-taking phone and he was not one to disguise his enjoyment.

Folded clothes, storybooks, English language books and assorted items filled her other shelves: everything in its place and easy to find.

Footsteps approached and Ashi came in as brisk and energetic as ever. She bent and embraced her awkwardly before sitting down and gazing intently into her face.

Tenzin knew what was coming.

'Now… Do you have your phone?' Ashi asked.

'At the bottom of my pack.'

Norba slipped in and stood just inside the room. He scowled and gave her a steely look. 'And so you walked?'

'After the bus, I needed my legs to move.' The actress in her smiled broadly. 'And here I am, safe and exercised and content inside my room with my family after surviving the trip. I have not brought any stories to give you nightmares.' She extended her arms towards her son. 'So come here and hug your mother and welcome her back. She's missed you both.' In truth, there were days she was enjoying the change so much she'd barely given them a thought.

Norba did as he was told and they sat, three on the bed. 'So how are my sister and her family?' he asked. 'I see no cuts or bruises on your face, so it appears you did nothing to challenge their views of India, its politics and future.'

Tenzin's sigh was that of someone grown weary to the haggling ways of the world. 'Such a long trip home just to be teased.' She smacked his hand. 'Your sister and family are well, and of course, if I had been cut or bruised, I would have waited until I was fully healed before presenting myself back to you.' She sighed again as though suffering and moved a few beads through thumb and forefinger before a mischievous thought entered her mind. 'But I am tired, so I will tell you everything about them tomorrow. For now, I only have the energy to tell you about a big man from Australia, like a hairy, white bear, I slept with coming home.'

*

From the centre of town up a steep, windy road they went, on either side small hotels and mostly closed cafés and travel offices and more dogs than people.

'First time in Leh, sir?'

'Yes.'

'Leh very nice, very peaceful.'

'Not like Srinagar in the west, eh?'

'No, not like. Srinagar once my home, but no tourists dair because much fighting, many soldiers. Business no good. People angry. Very bad.'

Two kilometres maybe before they turned right onto a gravel road beside a low-running creek. They slowed to walking pace, bumping and swaying past long rock walls before drawing up to a high metal gate that opened as if it had eyes. Into the compound they went and stopped outside the three-storey, brightly lit white hotel with honey-coloured wooden-framed windows, an outdoor courtyard and wide third-floor balcony. To Joe, it looked expensive, and deserted.

'Fifty rupee, please, sir,' the driver said.

All of a dollar, so Joe gave him a hundred.

'Thank you, sir.' He took the money with one hand, gave Joe his card with the other. 'That is me on card, Ahchook Spalzang, and mobile number. Wherever you go, I give you best price.'

Joe slipped the card into his jacket pocket. 'Good to know, thank you.'

As if there to greet royalty, an attendant in a Nehru suit – black trousers and black, collarless jacket over a white shirt – appeared, opened his door, stepped back and executed a little bow. 'Welcome to da Gomang, sir.' He grabbed Joe's bag, hoiked it over his shoulder and jogged up steps and in through the entryway.

Entering the place in pursuit, Joe slowed, smacked dumbstruck by a most appealing sight. Every bit of wall space, floor-to-ceiling, was covered in shelved paperbacks, Mostly English language novels, but a few Hindi ones too – to be read, provide extra insulation perhaps and keep a man like himself lounging in the attached reading room until seasonal lock-up time, surely. He did a quick calculation of his finances. Five thousand a night was doable if he was careful with other expenses. Looking around a second time, he could think of his future only in terms of a two-week stay here. Other places, other time frames faded: first this, then whatever. He stepped up to the reception desk.

'Welcome to da Gomang, sir,' the desk clerk said, his wide-smiling welcome like he'd just grown new teeth. 'First time in Ladakh?'

'First time, yes. Tell me – is this the Gomang Hotel or Library?'

Around the corners too, leading to rooms on his left, to the dining room on his right, more shelved books.

'For our guests, both.' He gestured toward the dining room. 'And restaurant too.'

'I'm looking for a room and I'd like it to be here,' Joe said, handing the desk clerk Tenzin's note.

As the clerk read the note, Joe tried to gauge whether his wrinkled brow and pursed lips indicated positive thought or petulance.

The clerk raised his eyes, his smile not returning. 'My name is Dorje. Can I explain to you, sir? If my aunt had her way, da Gomang Hotel would pay its guests to stay here.'

'I understand.' He was suddenly aware of his predicament, that the taxi had gone and it was a long, dark walk back down to the closest ho-tels. 'What is your normal rate?' he asked.

'But if she finds out you have not got a special price, well…'

'You'll hear about it?'

The clerk nodded an answer. 'And everyone in the family too… Dair is our smallest room on the third floor in a corner farthest from da stairs. How long, sir, will you be in Leh?'

'I hope two weeks. I believe you close at the end of the month.'

'We do, sir. Would two thousand five hundred rupees a night with breakfast be satisfactory?'

With the night gone coal-black, the access road unlit, a younger Joe might have leapt over the counter and embraced the man, such was his relief. 'Indeed it would be.' Joe extended his hand and Dorje, a little surprised, clasped it. 'Joe Broughton's my name. I'm looking forward to my stay here more than I've looked forward to anything in a long time.' In such an expansive mood, even as an old crock past his bedtime, he could still bang away at the hyperbole bell.

'If you see my aunt again, will you say dat to her too, please.' Dorje handed him a metal key.

*

Joe ate in the company of five empty tables, a vegetarian menu and a scampering Dorje who, in between stints at the reception desk, took his order and visited the kitchen, served, checked on him and took his bag to his room.

Labouring up the wide staircase to his room took Joe almost as much time as eating his yellow dhal, veg biryani and naan bread, and drinking his lemon tea. Four or five slow steps sent him breathless. Hand clasped to the banister, heart machine-gunning away, he rested before plodding on again. On the second and third tiled floors, he explored, touching the surface of things: framed Ladakhi landscape photos, more shelves and books replete with modern heat pumps, drop-down lighting and long, cushy sofas and beige armchairs arranged around a carved table and looking suspiciously ornamental through lack of use.

If anyone else was staying at the Gomang, they'd either gone to sleep, died or were out searching for the non-existent nightlife.

He found his room and inserted the metal key without difficulty. Yes, the room was small, in terms of pokey bathroom and single-shelf storage space, but everything worked and he and his girls could have slept stretched out together in the near wall-to-wall bed and still been left with rollover room. And no need for his headlamp, as a string-pull reading lamp over the bed was the strongest lighting in the room. Two windows: the bigger one affording a view of the lit-up Shanti Gompa on the crest of a hill behind the hotel, two lines of coloured lights criss-crossing the top of it. The smaller window overlooked the access road, a rare piece of flat ground, and what appeared to be a building site. All up, a fine spot to lay one's weary body.

Having checked out the neighbourhood by night, he lasted only minutes more and slept as if rehearsing for death before waking to multiple alarm clocks: a cow bellowing, dogs barking in competition like they were the majority residents, soon joined by the call-to-prayer echoing over the town. Once all that died away, he drifted off again before roosters crowed notice of dawn, the morning's first motor scooters puttered past at regular intervals and a helicopter whirred overhead, circling as though fugitive-spotting. Early morning Moonah was a tomb compared to this place, but only early morning before Moonah hit its noisy stride, while Leh quietened.

Grey light edged the curtains. A van chugged past, followed by kids chortling away. He stretched, breathing in the morning, his internal engine slow to start. The cat scratch itched on the back of his hand. He'd have to soak it and find a Band-Aid or two, hopefully at the bottom of his washbag.

He rolled himself out of bed finally, left elbow and knee stiff and sore from the fall but functioning. He pushed back the curtains to meet a bright, long-shadowed morning; the Shanti Gompa bathed in sunshine that, as he watched, moved sharp-edged like a creeping yellow tide down the hill. Already, people were zigzagging up the long run of cement steps to do whatever they do at such a time. From the other window, he looked down at large mounds of sand and rock by the side of the road. The spiritual and the practical on show either side; just pick your window.

Work had already begun; workers assembling makeshift scaffolding, pickaxing the rock and shovelling the bits with sand into sacks for others to carry on their backs to the building site twenty metres away. Minutes later came the handsawing of wood and hammering of nails. No power tools, backhoes or cement mixers. Obviously no trade unions or work safety regulations to adhere to either. Down there, pure third-world labouring: dawn to dusk, physically taxing and surely dangerous.

He stepped back and stretched his bones with a few back bends and toe touches, which got no further than his knees, but that was a start. Flexibility would improve as the day wore on, he told himself, and he should not overtax his injured and yet-to-acclimatise parts.

On his way to breakfast, he diverted to the open balcony, the sky out there like an upturned sea, He donned his sunnies and skirted past closed umbrellas, plastic chairs, sun lounges and tubs of geraniums to stand at the balustrade viewing the snow peaks to his right secreted in shadow or illuminated suddenly, blindingly, as sun broke through cloud. To those peaks, proof to Tibetans of God's existence, he muttered, 'If you're up there, heavenly overseer – Buddha, Christ, Brahma, Mohammed or Yahweh – just a quick thank you for getting me here', the sounds of motor scooters, hammering and birdsong providing accompaniment.

Leh was directly below. To his left, jumbled rock, scree and squat, flat-face houses butted into the side of the nearest hill as if sprouting from the earth. It was as though the scree had moulded into organised rock and builders (half-mountain goat, surely) had sunk timbers, constructed rock walls and fitted them with iron roofs topped in straw. Over every roof were prayer flags catching the wind, the prayers dispatched into the laneways and up the hills and mountains at night. Prayers first and foremost to keep the earth settled and still, Joe presumed, for town planning bodies, building codes and insurance consultants had clearly avoided Leh. So what chance survival if an earthquake hit? Live in hope and believe in the power of those multitudinous flags, his view from the balcony told him.

The word 'hope' stayed with him. When young, with life a series of endless possibilities, he'd brimmed over with hopes and dreams. Now in old mugginshood he had few. But as he sat down in old man comfort pose, legs stretched out, arms folded across his chest, he felt a tingling tremor of happiness in having realised one of his few remaining hopes. It hadn't been easy, but tick – best-case scenario accomplished. He was now overlooking exactly what he'd set his mind on in Moonah. And it was even better than he'd pictured it. So, master traveller, he commended himself, well done and how to celebrate? In the past, the dividend for small wins was a dram of the Dew in a frosted glass. For bigger achievements – like standing on this balcony absorbing all that he was – a glass of champagne seemed appropriate. However, well out of champers range, it would have to be a pot of tea with perhaps a sneak tote of the Dew just for tradition's sake.

But first another look around. He stood and went to the balustrade; poplars next to him glittery in the sun and just starting to shed their leaves provided a privacy screen. Below and to his right, more construction; the chop and clink of pickaxes working to dig foundations and ditches along the side of the road. Underneath, in the hotel courtyard of largely tables and chairs precisely positioned under raised umbrellas, two employees chatted, though Joe could barely hear them. Where else in India would hotel workers chat so quietly? Further evidence of a hotel built and arranged with the reading traveller in mind – especially the late summer ones. Still no sign of other quests; and to make the place even more alluring, a king's breakfast awaited him. Hands propped on the balustrade, he basked in the sunlight and surroundings for just a bit longer, taking everything in a third time and nodding his head in satisfaction before turning and heading below.

On his way down, he decided to check for any correspondence in the computer room. And with a little help from the counter staff of one, with his PhD in IT, he got into his account and opened up the single email.

Hi Dad

So impressed, also relieved, to get your email from Delhi. Evidence that you're adjusting well to the 21st century, the mastering of Worldwide Web use on foreign computers just another one of your many achievements. Soon Facebook, Instagram, Twitter and more will be part your digital arsenal. I'll be coming to you for advice, which will be easier to do once I'm home.

I'm not sure you were all that impressed though having to take a bus over the Himalayas. I've not heard of anyone doing that before, so I'm aching to hear how it went. And don't put me off, Dad. Debrief in full. I'd like at least an hour's worth of deep analysis, the triumphs and disappointments, accounts of interesting passengers and, not least, how you'd rate the trip on a one-to-ten scale for those a bit south of middle age. Okay? Do that and Tom and I will cook Christmas dinner for you in three months' time. Or, if your oven is having an off-day (why would I think that?), we'll order it in with help and advice from Uber Eats.

So, from mountains to desert.

Hottest month of the year here as we breathe in the heat and duck for the shade, the sun an additional challenge for our refugees, not that they need any more. But there are now fewer here than at any time since I arrived. Some have decided to return to the rubble of their villages now that the fighting is mostly over, though who knows what's ahead. Some have decided to strike out for Lebanon or Turkey with little more than what they can carry. And others, mostly from the elderly, die, though the young too have died in numbers. But we've saved lots and lots of people and that's what must be kept at the forefront of our minds, especially when we see children dying from wounds or diseases they've carried for long distances in getting here. Medical staff must keep their emotions in check, we were constantly being told in training.

Good luck with that, Brandy.

Anyway, brighten up, girl, the situation here has improved and that's one of the main things I wanted to tell you. The other is that hardened traditionalist Tom wants to get married, and he's made it apparent I'm the one he's got in mind. I've hinted at an inkling of interest (though I've had no complaints with the present arrangement) if (1) his cooking (or Uber-ordering) skills are up to scratch on Christmas Day and (2) he's prepared to ask your permission. At heart, I guess I'm a traditionalist too. Anyway, I thought you could use some lead-in time to prepare your answer.

So settle yourself in for some more foreign keyboard mastery in keeping me up to date, okay?

Oh, last thought: don't go all weird on me up in those Himalayan clouds – you know, hang out too long with the Buddha, join a monastery, take up residency in a cave. At Xmas, I fully expect you to be as I've always known you, unchanged.

Miss you and love you, Dad, as I know you know, and as I'll keep telling you until I can happily drop the 'miss you' bit (only that bit) at Christmas.

Lol, Brandy

An email that felt like an embrace. Best on ground – wherever the ground – she was, always. Yet he was pleased he could turn the computer off and disengage. That some sort of late-model Orwellian whizz-bang surveillance screen wouldn't be teleported the four thousand kilometres north-east in three and a half seconds to hover over him drone-like showing Brandy, hands on hips, impatiently awaiting his reply. Though he had to admit the small screen in front of him had served its purpose well, as he anticipated the hotel's breakfast would, while he thought over what he would include in his reply and what he wouldn't.

In the cosy dining room full of choices: omelettes, dhal baht, pancakes, bread for toasting, pastries, baked beans, juice, coffee and tea and a guest-occupied table among five empty ones, Joe wished the middle-aged Indian couple a good morning and they reciprocated. He sat at the opposite end from them, served himself and ate; low murmurs from the couple the only sound. In his email response, he would include Manali, landscape, villages and Tenzin. Certainly an account of his climb up the scree slope at five thousand metres would get coverage. Cat attack and what can happen up high without altitude tablets would not.

He returned to the computer room, logged in and feeling feisty, started his reply.

My Brandy,

cc – Mark Zuckerberg.

Yes, take note, Mark at Facebook and all the rest of you digital demi-gods, I, Joseph Broughton, epitome of 21st century man and digitalisation merging in complete harmony, am hereby launched.

So, favourite daughter, what a top email from you, so much to savour, inquire about (i.e., Uber Eats) and reply to. But first and most importantly, with regard to what this Tom bloke has 'got in mind', it's been my experience that the merits of prospective life partners can best be judged by what sort of flowers they give you before any relationship-advancing questions. Daisies are at the floral summit for such occasions. I know that you're working in a desert, but daisies are easily grown from seed and nurtured with little water. Yellow is the colour that signposts the most successful relationships. Don't ask me how I know, I just do.

Also a passage from a poem, or a relevant literary quote on the day would add gravitas to the occasion.

One last thing you might like to think about as well is, should this Tom bloke earn a bonus point or two for determination and stoicism by kneeling down in the midday sun before the yellow daisy handover, while you, of course, remain in the shade?

Do let me know if these essentials have been included, okay? Because they could influence my Xmas answer.

In a fine frame of mind after his burst of email creativity, he went on to eclipse his effort of the previous day by adding three lines detailing his happiness for her Tom plans and their upcoming Christmas together and thirty more lines about what she mostly asked for. To end the longest email in the history of the Broughton family, he added,

And finally, regarding me going 'weird', it's too late for the warning. Old age has its expectations and weirdness is first and foremost, especially in a place like Ladakh. Views and the quiet inside monastery walls here I suspect are unmatched anywhere in Moonah. So I'll send you a photo once I've been shaved and shorn, fitted in my burgundy robe and shown to my cell – or possibly my cave: though I'll have to borrow a phone or camera to record the transformation, won't I?

Anyway, best sign off before some Nigerian scam merchant keyboards in on me and my riches – the rotters.

Love you.

Dad

It took him ninety finger-cramping minutes – well, for the first draft anyway. Subsequent deletions and additions took him another forty minutes, with Tenzin getting a bit more favourable commentary.

Climbing the staircase again, punctuated with rest stops, he decided against the thousand-step climb to the Shanti Gompa that day until he had acclimatised sufficiently to get up the twenty-one to his room without a coronary alarm going off in his chest.

He donned his sunnies and returned to the balcony, arranged a sun lounge and umbrella to his liking and sat and stretched out.

It was a morning of travelling clouds and intermittent sun. He followed certain of those clouds on parts of their journeys before noticing how the inflammation had spread across his hand and tiny blisters formed. He went to his room, ran hot water in the sink and soaped and soaked and dried the wound. Then he searched his washbag for first-aid cream and Band-Aids amongst the broken combs, used cake of soap, withered toothbrush, rolled-up tube of toothpaste and a vast array of tablets for every degree of pain and range of ailment diagnosed in the annals of Himalayan medical history, surely. But no cream, no Band-Aids.

Still, not a problem: more an excuse to activate his lazy bones and nose around the neighbourhood and middle of town to get a feel for Leh. That good Tibetan woman, Tenzin, worked at a store named… Memory blackout: probably the only ailment he didn't have a tablet for. She did say something about the main part of town, so seeing the name should prompt recall, surely. Failing that, he could get a piece of cardboard and write, 'I'm looking for Tenzin, aged sixty-six, works in a general store. Can you help me?' If nothing else, a hairy, sign-waving septuagenarian might provide a photo op for the camera-actives down there looking for something more than monasteries, monks, nuns, rock dwellings and the dry sweep of hills and mountains to immortalise.

So he left the Gomang in his sunnies and new Trekker footwear, descending past the low-running creek, taxi vans and rumbling Royal Enfield motorbikes, the mangy dogs, scrawny cats, drying cowpats and two young women going uphill bent double under huge bundles of sticks. Other than shop-tight sections of the road, every spot had a view of mountains. A few travel offices and cafés were open, the proprietors sitting outside on plastic stools working their phones before greeting Joe and encouraging him to support their businesses.

'Just walking now, maybe later,' he responded to all.

A few other tourists and cows and yaks with jangling bells around their necks were about. But nothing and no one was in a hurry.

The road flattened out some and merged with the main road. Turning left, he came to the main square with its wide, mosaic-tiled thoroughfare and elevated planters providing seating around marigolds, geraniums and small shrubs with tiny yellow flowers. Conjoined three-storey buildings with interior staircases lined the square either side, mostly made up of food, gemstone and tourist shops, Tibetan refugee stalls and Kashmir pashmina wool outlets. Rows of men, a couple twirling prayer wheels, sat cross-legged, backs perched against shops. Next to them were open sacks of nuts and spices and fruits for sale.

A few tourists strolled gawking curiosity – as he did – at the sleeping dogs, long-scarfed women, pairs of younger men linked by little fingers, old monks with walking sticks, bearded Muslims and a policeman or two, the great mix prompting Joe into mind-singing mode: 'What we need is a great big melting pot, big enough, big enough to take the world and all it's got…' On the left, opposite the thoroughfare's ninety-degree right turn, was a mosque with dirt tracks running up both sides.

He veered off up past the mosque, ducking into a laneway dim as dusk and just wide enough for two people to pass shoulder-to-shoulder. The temperature dropped and, despite taking off his sunnies, it took a while for his eyes to adjust to the semi-darkness enveloping the concrete residential blocks and low-roofed workshops, poky tea shops and stalls – the items for sale small and useful, nothing valuable. Everything close: tinkling chimes, tethered goats, eateries with tarpaulins laced overhead, dogs nosing about the gutters for scraps, plucked chooks and slabs of fly-attracting carcasses hanging from steel hooks.

Dogs loped past him, ribs standing out like cages, distended teats swinging. A tangle of power lines hung low and heavy overhead. Eliminate those lines and it was a laneway frozen in another time.

How people could live and work sunless and freezing in such tight quarters during the long months of winter, Joe could not begin to imagine. In some ways, the laneway reminded him of Dickens's London: the cramped, colourless spaces, the smells and dimness and lingering smoke; the poor and unlovely in their worn clothes, wrinkled old men and women with blackened teeth and ulcers on their shins. Though, of course, no evidence of the pickpockets, shivs and gin bottles from Dickens's time. No hint of angst or aggression either: the Ladakhis smiling up at him, their eyes lingering, a few greeting him with 'Namaste'.

'Gazed at like a comet,' he muttered to himself, trying to recall the Shakespeare play that line came from.

He wended his way onwards before a retaining wall broken into blocks of rubble appeared, allowing in welcomed sunlight. In front of it, a barely serviceable wooden bench pulled him up. He stood considering it then went and pushed down hard on its planks, testing. Satisfied with its strength and position, he sat and looked out at small shops lining a steeply rising road that ended at an entryway to the ancient nine-storey Leh Royal Palace, far and away the biggest structure in town. Like the Shanti Gompa, on his to-do list as well once the workings of his heart and lungs reached high altitude standard.

After a while, he swung around to face the laneway. Across from him a gaunt-faced old woman – haggard eyes, hollowed-out cheeks so sunken they almost touched one another – sat on the ground, legs folded, begging bowl and a small, bony dog curled up asleep in front of her. No extended hand, no voice seeking his attention; just lips chewing on an empty mouth. He went over and dropped ten rupees into her empty bowl, the dog lifting an eyelid. As he backed away, she picked herself up, money in hand, and shuffled off twenty metres or so and entered an eatery. Minutes later, she returned holding a plastic spoon, a piece of naan bread and a small food container. She smiled her thanks to him, her right eye clouded and blue, nails yellow and cracked. She sat back down and started spooning what looked to be potato or cauliflower soup into her mouth. After three spoonfuls, she cupped her hand, poured broth into it and encouraged the dog to lick it up. Then the two alternated – a spoonful for her, a palm-full for the dog. Soup finished, the woman tore the naan bread into two pieces to be shared. That finished, woman and dog reverted to their original poses.

Joe looked upward in the direction of the Gomang, his refuge from upheaval still in the direct path of the morning sun. He reached into his pocket for a twenty-rupee bill and went over and dropped it into the woman's bowl. Slow-eyed, she gazed up showing a gap-toothed smile and muttered something to him – maybe a thank you, maybe an invitation to visit the site more regularly.

Orientation done for the day, how was he to find his way back to the main square? He walked along to the eatery and sat outside on a plastic chair at a plastic table. He ordered, and in minutes a girl server, in faded jeans and a 'Make Me Happy' pullover, placed a bowl of cauliflower soup, a plate of naan bread, a small brass pot of Tibetan tea and a white cup in front of him. He met the server's eyes and asked for directions.

She smiled her understanding. 'Lost?'

'Yes.'

'Go.' She pointed with her chin to the crossroad ahead then finger-pointed right. 'Follow to big road. Go right and follow. Soon market place and after that main square.'

He thanked her and looked down at a fly succumbing in his soup. Extracting and flicking it away, he polished off the soup and every bit of the bread, washing it and anything else down with the tea.

An hour later, after entering the main square again from the opposite end, he sat down on the first elevated planter he came to and stretched his legs out. As he scanned his surroundings, a big, red-lettered sign over an open door caught his attention. It said, 'Singay General Store'.

12

Joe noticed first the lack of promotional colour and the dim lighting that failed to penetrate beyond the first rows of canned goods stacked shoe to eye level along aisles of shelf board. At the front counter were two customers having their purchases tallied up on an old-style cash register, its ringing and opening and closing drawer taking him back to the stores of his Popsicle and Bazooka bubble gum-buying days.

A middle-aged man stood stony-faced behind the register minding the counter. Customers gone, his laser point stare fixed on Joe, like Joe was fifteen again and about to fill his pockets with shoplifted goods. Hardly the sort of welcoming look he had grown accustomed to in Ladakh.

Joe glanced away and scanned the first two aisles again before approaching the man and saying, 'I'm looking for a woman named Tenzin. I believe she works here.'

The man nodded slowly without breaking his eye grip. 'Yes: my mother.' He eyed him a bit longer. 'You are da man who slept with her?'

'What?'

'On the bus from Manali.' He held his stern pose for seconds before his face broke into a smile. 'Good for you to do. Thank you.'

'I…' Joe fell short of words.

Son of Tenzin pointed towards the last aisle. 'At end.'

Joe spotted her sitting on an upturned bucket, shawl around her shoulders, mumbling something amongst the canned goods she was restocking on the bottom shelf. He wondered about her hearing as he drew close, before she looked up and smiled. 'Ah, Seventy-three – you find.'

'Yes – hello.'

'*Dhrog-po*. Boyfriend?' the son asked, looking in from the start of the aisle.

She grinned. '*Hon*. Yes.'

'*Jegs*. Hairy.' With that he returned to the counter.

Tenzin clasped her knees, lifted herself up and pointed outside, saying, 'Come, come. We talk private.'

They went out and sat together on the same elevated planter Joe had occupied earlier.

'Hotel good?' she asked to break the silence.

'Yes, very good. Thank you for recommending it.' He felt a bit flushed, like a flu bug was after him and put it down to the day's high-altitude exercise.

Two monks, two nuns, assorted women in headscarves and an old man walking an old bicycle passed.

'Happy in Leh?'

'Yes, very happy.' He couldn't remember ever being in a place that took him so far away from what he knew. But he kept that to himself.

More people passed.

'Want to buy food?'

'No – maybe later. Right now I just want to buy some first aid cream and Band-Aids for this.' He showed her the back of his hand.

She stared, mouth open, concern crinkling her face. 'Ohhh.' She took his hand and placed it on her lap. 'Cat?' she asked, her fingers stroking the inflamed edges.

'Yes.'

'No good.'

'Infected, I think.'

'Stay here, I come back.'

And in half a minute she did, though empty-handed. 'Come, come, we go.'

'Where?'

'Hospital not far.'

'I'm not going to any hospital.' He stood, about to make his way back into the Singay, when she grabbed his wrist and leaned back as though holding an escaping animal in check.

She scowled up at him. 'You do not know Leh, Seventy-three. I know Leh. Many cats in Leh and when people have bad cat scratch must go to hospital. If not go, maybe hand fall off. So I take you!'

'What she say is true,' son of Tenzin said, again monitoring them chaperone-like outside the store entrance.

'Do you sell first aid cream and Band-Aids?'

He shook his head. 'Not dis morning.

As Joe vented his frustration, Tenzin tugged him towards the road. Arriving, and breathing hard from the effort, she glanced out at the traffic, As if summoned by thought, a taxi van pulled up. Who should stick his head out of the open window but Ahchook Spalzang, obviously Tensin's go-to driver.

*

Sonam Norbu Hospital, a long, drab, two-storey concrete building, was accessed via a potholed road running through a field of rubble, as though an aerial bombardment had decimated the hospital's outer perimeter, but left its core intact.

They stopped outside the entry and Tenzin turned to Joe in the back seat and asked, 'You have money?'

The ride was about half the distance of the previous night's to the Gomang, but Joe took out a hundred-rupee note anyway and handed it to her.

'No, no – thousand.'

Twenty dollars for less than a kilometre? Was she charging an escort fee as well? Scowling, he handed over what she asked for and she immediately passed it to Ahchook, along with a monologue Joe had no hope of understanding.

'We go,' she said, turning to him again.

They got out and entered the building. Tottering along at surprising speed, she led him through a lengthy corridor to a counter in a waiting area half-filled with locals; a number of babies and children in their parents' arms. Tenzin pointed and Joe sat in a plastic chair while she went up to the counter. On the wall to his left, in red block letters, 'LEPROSY

CAN BE CURED', as per a sign on the Delhi to Leh road. He glanced around at those sitting nearby for any telltale signs.

Half a minute later, Tenzin returned. 'You have money for hospital?'

'I have travel insurance. If they need money, I think I'll have to go to a bank. I've been told Leh has ATM machines.'

'Two hundred rupee you have?'

'Ah.' Four dollars: rivalling Indian army medical ward rates. He took the money out of his wallet, handed it over and Tenzin returned to the counter.

She paid and filled out forms. He signed them. They turned and she grabbed his wrist and led him further down the corridor like he'd lost half his brain and needed guidance. He looked back at those waiting. Was the money a bribe for preferential treatment?

'What about these people?' he asked.

'Different for Westerners. Is okay. Come, come.'

He disengaged her hand from his wrist and followed, passing open rooms with patients, a dark room taken up with a 1950s model X-ray machine, another room with a partially attached door. They turned and entered a room with an examination table and a middle-aged Indian woman behind a desk reading a magazine. Tenzin indicated where Joe should sit on the table, and he did. She talked to the woman briefly before the woman got up, grabbed a tray, soap and small towel, filled the tray with water from a sagging sink semi-detached from the wall and went to Joe and started washing his hand and dabbing at the infection. Something he was perfectly capable of doing for himself.

Minutes later ,Ahchook entered the room carrying two cellophane bags. Plopping them down next to Joe, he took out a roll of toilet paper, four canned drinks, straws and four pastries from one bag. From the other emerged a hundred-rupee note, tablets and an ampoule that he passed to the woman.

She pulled out a syringe from her front pocket, ripped the packaging off, and inserted the needle into the ampoule, drawing out the contents.

'Which arm?' she asked Joe, smiling up at him for the first time, like this was measuring up to be the best part of her day.

'What is it?' he asked, feeling he had every right to know.

'Antibiotic. Also tablets one time a day.' She pointed.

Ahchook took off with the toilet paper.

'What hand you write?' Tenzin asked.

'Left.'

She unbuttoned his right sleeve, but got no further, as Joe took over and rolled the sleeve up.

The woman jerked the needle into his arm then went back to her magazine, placing the syringe on her lap.

Ahchook returned and nodded to Tenzin, who said to Joe. 'Toilet good now. You can use if want. Must stay in hospital for twenty minutes. If you okay den, we go.' She popped open the drinks and took one of them and a pastry to the desk, saying, '*Dhanyavaad.* Thank you.'

'*Tujay-chay.* Thank you,' came the response.

'What is this, a BYO hospital?' Joe asked, realising in the next instant the acronym might as well have been uttered in Pitjantjatjara. 'A bring your own food, medicine and toilet paper hospital – yes?'

With the other two eating and drinking, only Tenzin paid any attention to him. 'Yes.'

'Right. That's decided then.' His next email to Brandy was already in the planning stage. However bad the Jordanian refugee camp medical facility was… That would be the essence of the first sentence. It could prove a lengthy email from there on.

Half an hour later, as Ahchook was driving them up the road to the Gomang, Tenzin turned to Joe in the back seat, her flexibility surprising, and pointing to his bandaged hand, insisted that he rest and get better. As well, Dorje was working at the hotel and she would tell him to take care of Joe.

'Fifty rupee, please,' Ahchook said outside the hotel. Joe passed over a hundred and, as Tenzin got out and entered the hotel, Ahchook asked, 'What you do tomorrow?'

'Tomorrow I want to walk and do things around here. But the next day there are gompas I'd like to…'

'Yes, I can do,' Ahchook interjected.

'…visit: Stakna, Hemis, Thiksay and maybe Shey if there is time.'

Tenzin returned and said at the window, 'Dorje know.'

Joe nodded. Once inside, he'd issue a-need-for-care disclaimer. 'What's the price for the four gompa tour?' he asked Ahchook.

'Two thousand and I bring for you cold water and candy. Must go early. Maybe eight o'clock.'

'Good. Day after tomorrow I'll be right here.' Climbing out, Joe conked his head on the door frame.

'Ohhh,' Tenzin voiced, offering him a helpful hand.

'Day after tomorrow, better you in da front seat,' Ahchook suggested.

Joe ignored both comments and Tenzin's hand, but did say, with some sincerity, 'Thank you for your help, Tenzin. You're a good person to share a taxivan and hospital room with.'

Tenzin laughed, surely recalling when they last exchanged such sentiments.

'And,' Joe continued, 'I'll visit your store tomorrow and buy a few things, including first aid cream and Band-Aids that I suspect will be back on the shelves.'

Tenzin produced a catlike smile, got back into the taxi van and, as it pulled away, immediately started jabbering away to Ahchook.

The next morning, Joe descended into town, toured the laneways and had lunch. He went into the Singay General Store and, without asking for help, quickly found first aid cream and Band-Aids prominently displayed in the first aisle.

'My mother not here now,' son of Tensin said while ringing up his purchases.

'Say hello to her for me.'

'Anything more from you I can say?'

'No, no more, thank you.' He forced a courtesy smile of sorts.

With just a single brief stop, he climbed the road back up to the Gomang and sat down in the computer room feeling good about himself. Forefingers ready, he started.

My Brandy

Let me tell you about a BYO hospital I experienced yesterday, that in your role as an international nurse specialising in remote area treatment, you need to avoid at all costs…

Fifty-seven lines and two hours and ten minutes out of his afternoon by the time he finished: a new record. He decided a pot of tea on the balcony would be an appropriate way to celebrate another stint of foreign keyboard mastery.

13

'*Alhamdulillah*. Praise be to God,' he whispered, thinking about the two nights spent in Kargil, the second one so much better after Waqas Commando left that day for Leh. The town was mostly a Muslim one, everywhere pictures of the Boxer Prophet, and it was so much drier and poorer than Srinagar. Depressing was the best word for the place, made more so by Waqas Commando with his continual scowl and cutting words. In their small room before Waqas Commando arrived, he'd recalled a friend of the family saying once that whenever he hated anyone he prayed they would be reborn in Kargil. Now Sameer understood why.

The bus wound, climbed and descended, Sameer rarely diverting his eyes from the desolate landscape – bare mountains, bare gravel slopes, bare sandy plains – as if it were leading him into a place where all life ended. And in a sense he supposed it could be, for there had been only the sketchiest mention of him returning to Hizb base camp following the mission.

He should have felt honoured and excited at being given a role in… well, whatever the mission was. But at this stage he felt only puzzlement. All he knew was the mission had something to do with a plane, a shoulder-bearing missile launcher and the fact that his relationship with Waqas Commando was less than comradely.

Dented road sign: 'Be gentle on my curves.'

He could appreciate that in tightly packed Srinagar with its thousands of Indian soldiers, dozens of roadblocks, its armoured vehicles and constant surveillance, carrying missile launcher parts around undetected would be near impossible – never mind being able to assemble the weapon and use it there.

Yet since departing Srinagar he'd not seen a single Indian soldier, military vehicle or encampment and he couldn't help but sense a small change coming over him. Far away as he was from Hizb training and fighting, and without his comrades, heavily armed Indian soldiers or the Srinagar Muslim community close by to fuel his hatred of Indians, it was as though a small crack had opened up inside him allowing a little of his long-simmering hatred to leak out.

And there was something else that concerned him, though he thought that it shouldn't and that it could only be through a weakness in him – pride most likely – that it did. Yes, he'd been sternly instructed and ordered forcefully to do things by Hizb commanders. That was the norm. Yet he'd also been trusted and given weighty responsibility, like leading the four now-martyred fighters overnight to the Indian military base outside Srinagar to stage their momentous attack. For which he'd been praised and feted. He was a proven freedom fighter – not a child, not a servant – and should have been treated as one by every Kashmiri freedom fighter, including Waqas Commando.

In Srinagar, as well as being given a key and directions to the Kargil meeting place, his mosque contact said he'd be given more information on arrival. But other than being entrusted with a bag of launcher parts, given Stinger instruction (more performance than instruction) and an address and approximate time for their next meeting in Leh, nothing else had been provided. He knew little more now than he did on leaving Srinagar.

Maybe Waqas Commando felt he was too young and inexperienced to be trusted with the details; that if he were apprehended, imprisoned, tortured, he could utter only the words Stinger and Waqas Commando, which he knew to be an alias. Or maybe Waqas Commando didn't know the details himself and wouldn't until he was contacted in Leh. But at least whoever was in charge of the mission should have trusted Sameer enough to tell him why he wasn't being told. Working together, supporting and depending on each other called for no less. Mutual trust, mutual dependence had been drilled into them in Hizb camp.

Admittedly, this was only his second mission and he wasn't the most patient of young Kashmiris in Kashmir, was he? Things would change once he was in Leh, he told himself, though not wholly convinced they would.

The bus continued to labour up hills and rattle and screech going down them. In the back row bench seat on his own, as invisible as he could make himself, Sameer stared out the window, periodically glancing around at nearby passengers to determine if anyone resembling an authority figure had suddenly risen from the bus floor, escaped from someone's baggage or slipped in through a half-opened window. Yes, he acknowledged to himself, such thoughts were an indication of how jumpy he was. Strange country, strange people, strange thoughts and sharing a room with a person he hardly knew and didn't particularly like maintained his edginess. The way he was feeling, he even fantasised about a passenger coming to the back and handing him a message, or whispering to him that the mission had been aborted. Or he'd simply be told to get off at the next town and return to Hizb camp.

If he survived and there was a next time, he vowed, he'd request a mission where he knew the fighters first-hand and given responsibility right from the start. 'Alhamdulillah,' he whispered again to reconfirm why he was on that bus. To assist him to do that, he turned his mind back to Ifra tapping the cobblestones with her walking stick, to Parvais the moment he was shotgunned. Then forward again to Hizb training camp.

Three instructors alternated raising large, framed photos of martyred Hizb fighters into the air and shouting questions.

'Where are our martyrs?'

'Alongside each of us!'

'What do our martyrs do?'

'Make demands on each of us!'

'Louder!'

They screamed the answer again.

'What's their most important demand?'

'Rid Kashmir of the Indian occupiers!'

'How?'

'Worship Allah, train and fight to the death, achieving martyrdom in his name!'

The self-sacrifice of martyrdom immortalised on video and adored by fellow freedom fighters. As his eyes followed the dry, lumpy terrain of this nowhere place, he worked to close his mind to everything outside the vague construct of the mission.

*

At the front of the bus, immediately behind the driver, Anil Hanif leaned forward and reached into the bag at his feet. He took out a mirror and held it up as if to groom his leathery face, the thick black bush of his beard. But instead he turned and angled the mirror so it took in the shoulders and head of the operative at the back of the bus. Fresh-faced, the operative looked barely old enough to sprout his first whiskers – anywhere. More like a boy provided with money enough for food and transport and given the freedom to visit family in the next town for a day or two. Hizb casualties must be running high, he thought.

Road sign: 'Three enemies of the road: liquor, speed and overload.'

Anil Hanif returned the mirror to the bag and rummaged around for his packet of nuts. Not there, so he must have left it in his bag riding in storage below, the nuts the only item in it approved for public viewing and consumption. Despite himself, that thought made him smile. He glanced at his watch then fixed his eyes on the landscape, as empty and boring as always. Still, he just had to get to Leh for things to liven up and his view of Ladakh to improve considerably.

14

Another perfect morning in Joe's comfort mountains and his short-term goal (as if long-term didn't figure in his plans any more) was simple: avoid entering a medical facility for the third time in four days. The odds were heavily in his favour. As a rest and recovery home, the Go-mang was unsurpassed – at least for his requirements.

The previous afternoon, after finishing in the computer room, he'd climbed the entire staircase with just a single three-second stop. He'd scoured one of the bookshelves for familiar titles then gone out and sat on the balcony and watched the neighbourhood in action: hand tool construction of a house, future Gavaskars and Tendulkars playing cricket with stacked concrete bricks on building site loan serving as wickets, women in long scarves, loose pants and double aprons sauntering past, and further along girls washing clothes in the creek.

Reading, eyeing the mountains and being offered pots of tea with biscuits rounded out his afternoon. A case of Aus-American-Canadian impersonating Brit colonialist – in pose and tea drinking, if not in breeding, age and clothing style. If he'd been any more relaxed, he might have melted away like the *Wizard of Oz's* Wicked Witch of the West, the scariest character ever from his childhood, and to this day still capable of turning his dreams into nightmares, though not last night.

Without surprise, he'd slept like the dead he was soon destined to join and woke to the call of prayer at complete peace with himself and the world, his hand near painless, curtains open, the sunlight moving in a line down Shanti Gompa hill. Following ablutions, with sunlight pouring through the window, he dressed and loaded up his daypack, anxious to eat, for the hotel gates to open, for Ahchook to drive in and the tour of back-road gompas to begin.

As he passed reception on his way to breakfast, a voice rang out, 'Good morning, Mr Brewton.'

He stopped and turned as a middle-aged, bushy-bearded man emerged from the back room and stood at the reception counter emitting an air of courtly courtesy. 'Did you have a pleasant night?' he asked.

'Yes, very pleasant, thank you. Is Dorje not here?'

'No, Mr Brewton. For two days go then come back.'

'Oh, right. Well then, please call me Joe. Dorje does.' He approached the counter hand extended.

They shook hands and the man said, 'My name is Anil. Anything at all I can do for you please let me know.'

'I will.'

'Enjoy your breakfast.'

'I intend to.'

When the gates opened, Joe took the person in Ahchook's front passenger seat to be a new arrival to the hotel. Only when Ahchook drew up alongside him did Joe get a clear view of Tenzin offering up a grin, a wave and quick to announce herself, 'Good morning, Seventy-three.'

For a few moments, he questioned the value of becoming the accidental friend of such a headstrong woman. 'Joe,' he reminded her.

'Joe. I have friend monk at Stakna Gompa. So if okay I go with you?' In the next instant, she was out opening the back door and pulling herself into the seat next to two bags of food. 'Better you sit in front so don't break head.'

What choice did he have? He did as instructed and they were off over descending laneways, avoiding ambling cows, and out to the main road – all curves and low stone walls – passing a large military compound that turned Joe's head, the memory of Travindra Singh filling his mind. He checked his daypack to see if he'd brought his Diomex. He had.

Tenzin leaned forward, reached for his hand and from a cellophane bag poured nuts into his palm. When Ahchook extended a palm, she did the same for him.

On the outskirts of town they crossed the Indus River and into the bowl of the river plain they went.

First road sign instruction for the day: 'Short cut make short your life'.

Then, a few hundred metres further along, 'Leprosy is curable.' Could anyone anywhere in Ladakh be unaware of that?

More rock walls on the left ran along the road. A scattering of stone hut-houses – small doors, single slit windows, insulating straw, prayer flags over the roofs – appeared between river and road.

Whatever the outcome of global climate change, one thing was certain. The Ladakhi Rural Fire Brigade would remain, along with those of the Sahara, Arabian and Gobi Desert brigades, the least active in the world. Joe had not seen a tree since leaving town. From the treeless terrain, via the rear-view mirror, he watched Tenzin working her beads, pulling on her braids, eyes peering upwards at the slants and jutting slopes on their right. When she spotted him in the mirror, she waved, beaming a smile.

Road sign: 'Shooting stone slide area. Stop, look, go.'

They ignored 'stop', obeyed 'look' and 'go' as close-up mountain dimness consumed them, like they were moving through half a tunnel.

After a kilometre or so, the mountain eased back allowing sunlight to trickle through the gaps again, and they emerged with 'shooting stones' still to avoid. Without slowing, Ahcook swerved around them with stunt driver precision, and on a straight course again pointed left to a knoll in the middle of the river plain. Atop the knoll a paper-white gompa perched on a cradle of rock against the clean blue sky.

'Stakna,' Ahchook said.

Joe recalled seeing it from the other side while on the Leh bus and mentioned that to Ahchook.

They turned off and bumped along a rutted track past another small stone house, a most unlikely sign on its window declaring 'No smoking, unless you're on fire', as if the place was a venue for remote gatherings and entertainment. What was it with the Ladakhis' penchant for signs?

They climbed a series of gravel switchbacks to a parking area below the gompa. Two other taxivans were there, the drivers sitting at the wheels. Ahchook went in between them, turned off the engine and opted to stay for a drivers' chat.

Carrying the food bags, Joe and Tenzin got out and walked the rest of the way up to a viewing area overlooking the broad sweep of river plain. Intersecting the plain and running parallel to the Manali-Leh Road was the Indus River sparkling in the sunlight. Beyond the road, between steeply spurred hills, a thumb-shaped basin rose gently upwards. At the centre of the basin, yellow smoke funnelled up from what had to be a flare, the breeze blowing the smoke parallel with the Leh Road.

Just four other people at the viewing site: two Indian women, an old man whirring a small prayer wheel around and around in his hand and a young, bearded man in traditional Muslim Shalwar Kameez clothes and rounded Pakul cap snapping photos with his phone of the fine view.

Tenzin grabbed Joe's hand, turned it palm up and from a cellophane bag shook a handful of dried apricots into it, then into her own. They munched together, viewing what the others were.

Out of the open sky came the hum then rumble of a C-130 military transport plane. It passed overhead, banked into the breeze and when over the basin a dozen paratroopers dropped from its belly at quick intervals, chutes opening. On landing, they gathered up their chutes and, weapons in hand, sprinted to an embankment, dropped down and started shooting at something only they were aware of: the 'rat-ta-tat, rat-ta-tat, rat-ta-tat...' echoing over the plain.

Another C-130 roared over, banked and dropped a dozen more paratroopers into the 'battle' zone.

Minutes later, 'victory' achieved, the shooting stopped and the soldiers congregated around a single figure. Troop-transport trucks arrived. The soldiers boarded. The trucks departed and all fell silent again.

'War games – not something I'd have expected to witness from a monastery,' Joe said, still a bit stunned by it all.

Unusually, Tenzin stayed quiet, a pensive look on her face as she watched a monk with a walking stick hobbling along a path back from the river to the monastery. 'Come, come.' She grabbed the food bags, turned and walked briskly back down the entryway they'd just come up, Joe having a job to stay with her.

At the junction where a second path led down into the valley, Tenzin stopped and turned to Joe. 'My friend come now. His name Lob-sang. You say it?'

He did and she smiled her approval.

A minute or so passed before a leathery old monk – stooped like he was carrying his years on his back – rounded a corner. He struggled up the slope walking stick assisted. When he looked up and spotted Tenzin, he smiled, saying something to her. A second effort brought him along-side them.

There wasn't much of him: thin like the wind could blow him over, which it might have as his left arm was swollen at the elbow and bent as if about to be fitted for a sling. Blood ran down his left calf. His pinched face was a mix of protruding bones and deeply wrinkled skin, augmented with a crooked nose and half-lidded, yellowish eyes.

'Ohhh,' Tenzin exclaimed, eyeing the blood. She said something to Lobsang and with a slow grin he replied.

'Fall,' Tenzin informed Joe before introducing them.

Joe clasped his palms together in front of his face while Lobsang extended a gnarly right hand. They both laughed at the confusion. Joe obliged and shook hands and the three climbed the entranceway towards the courtyard and monks' quarters, Tenzin pointing again to the monk's calf and swollen elbow, their topic of conversation obvious.

Lobsang veered right and stopped outside the first room, a small bench out front. Tenzin put the bags of food on it, the two exchanging more words.

Before opening his door, Lobsang faced Joe and surprised him by speaking in slow English. 'Please excuse me. I wash. My good friend Tenzin show you monastery. And you…' He pointed to the bench '… please come back and talk.'

Joe nodded. 'Yes, okay.'

Across the courtyard, they took their shoes off, and up stone steps they went and entered the monastery's temple room with its white walls and a floor that creaked beneath their weight. On display, an array of drums, vases, gold and plaster Buddhas and junior Buddhas, burning candles with an odour that made his eyes water, racks of smouldering incense sticks, mandalas and sacred texts bound in red and yellow silk. Paintings of gods haloed in flame and demons with knives, bowls of blood and terrible stares hung from the walls; the area hardly a testimony to the virtues of renovation and updating the past. Joe doubted he'd ever been in a place so old, or mustier and dustier.

He asked his tour guide Stakna's age.

'More than you, Seventy-three. Maybe one thousand years more.' She took his wrist and led him to the start of another challenging climb. After a rest stop halfway up, Tenzin held on to Joe's arm and let him do most of the work in getting them to the upper level. While glancing out at the river, road, the dried-up greys and yellows and vast war-game basin on their left, they passed a number of chambers, wooden pillars carved in figureheads, richly coloured paintings of dragons and gods on the walls. They entered the prayer hall. In a small alcove off to the side, a soldier in fatigues knelt chanting and praying quietly, seemingly oblivious to their presence.

Just something else oddly military at Stakna for Joe to ponder.

They browsed the displays and left, continuing along the passageway to the butter lamp offering room, dim and cool in yak butter candle-light and so still it seemed artificial. An avenue of low pews led to an altar with a three-metre gilded Buddha draped in scarlet cloth gazing out at them with an absent smile. On either side of him were incense sticks, bowls of water and rows of butter lamps casting shadows on the walls; the aromas of incense and melted wax strong. Further along statues and glass cabinets that housed frayed texts, yellowing scrolls and plastic flowers under black and white framed photographs of past lamas in ceremonial robes. On the walls above, more framed photos of long-ago monks and statuettes of the Buddha and Tara, the bodhisattva of compassion who had delayed nirvana to assist others towards Buddhahood, her serene face supposedly embodying extreme kindness.

Tenzin paused from guide talking and gave him a look. 'Good to see all da things?'

'Terrific.'

'Not yet see bardos room. But dat room dark, so not good for seeing if not ceremony for dead person dair.'

'You're an excellent guide, Tenzin. In Australia you'd be paid for doing such work.' When she eyed him quizzically, he took out his wallet and pointed to it. 'Money for showing me things, yes?'

Now she understood and shook her head. 'Money box next to monk rooms if want to put.' She grinned, eyes twinkling. 'Or maybe we go eat…together…in Leh sometime.'

'Is this afternoon too soon?'

She took on a decision-making pose, furrowed brow, lips pressed together and watched him, until her face lit up and she answered, 'No, not too soon. Good dis afternoon. I am hungry after exercise.' She took his wrist. 'So come, hurry.'

Always charging off elsewhere she was, like someone else from his deep past. Getting down the flights of steps to the courtyard took nearly as long as touring the rooms and halls. But, other than the soldier and resident monks, no one else was about so they took the steps slowly, as though excessive movement could prompt heart attack, Tenzin counting the steps as they descended.

Next to the bench, Lobsang and Ahchook were sitting together in two plastic chairs talking, the sun on their faces, Lobsang's calf bandaged; his damaged arm wrapped in cloth and cradled on his lap.

Two monks passed with baskets of washing. Smiling without appearing to notice the injured Lobsang, they entered their rooms leaving their doors ajar.

From above came a chorus of laughter, then everything went quiet again.

Tenzin and Joe sat down on the bench and Tenzin immediately started talking to Lobsang. Eyes – at least Tenzin's and Ahchook's – were aimed at the damaged arm, and whatever Tenzin was saying, the nodding Ahchook was agreeing with.

After a minute, Tenzin turned to Joe, her face a picture of frustration. 'What is word in English when somebody need to do something but will not do?'

'Stubborn?'

'Yes dat.' To Lobsang she said, 'You are stubborn.'

Lobsang's face lit up with amusement, like Tensin had just told a good joke. He spoke again in Tibetan or Hindi, or in some other language Joe had no hope of following, though the word 'Mandi', a town on the other side of the Himalayas he'd passed through on the Leh bus, was included. Tenzin replied and proceeded to talk without pause until the praying soldier descended the steps, both Lobsang and Ahchook, as well as Joe, taking notice of him. He carried a long, thin bag strapped to his shoulder, like that favoured by professional snooker players to protect their valuable cues. After the soldier left the grounds, Ahchook got up saying something then followed him out.

Lobsang stood, grimacing a little while refolding his robe around himself and sitting back down again. 'We talk English now?' he asked, looking over at Joe and smiling, though he had to be hurting.

Joe nodded and Lobsang started the questioning by pointing at him. 'Australee, say Tenzin. Good place, Australee?'

Maybe half an hour passed, Lobsang questioning, Joe answering simply, slowly, Tenzin and the returned Ahchook turning first Lobsang's way then Joe's way as though watching a tennis match between the old and slow. Without doubt, it was the longest, most concentrated session of pure talk Joe had engaged in since his travel plans rant at Nima's a fortnight before his departure. And he couldn't recall speaking at length in the close company of more than a single person since Ahmed's funeral day.

Finally Ahchook broke in, asking Joe, 'Go to Hemis today or another day?'

He doubted a second, third or fourth gompa experience anywhere in Ladakh could match Stakna's. Tibetan lama with his tranquil gaze, robust Tibetan/Ladakhi widow and taxi driver of whatever extraction sitting either side of him in the sun, warmth radiating from the walls, occasional tinkle of a bell, rotation of a prayer wheel, a fantasy image of himself as a monk, shorn and shaven as per his email to Brandy, living a life so quiet he didn't need ears. After a quick scan of the courtyard and a passing monk, the Broughton-turned-monk reverie continued: prayer beads clicking in his hand as he walked out to the river, sitting down under the valley's shifting patterns of light, watching for the mountains to move, the sky to smile down on him. In a conflicted, money-mad world, here was his personal Shangri-la 2019, a place entirely devoted to the benefits of high mountain serenity: simplicity, compassion, study and reflection being the prime dot-points of monastery business. And he felt another Wordsworth 'spot of time' moment coming on: a deep, tingling wave of contentment and gratitude for the day and the people he was sharing it with. Had there been accommodation available, he'd have asked Ahchook to return and pick him up later in the week.

'Would another day for the other monasteries be okay?' he asked.

Ahchook's nod and smile indicated it was.

Then, in unison, Ahchook and Tenzin turned to Lobsang, pointing at his arm, gesticulating and imploring him to do something that Joe could only guess at, while the old monk just sat there still as stone, a grin on his face. Talk stopped finally. And Joe, all monk and horizon-struck, engaged again with the silence, knowing he'd ticked another very big box in coming to Stakna. And he asked himself, apart from Nima and Brandy, how long had it been since he'd been in the company of people who just naturally made him feel better?

When did Ahmed die?

'Sorry, Seventy-three, for you not knowing,' Tenzin said, breaking the silence. 'Lobsang arm break, I think. So must go hospital, but he not think dat.' She turned in Lobsang's direction again. 'Stubborn Lob-sang.' And she unleashed another appeal, this time without Ahchook's help.

It got the same response, and all went still again before Lobsang stood and continuing his English, said, 'Thank you my friends for… worry about me. I go now in my room and come back and go to hospital with you.' He looked at Ahchook and said something else.

To which Ahchook replied, and after Lobsang said something else he went into his room and Ahchook said to Joe, 'He ask about pay to go to hospital. I say you pay already for trip. He say thank you.'

'What about paying for the hospital treatment he gets? If he needs money for that, I can help.' Then recalling what his own bill had been, he felt a twinge of embarrassment having made such a 'generous' offer.

'Not need. Free for monks.'

Lobsang returned carrying a small bag with a few things in it. When Tenzin automatically reached for it, he allowed her to take it, and they made the slow descent to the car park, Lobsang asking Joe, 'You already see da hospital in Leh?'

Joe assured Lobsang that he had.

15

Sameer had seen three of them while in training at Hizb camp and had worked on one. Instructors had lifted them up with both hands, saying that when armed they weighed between five and twenty kilograms. Working in tandem, they went on to name and explain the parts: small batteries, detonator, colour-coded wiring, pocket trigger, Semtex explosive that along with nails, screws and bolts packed the many pouches. Once the wiring was disconnected and the pouches emptied, the trainees were divided into three groups, separated by a hundred metres or so and told to carefully reassemble their vest.

All were reassembled, though neither quickly nor comfortably. The main question was, did the trainees get the wiring right? If a group failed, they were instructed to repeat the task twice over. Each vest was then carried to one of three pits – Sameer uneasily carrying his group's 'heaviest' one – and lowered carefully to the bottom and a minute later detonated from a safe distance. All exploded, all groups passed.

He'd not seen another one since, until now.

As Chacha from Pakistan's Lashkar-e-Toiba, who only arrived half an hour earlier, lifted the vest from behind him for the fitting, Sameer extended his arms out, understanding this was meant as more than just another familiarisation exercise.

Vest on, shoulder and waist straps adjusted to fit the smaller person that he was, Sameer asked, 'Happy?'

'Yes. It fits now,' Chacha said, nodding. He removed the vest and stowed it in a case and placed the case under a bed next to the wall.

As he did, Sameer dropped his arms, slowly watching a fly punching at the window in an effort to escape.

'Sit, sit,' Waqas Commando implored, and the two did in the middle of the floor, straight-backed, legs folded, sunlight fanning in through the window above them.

When Sameer next looked, the fly was gone.

Water boiled, Waqas Commando got up, made and served the tea and sat down again. They sipped to the sounds of distant traffic, an occasional blaring horn, and passing voices from the laneway below.

Sameer spoke finally. 'What's the mission and what am I to do?'

'What did I show you in Kargil?' Waqas Commando answered briskly.

'A small missile launcher.'

'So why do you think I did that?'

Again talked down to; Sameer the schoolboy, the village twig-brain. He yearned to be away from there now, one half of him longing for Hizb camp reassurance, the other half the closeness of his family. He ignored the question and looked over at the bed by the wall – his voice barely above a whisper. 'I take it I'm to pack, wear and detonate what's under there.' His once-strong sense of mission and acceptance of martyrdom continued to wane in the company of Waqas Commando – the carping and bossiness making him feel more an errand boy than a freedom fighter.

'Pack and wear, yes,' answered Waqas Commando. 'Only if certain things happen, detonate. *Insha'Allah*, if God wills it, you're the insurance if something unplanned happens. Though it is unlikely you'll have to do anything but stay alert and do as instructed.'

Those last three words irked him. They hardly needed stating. 'The mission, then, is to shoot down a plane. So when and where does that happen?'

Chacha jumped in. 'It could be a few days or a week, maybe longer. We're waiting to find out. When we know, you'll know.' Chacha, maybe sensing the tension, at least treated him as an equal. 'You have heard what India has done in your homeland?' Chacha asked.

'You mean more than just occupy?' Sameer checked.

'Yesterday they disbanded your government, rescinded Kashmir's special status, shut down the Internet and all phone networks. It sent in thousands more soldiers and a glob of spit lieutenant-governor from Delhi to rule as your new emperor. All of Srinagar is in full lockdown with a twelve-hour military curfew. It makes me ask how many soldier-jailers the Indian army thinks it can fit shoulder-to-shoulder at Srinagar road blocks and street corners.'

A motor scooter passed below.

'Our mission takes on even more significance, serving as a first re-sponse to that latest Indian outrage,' Waqas Commando said, lips curl-ing slowly into a smile, as though looking into the future and liking what he saw.

Sameer hopped up. 'I'm going for a walk.' It was more to prove a point, strike out for a degree of independence than in his need for space and distraction. 'You must have things to talk about here,' he added.

'We'll all go,' Waqas Commando said, hoisting himself up.

'Please, there's the mosque down the laneway. I'd like to go there alone and pray. I am not a child. I don't need minding. If you do not trust me, trust that I'll behave like the Hizbul Mujahideen fighter I am and always will be until victory or martyrdom, just like you, then shoot me.' First time he'd bitten back at Waqas Commando and he didn't re-gret it. He turned and moved towards the door half-expecting not to get there.

*

Prayer in the mosque had its desired effect. But though point proven and feeling calmer, Sameer didn't want to return to the room right away, particularly to Waqas Commando. So he walked on past their building block and continued along the laneway feeling most the absence of In-dian soldiers. As a military base was on the outskirts of town, he'd ex-pected to see and pass them, especially around the mosque, but no, he hadn't – at least any in uniform. Whether that pleased him or not, he couldn't say. He was curious about the sort of weaponry they might carry in such a remote place, and whether or not they gave him, a strange-faced, fighting-age Muslim, a second look. For he didn't fear them, or at least wouldn't have, had he been in close proximity to them. Leh was not only far away from Srinagar, it also appeared to lack Srinagar's religious divisions, its oppression and violence and continual military patrols. Without heavily armed soldiers following his every move and curfews to be constantly mindful of, walking had never been so relaxing for him. Here, Buddhists, Muslims and Hindus shared shop and stall space, and, as far as he could tell, building-block living space as well.

Leh was what he wished Srinagar could be, at least in its friendly, conflict-free lifestyle – no checkpoints, intimidation, strip searches, beatings – if not in its poverty and stark landscape. And as he wandered along eyeing the pedlars and browsers, he fantasised about living here with his family, worshipping untroubled at the mosque, returning to school, learning a trade, marrying and fathering children. Ifra in need of constant care, Parvais dead, he was the only one left who could provide happiness for his parents; the best way by giving them grandchildren to dote over and watch grow. Strange how he'd not given thought to that until recently; the tendency being maybe that the greater the distance from family, the more likelihood there is of family thought.

Moving into sunlight, he brought his mind back and reminded himself again of why he was in Leh. On the issue of his primary duty, a topic he'd fixated on the past few days, he recalled his Hizb instructor saying one day that family and country were one; that what was good for one was equally good for the other. Death, for example? he thought. On that, he could use more convincing. He might raise the issue again if and when he got back to camp. He wandered on, family filling his thoughts.

He slowed eventually, reaching into his daypack for sunglasses and putting them on. An empty bench – as good for lying on as sitting on – was to his left and with it a view of a monster historical building atop the nearby hill. To his right, a woman sat on the ground, legs to one side, child beside her, a begging bowl by her knees. He took a coin from his pocket and dropped it into the bowl. The woman raised her head, squinting. She didn't look well – bony, lips cracked, a yellowish tinge to her skin and eyes. She muttered '*Tujay-chay*' in a gravelly voice before her head sank back down, like she no longer had the strength to hold it up.

He strode to the bench and sat, the child following him with a shy sideways look. Moments later, she leaned into her mother. In the interlude that followed, Sameer thought how good it felt to be outside on his own just doing what he wanted amongst neutral people who had no idea who he was and why he was in Leh. The whys continued: why he didn't want to return to submission in that cage of a room, why some of his anger had been transferred from Kashmir-based Indian soldiers to Waqas Commando, and why, though he very much wanted to, he couldn't return to Hizb camp and explain that, because of his dislike of Waqas Commando, he'd abandoned the mission and returned. Or he could, but a bullet to the back of his cowardly head would be the likely result. And, reflecting on his bomb-vest fitting earlier, if he stayed, which he knew he would, there was a chance he'd die by explosives detonation anyway. At least in staying and being martyred, his family would forever be held in high esteem by Hizb's hundreds of thousands of supporters. Recently, he'd thought that dying in battle would be the best thing he could do for his Ma and Baba. But then how valuable was being held in great esteem when both their sons had been killed, their daughter semi-blinded and no one was there to care for them in their old age.

Going around and around, questions without answers, like problems without remedies that he needed to forget about and move on.

He glanced up. A big white-haired, bearded Westerner was walking down the middle of the laneway a little stiff-legged, like his knees needed replacing.

<h1 style="text-align:center">16</h1>

Lobsang was hospitalised. Not solely due to his broken arm, but also for an irregular heartbeat and an infected wound on his shoulder found after his arm had been set in plaster, or so Joe was informed.

'Well, thank you for the information,' Lobsang replied to the doctor in attendance. He'd be on his way. If either condition worsened, he'd return.

Or at least that was the gist of his response, as told to Joe by Tenzin. After which, she wasted not a second in turning her attention back to her monk, testing his serenity, the topic of her monologue all too predictable.

Minutes later, as the doctor led Lobsang, Tenzin and Alchook one way, Joe went the opposite way, saying he'd probably see them in the next day or two. He wanted out. Ladakhi medical wards were about as alluring for him as ice baths, though he kept that sentiment to himself.

It was only mid-afternoon, so once outside under a mellow sun, he walked towards the town centre intent on enjoying another hour or two of random observation. Retracing the route taken days earlier, he reached the square lined with produce sellers. It struck him how small most of them were – that when squatting on their heels, their knees were almost level with their ears. Yet he envied them their ability to squat so long and naturally, the flexibility and strength in those knees. He veered left away from the square and climbed up past the mosque into the dim laneway and went on, his mind drawing up an image of the bench he'd tested out and found satisfactory for his needs on his previous visit.

Ten minutes later, after passing two monks sitting on a pile of stones for whatever reason, he arrived in renewed sunlight. On the far end of the bench sat a young man – pancake hat, sunglasses, not-yet beard, patched jacket and trousers and worn boots. He was watching that same beggar woman Joe had encountered days earlier, this time without a dog, but a toddler instead pressing its face into her sleeve.

He went over and dropped coins into her bowl. Eyes down, she didn't move and said nothing. It was as if she was sleeping sitting up, despite the toddler's movements. So Joe retreated to the bench. As he sat, the young man turned, sunlight glinting off his blue-lens glasses. Their faces met.

'Hello,' Joe greeted.

Sameer had about four seconds to decide whether to respond. His training said get up and leave. But the old Westerner was just being friendly and was hardly a threat. And Sameer had talked to no one but self-appointed overseers since leaving Kargil, and there were things about the man that interested him, especially his bushy eyebrows and long, full white beard that reminded Sameer of his imam back in Srinagar. 'Hello,' Sameer said quietly. Had the old Westerner been wearing a *taqiyah* cap, *thobe* robe and sandals in some darker place where his skin colour wasn't so prominent, imam and old Westerner might have passed for brothers.

Joe waited in case the bench-sharer followed up with something else. He didn't, and Joe listened to the debate rising inside him: speak or stay quiet? He stole a couple of quick glances at the lad, alternating between him and mother and child across the laneway. Was it his imagination, or did the young gentleman possess a bearing beyond his years sitting there so straight-backed and alert – a true thinking man's pose – without a single electronic device to get him through the afternoon.

'Nice place this Leh. Do you live here?' Joe asked.

As well, English, especially as spoken by a Westerner, interested Sameer. Hearing it was like being back in school again, his class being drilled on proper answers to English questions. Besides Urdu and Kashmiri, it was the only other school-taught language he was prepared to study. Hindi was for obsequious dogs and Dogri and Bodhi for villagers who would never leave the place where they were born. He turned and faced the man, and in a flat, toneless voice said, 'Yes, it is a nice place. No, I do not live here.' With that, he looked back at mother and child.

Tempting as practising English was, though, he couldn't get involved in a conversation: Where do you live? What do you do? My name is Donald, what is yours? He was, as he kept reminding himself, a freedom fighter here on a kill-and-destroy mission and who needed to avoid prolonged contact with anyone who wasn't. So, comfortable as the outdoors, the bench and sunshine were, good as it might have been to practise English with such a friendly tourist, it was time to go, but in which direction?

'As peaceful a place as I think I've been to for a long time,' Joe said.

Sameer pretended not to hear.

A dilapidated flatbed truck chugged down the laneway and stopped in front of them. Two men clambered out and climbed into the back, leaving the noisy engine to idle away. When next Joe glanced over at the young lad, he was striding off down the laneway.

Close as the men were, Joe had little choice but to watch them work – small men with strong backs lifting rocks the size of washing baskets and dropping them in a mound on Joe's side of the bench, obviously to be used for repair work to the wall behind him. Ten minutes maybe before they finished. When they drove away, quiet returned. People passed. Joe looked across the laneway. The woman lay motionless on her side, child on its knees in front of her.

Joe stood and went to her. While the child cried the same word – '*Ma-an, ma-an*' – he knelt down and nudged the woman lightly as if to wake her then felt her forehead, placed two fingers on her throat detecting a pulse.

Arms stretched down from behind him and lifted the child up, Joe twisting around to see the lad he'd just shared the bench with. 'What's she saying?' he asked.

'Mother.' Sameer rubbed the girl's back, cooing something into her ear. 'Woman sick, yes?'

'Unconscious, feverish, but breathing. She needs help.'

Onlookers gathered. One keyed a phone and began talking into it.

'Ambulance,' Sameer informed Joe.

A stall girl rushed up, passing Joe a wet cloth that he placed on the woman's brow and gently wiped her forehead and cheeks, dabbed her cracked lips and chin. Still she did not move.

More people gathered. A siren wailed, closing in.

The ambulance arrived lights flashing red and blue – onlookers moving back, clearing a path. Paramedics jumped out. One knelt to assess the woman while the other retrieved a stretcher. In the next half minute, the woman opened her eyes and stared transfixed while being lifted onto the stretcher, strapped in and bundled into the back of the ambulance.

Still carrying the child, Sameer approached the driver and started to hand her over, but the driver shook his head and pointed further down the laneway, jabbering something sharp and quick. Paramedics hopped back in. The ambulance wailed, turned in a series of jerky reverse-forward movements and headed back out.

'There is mother of mother,' Sameer said, nodding in the direction. 'Where I go to put child…'

Joe picked up the begging bowl weighing his options. 'I'll come with you.'

Sameer seemed to fidget, suddenly unsure of something, before surveying the surroundings. His scan ended at the bench, someone sitting there. Without a word, he hustled off down the laneway past the tiny café, a huddle of rickety-looking stalls, dogs sleeping as if shot, before veering right into a dark swell of shadow. A narrow gravelly path wound past cement buildings with dim, open doorways. Stopping at one, Sameer went in, Joe following. Doors lined both sides of the hallway. At the third one on the left, Sameer knocked. The door cracked open, hinges squeaking.

An old woman's pouched face appeared from behind it. Seeing the child, she flung the door wide open. '*Pema,*' she cried out, and took the child from Sameer, though she hardly looked to have the strength.

A conversation ensued before Sameer turned and, ignoring Joe, left the building.

'For you.' Joe pointed at the bowl with its contents.

Her hands full, she stepped back saying what Joe took to mean 'come in'. He did, conking his head on the low doorframe. Getting through on his second attempt, he stepped inside and set the bowl on a wooden box, took some bills from his pocket and added them to the bowl. Without pausing, he ducked back out the door, hearing the woman say, '*Tujay-chay*. Thank you.' He left the door ajar in the belief she'd be leaving for the hospital soon.

Up ahead, Sameer approached the bench and slowed, feeling Waqas Commando's eyes on him. He stopped beside the bench, sat and waited for what was to come.

Seconds only before, Waqas Commando obliged, 'What have you become, Sameer, after such a short time outside? A medic? Someone whose job it is to help fainting women and crying children and lead Western tourists through the back alleyways of Leh? Have you registered as a guide with the tourist office as well?' Before Sameer had a chance to answer, if that's what he intended to do, Waqas Commando got up, saying, 'Your Western friend must appreciate your work. He's returning. We'll talk back in the room. Get there.' Looking up the laneway, he set off at a brisk pace.

The Westerner was the second-to-last person in Leh Sameer wanted to meet up with again, having just been reprimanded by the person he least wanted dealings with. He glanced around and spotted another gravelly path behind the small café. He went for it.

*

Back in the room, Waqas Commando pointed to the floor and instructed Sameer to sit. Then he sat down on the edge of the bed beside Chacha. Thinking silence ensued, sounds from the laneway seemingly louder as the two on the bed stared at the one on the floor, who returned their looks before lowering his gaze.

'We've received communication,' Chacha said finally.

17

She looked up from the counter, face brightening, and became instantly Tenzin. 'Seventy-three, I not see you for many days. How many you think?'

Joe shrugged and stepped aside for a customer, whose purchases were placed on the counter, tallied up and paid for, the items slotted into a cloth bag and taken away.

'Ahchook see you – two times, I think.' She put on her hard-done-by look, narrowing her eyes, folding her arms across her chest, lifting her chin and waiting for an explanation.

'We saw the rest of the local monasteries one day and took a trip a couple of days later to Likir and to the big monastery further on at Lamayuru. Lots of old sights for old eyes out there. Knuckled hills and stark mountains: up and down and around the long, deep quiet of the antique landscape, stopping at rock temples and viewing elaborate cave art going back a thousand years. Yet still aqua-coloured rivers and river bank trees to lend some colour to the chalky dryness.' He stopped, having gone off on a flowery spiel more typical of a tour guide than a tourist. Maybe because Tenzin was the first person he'd talked to since returning and he was still hyped by the experience, though he did wonder if she understood much of what he said. She hadn't changed her pose. 'So all up it must be five days since I last reported in.' He waited.

'You are Australee tourist. I am Ladakh… What you say?' It came to her: 'Resident.' She grinned. 'Good word – yes?' She didn't wait for an answer. 'But you see more of Ladakh dan I see. You go next time, take me with you. Ahchook give us cheap price.'

'Okay.' What Ahchook had charged, beyond the cost of petrol, was the equivalent of a couple of meals in town – though Joe gave him more. 'I thought you'd be working, otherwise I'd have asked you along.' Actually, he wasn't sure he would have.

She appeared to accept that, letting go of her arms and visibly deflating. 'Someone in family work for me so no problem. Also I can be your guide – like tour guide. Den Ahchook can sleep for his driving. Also, you den owe me two lunch at café.'

'Ah, yes. With Lobsang in hospital, we didn't have lunch number one, did we? What about today?'

'I cannot. No one in family can be here because busy. But tomorrow I can.'

'Good. What if I meet you here at one o'clock?'

She considered that with a furrowed brow, as though it was a difficult decision to make. 'Yes, okay. Three Wise Monkeys good place. I know owner. He give us good price.'

Actually, he preferred having lunch with her than asking her along to wherever 'next time' would take him, which presented a problem. He'd got used to walking solo back home and had drifted off into his own mountain hermit world in all that Likir emptiness while meandering over a stilled track from one barren point to another. Resting on boulders, he'd shouted out, 'Brandy, can you hear me?' and listened to his voice echo along the valley. And later he'd visited the Lamayuru monastery with a quiet Ahchook by his side, not speaking unless asked a question. Two terrific days they were: days that filled out his Ladakh stay and provided plenty of material for another long email to Brandy.

'Is Lobsang still in hospital?' he asked.

'Yes, but tomorrow he leave. I meet Ahchook in morning at da hospital. We take Lobsang to Stakna. You want to come?'

He almost expected her to add, 'See how sharing a trip together is done in Ladakh?'

Of course, going along meant another hospital entry, but after five days' break, he felt up to it. And of all the monasteries he'd visited, Stakna was his favourite. As well, Lobsang was the only monk he'd spoken with at length. He'd welcome the opportunity to repeat the experience – extend it even. 'I would, yes – thank you.' He thought he detected the start of a smile on her face.

'You welcome, Seventy-three. And maybe you want to buy some food for tomorrow. For monks and Lobsang and Ahchook.' Now she smiled full-force. 'For you and me. I give you best price.'

*

New arrivals Habib and young Abu, like father and son though they weren't, sat on the edge of Chacha's bed cleaning and reassembling their Kalashnikovs. Sameer and Chacha sat on the floor and Waqas Commando got down on his knees between them, unrolling a poster-size roughly drawn map and placing stones at the corners to hold it flat.

'Our day has come. *Insha'Allah.* Vengeance is near.' That said, Waqas Commando began explaining and pointing. 'The planes fly out of the mountains here and descend over the monastery here. There's a river here, the main road is here and just to the other side of it is the drop zone here. Our problem is this: traffic travels over the road and military trucks will be waiting to pick up the soldiers, so we can't launch there. The monastery is up on a knoll overlooking the entire river valley and there are no roads that branch out beyond it, only the one that leads into its car park. Here, just before the car park, is an abandoned house. There are no locks on the doors. So…' He looked up at Sameer. 'Knowing all that, Sameer, and from studying the map, how should we go about the attack?'

Sameer knew he was being asked just so he could be contradicted.

*

Lobsang's stay hadn't stretched anyone's food budget. His head freshly shaved, he looked thinner, more vulturesque than ever shuffling out to Ahchook's taxivan, arm in a sling, robe hanging off him like a coat on a peg. Joe stayed close and joined him on the back seat ready to offer support. But Lobsang didn't need it, seemingly growing more upright and animated the closer they got to Stakna. And from the smile on his

199

face while looking left, looking right, as they bumped along the monastery access road, it could have been years he'd been away from his home rather than a mere five days.

For Joe, with his short-term random family close, it felt even better than the first time rolling up to Stakna, Lobsang repaired, everyone cheerful and expectant. Joe thought he might take the walk out to the river. Perhaps he'd borrow a walking stick and take his time, stopping at intervals to look at the lookable, listen to the silence, the pulse in his ears.

Tenzin swung around, breaking his train of thought. 'What you want to see at Stakna we not see before? Tell me, Seventy-three, and I show you.'

'Nothing – nothing more.' No sooner considered than the walk was already under threat. 'I'm still digesting everything you showed me last time. I might just sit in the courtyard and watch the sun and the monks pass by. But you go on, do what you want. Don't worry about boring, old stone-foot here doing nothing. Doing nothing is what I do best.'

She scowled. That wasn't what she wanted to hear. 'You think, Seventy-three, think…'

He did, fast.

'…and I ask you again at monastery.' She turned back round.

They passed the house, Joe in thought, Lobsang staring and saying something to Ahchook, who glanced back at Joe. 'Lobsang thinks something at house change, but not know what.'

Three minivans were parked side by side in the car park, but they went further on and parked at the end. They got out and with the morning sun on their faces began the slow walk up to the monastery. Halfway along, Joe spotted a vulture wheeling between river and monastery. He stopped and watched it, wondering what it was watching. If not them, what?

At the viewing site, all the river plain clearly visible, Ahchook stopped and pointed, shouting something. The three went to him, looking out. Dozens of people – mostly monks – were scattered like seeds over the plain moving slowly towards river and road.

'Why?' Joe asked on impulse, eyeing Lobsang.

From behind them, gravel crunched. They looked around and froze. Two men approached in jumpsuits and black balaclavas gripping assault rifles across their waists. Behind them, descending from the courtyard, three others: one with an assault rifle strapped across his back, another carrying a large cloth bag, the third shouldering what might have passed for a bazooka mid-last century, but had to be more than that now.

The gunman closest pointed his rifle, moved it back and forth from them to those spread over the plain. 'Go! Go down there now…with them!'

Shocked eyes darted from gunmen to plain and back again. Who would move first?

'Go!'

Ahchook split off and walked slowly back down the entranceway, the others following, Lobsang muttering to Joe, 'Pakistan, I think.'

From the mountains to the north came the hum of an aircraft that grew deeper, louder, took on altitude. They spotted it glinting in sunlight as it banked, changing direction slightly.

'Mountain Tamers,' Lobsang said.

Joe recognised the name.

'Why those men here.' Lagging behind without his walking stick, Lobsang looked back at the gunmen, one monitoring them, the others – assault rifles leaning against the viewing wall – working the bag open, taking out a small missile and slipping into its launcher.

Lobsang stopped, eyes flicking from Ahchook to Tenzin to Joe, and said enigmatically, 'One day in Tibet, Chinese jail, old monk I know must go to officer for punish.' He paused, looking up for the plane and finding it again.

'Go!' the shouter shouted, waving his gun.

Lobsang didn't, the others wouldn't without him. 'Old monk smile, not stop smile, and say to officer, "I am old. Death come soon anyway. Go home, Chinese. We do not want you here." Guards hit him and hit him with guns, take him away. I never see him again.' Lobsang smiled and turned, taking his arm out of its sling. 'I am old monk now,' he said, clasping his palms together in front of his face and walking back towards the gunmen.

'Stop!'

Lobsang kept going, appealing, 'Do not kill Pakistan. Respect monastery please. We, you are same in these mountains. Please do not kill Pakistan.'

Two gunmen – one the shouter – exchanged sharp words. As the one stepped towards Lobsang, hand outstretched, the other pointed his gun and fired – 'Tat, tat, tat, tat, tat.' Lobsang hurled backwards as if yanked by an invisible force and crashed to the ground.

'AAAHHH!' Tenzin's scream covered the valley, echoing back over them. Jaw clenched, body curved forward in headbutting pose, she took off for the killer gunman, who shook his head at the pathetic response. Taking his time, he pivoted, butting his weapon against his shoulder, curling his finger against the trigger and…

'Tat, tat, tat, tat, tat.' Spurting flashes, whip crack of gunfire from above. Killer gunman collapsed. The others scrambled for their weapons. 'Tat, tat, tat, tat, tat.' No cover, nowhere to run. A gunman sprayed bullets wildly from car park to courtyard, 'tat, tat, tat, tat, tat, tat, tat, tat'. His head kicked back, forehead a fountain of blood as he went down. 'Tat – tat – tat – tat – tat.' Weapons hit the ground. Hands clawed the air. 'Tat, tat, tat, tat, tat, tat.' All five down – so too Tenzin.

Echo faded to untouched silence – five, ten seconds.

No plane.

Heartbeat all Joe could hear. Body cold, stomach liquid; trembling hands, lips, voice, he muttered, 'Ahchook?'

'Yes?'

Just below his feet. 'Okay?'

'Yes… You?'

'Yes.' Meaning only he hadn't been shot.

They raised their heads as a hunched soldier advanced along the far edge of the entranceway – dashing a few metres, dropping, aiming. He signalled them to stay flat, slapping the ground with an open palm. That soldier, Joe recognised: the one in fatigues praying in the altar room alcove that day then leaving with a long bag strapped across his back. A Mountain Tamer security plant – had to be.

*

On his back, head lolling to one side, Sameer assessed, sizzle of pain spreading like he was being lowered into fire: leg, groin, shoulder. He slipped a hand ever so slowly to his groin, pressed, released. Just his eyes moved to view his hand covered in blood – dark and thick. Confirmed, he was bleeding out. He inched both hands inside his jumper, over his vest. No response from the shooters. Wiring felt intact, so too the detonator tabs. He feathered the switch, took the tabs between index fingers and thumbs ready to detonate and stretched his eyes again. No movement from the others: brothers and Waqas Commando, old monk and old woman – may their God watch over them – all spilling blood, as he was. He could make out the big, white-haired Westerner lifting his head. Someone else down there was doing the same. Then they went as still as the others. On the down slope they were, far enough away, and just needed to stay there.

So to wait, thoughts of his family, while praying to stay alive long enough to salvage something from the mission.

A footstep, and another, another: the light crunch of gravel barely discernible over his lungs working for air. Then nothing. One soldier only   a pity. The next sound, whether from assault rifle or gravel, would determine his chances.

'Crunch…'

Sameer counted the steps, consciousness starting to ebb: two – three – four – five – six… 'Allahu Akbar. God is Great!' he screamed and detonated.

A flash, a thunderous blast, a fiery ball of orange-yellow flame shot high in the air sweeping out over cold stone.

18

He'd thought himself too old for tragedy, and if by some remote chance it happened again to him, it would involve Brandy or Nima: but no.

A blur of distant days and bad nights passed. Ahchook, as Ahmed had been, Joe's daily companion now, staying close. Time spent back in hospital getting cuts and abrasions treated (internal wounds the far bigger issue), being counselled by the Mountain Tamer doctor, Travinda Singh, officiously holding a pad and biro, and interviewed by policemen, military investigators and journalists similarly equipped. Outside, Leh seemed barely real to him, as if he were drugged or hadn't slept in a week. Then his horror and anger, suppressed for a time, would pierce through again, join his trembling hands.

How, for Christ sake, could such a thing happen at such a place: one moment a remote sanctuary of the highest human order, the next a killing ground as horrifying as the streets of Kabul, Aleppo or Baghdad? Was there nowhere left to escape the world's madness? Would gunmen target the Dalai Lama next, or the Sisters of Mercy, or the Pope? Questions he asked his interviewers after explaining that with the exception of his wife he'd never seen a dead person before, nor imagined what modern-day bullets and suicide belt explosives could do to people, especially those he knew and felt so close to. And they nodded, and they wrote in their pads with steady hands, and they lifted their heads blank-faced and waited for more. Only Travinda Singh, drawing him and Ahchook aside, verbally responded, talking at length about who the killers were, what they represented, what their likely motive was, how such horror could affect those who survive it.

Still, in spite of everything, the sun rose, kids passed the Gomang going to school, workmen fronted up to the building site across the road and Dorje was back behind the reception counter greeting him sombrely as he passed into the dining room.

Along with the shock and anger, Joe carried a consuming disappointment in himself that strengthened during the three 'therapy' trips from the Gomang to Stakna's 'bardos' room: first one the hardest. Human abattoir – impossible to forget – disposed of, workmen and their ramshackle flatbed trucks and cement and rocks and gravel and brooms were already making inroads into restoring the viewing area. Further along in the bardos room, Tenzin's, Lobsang's and the soldier's black plastic-bagged remains lay side by -side on the floor (distinguishing what was soldier, what was bomber a matter of guesswork, surely) encircled by praying monks, Tenzin's family and a wide ring of maybe two hundred butter lamps, their flames trembling, as was Joe, in the draft. No thought was more prominent in his mind as he stood there lost in sorrow than the First Noble Truth, life's capacity to produce suffering.

Death stabilised by three days of ritual and prayer, at least for some.

And on that final day, a half hour's drive from Stakna and half an hour's climb took them to an area fifty metres below a Tibetan Buddhist burial site. They sat on Ahchook's homespun blanket, mantra-murmuring monks and friends of the dead scattered around them. Further up on the ridge, overlaid in prayer flags and dozens of impatient vultures, the body-butcher/body-breaker in a black hood and heavy scarlet coat went about his work with a knife.

'Called bird burial, Joe,' Ahchook said. 'Or sometimes sky burial.' He went on to narrate an 'as-it's-happening' account. 'Tibet people believe vultures take soul to heaven so can wait for next life. So bird burial not bury body, not hurt land. So everyone happy to watch. But family not suppose to, so stay home and pray.'

Joe's send-off trifecta complete: Christian services in the past, Ahmed's Muslim service, now the prolonged Tibetan Buddhist one, he thought, tremors of emotion running through him. He could write a book, title it *The Medical Facility and Disposal of Bodies Guide to Touring*

Ladakh. No doubting its uniqueness, at least for Westerners. Though, based on past writing experience and lack of marketability, the book would necessarily be for personal use only.

Strange the things and places his thoughts took him to as he sat there with Ahchook, watching.

After a while, body-butcher and his helpers retreated, their places filled in an instant by swarms of frenzied vultures, jumping on top of one another, wings beating the air, beaks plunging down and ripping off flesh.

Gradually, the vultures took to the air and circled as though a second bird burial was imminent. Body-butcher reappeared as body-breaker carrying a sledgehammer across his waist as the Stakna gunmen had carried their guns. As he beat the bones, helpers bent and scooped up the remains, dropping them into bowls, mixing and rolling them into balls.

'Besides the obvious, what else goes into the bowls?' Joe asked, mostly to convince Ahchook he was weathering the burial as well as anyone, though he knew he wasn't.

'Yak butter and barley flour mix with the bone powder.'

And this was part of Travinda Singh's program to counter his trauma, do him good.

Finished sledgehammering, Body-breaker reached into the bowl, grabbed balls and threw them underarm one after the other into the air; most caught, or if not, fought over on the ground.

Then it was done, the ridge picked clean of Tenzin and Lobsang, the spectators appearing satisfied that it went so well.

No surprise that Joe – Ahchook staying close – was the last one down the hill. Even the body-breaker, his helpers and their stretchers and implements overtook them halfway down and had left, along with everyone else, by the time they arrived back at the taxi.

They climbed in and sat a while, Ahchook saying, 'Joe, you come to my house, eat, meet family and we say thank you for Tenzin and Lobsang.'

And that night they did around a small table where feet and knees and elbows touched, where downturned eyes and Ahchook's brief eulogy dealt with the day.

He could not have been better catered for by Ahchook and wife, Dolma, who, when standing, were like planets for their two shy, young daughters to orbit around.

Later, while dropping Joe off at the Gomang, daughters in the back, Ahchook asked, 'What you do tomorrow?'

Ahchook had obligations other than looking after him, like supporting a family. And Joe wanted nothing more than to spend some time on his own. 'I'll stay close to the hotel for the next few days, do some walks.' Not the first time he'd said that to Ahchook, as he recalled.

'Okay.' Ahchook smiled. 'But want to go somewhere or maybe talk, call me from hotel, okay?' For the third time in their short relationship, he handed Joe a card with his mobile number on it.

And Joe replied as he had previously, 'Rest assured, Ahchook, I'll only ever travel with you.'

And so the next few days passed – Joe, short of sleep, sitting fixated and remorseful on the Gomang balcony after a light breakfast or just coffee, As Travinda Singh predicted, the self-blaming that started in the hospital was well underway now, roiling his stomach, monopolising his thoughts. In other versions of the killings, he ran and tackled Tenzin, rolling over so his back hit the ground, then rolling again to blanket her from harm. He was closest to her. He had the best chance of stopping her. So why didn't he?

Fight or flight – or in his case, cower. All hail the reed man with shivers for a spine and putty for legs. Where in him the backbone, the pluck, some semblance of inner strength needed to do what needed to be done? That impossible question took him back to high school in North Long Beach, of once wandering inadvertently into gangland territory and being confronted:

'Welcome to Tiger-land, maggot brain, proud promoters of war on the streets, over streets, for over a decade. Hope you brought your first-aid kit.'

Terrified, he bowed his head reverentially and clasped his hands together as if about to enter church and was beaten, left dazed and bleeding to be escorted back to neutral ground.

All those years between North Long Beach and Leh to work on a braver self, and when again confronted, again he dissolved.

Chinese proverb: 'A traveller has no shame.'

Not entirely true.

No shortage of balcony attention, though, as staff arrived regularly with fresh pots of tea and warm cakes. They knew; every news follower in the country knew. *The Reach Ladakh Bulletin* and *Times of India* – day-old guest copies in the reading room – had headlined the attack 'Fatalities as Stakna terrorists thwarted' and 'Death in Ladakh as terrorist attack on military plane foiled'. And though, unlike his three companions, he remained unnamed – described only as a seventy-three-year-old Australian tourist – how many of those sorts were walking through the main square, over the laneways and roads of greater Leh?

He took long rambling walks anyway into late morning and afternoon. On the third morning, to avoid clusters of watchful Ladakhis and Indian soldiers in full combat gear now patrolling the streets, he went uphill away from town, turning here and there to the gurgle of glacial melt running down channels towards Leh and the small fields below. He stopped at a small, three-strand wire-fenced paddock, a sign on the gate written in three languages, including perfect English: 'THE HOME FOR HELPLESS DONKEYS – This is a sanctuary for sick and old donkeys. If you find a sick or neglected donkey on the street please bring it here. Reward given.'

What more reward could there be in a place like Leh than a smile, foreheads pressed together, the satisfaction of knowing your actions had saved a life, regardless of what sort it was? Six donkeys no longer neglected, either stretched out asleep in the sun or ambling up for a snack.

And when that wasn't available, one stuck around long enough for a few soothing words and a rub to the forehead before ambling off again.

Next day, armed with a bag of carrots, Joe arrived determined to do his bit for donkey welfare – at least in the short term.

Soon carrotless, he rummaged in his daypack for anything else that might prove donkey-attracting, when he came across *Cloudstreet* – many of his favourite parts still bookmarked. Leaning against the gate, he opened the novel and read the last three pages starting with, 'But here, here by the river, the beautiful, the beautiful the river, the Lambs and the Pickleses are lighting up the morning like a dream. Students stop to watch. Council workers grin and nudge each other. It's a sight to behold. It warms the living and stirs the dead. And speeds the leaving…'*

Again the old donkey with particularly mournful eyes and patchy coat stayed to the end, nudging his shoulder, allowing Joe to convince himself its actions had more to do with Winton's quality prose than the possibility of getting another carrot.

Abandoned finally – donkey finding a spot to collapse and digest its lunch – Joe pushed on up the road following his shadow, the workings of his high-altitude lung power now a template, he reckoned, for the rest of the world's mountain-touring septuagenarians.

When he stopped, it wasn't due to breathlessness or pain, but to sit amidst the rock earth under the huge, blue sky and mull over what he would write to Brandy. He was in a quandary. He owed her an email and had thought to write that an unlikely incident had taken place at a nearby monastery and that he'd tell her about it when they were together again at Christmas.

But of course nowadays, when nothing digital was exempt from immediate research and response, the recipient of such news would just go online for more details, wouldn't they? And having done that, Brandy would likely board a plane in a panic and get to Leh convinced her father was next in line for a funeral of his own.

So he would hold off writing anything more substantial than just

* Tim Winton, *Cloudstreet,* Penguin

'Big demand for the one hotel computer. Plan on heading home soon, and on return to Broughton Manor will write my fingers raw filling you in on everything.' Once home, he'd write a general account of what happened and have Nima verify that he was fine and that time and distance, her strong coffee and good company were playing their roles in settling his aftershock. Though he didn't know if they would or not. He had a habit of holding on to his unmanly grief. Still, it sounded the right thing to say. He'd then write till raw about what they would do over Christmas.

A good plan, he thought, one that would require another visit to town and the travel office – but not today. He stayed, adding to his plan the more immediate need of another bag of carrots and the novel *Lonesome Dove* for a second donkey reading the next day. Helpful, he thought, in distraction, in easing the guilt, shock and sorrow weighing so heavily down on him. And for the nights too, hopefully, that had turned harrowing – like being immured in a concrete vault, sleeping fitfully, snapping awake sweat damp and trembling, mind immersed in balaclavas, assault rifles and bullets tearing through flesh, in severed limbs and headless torso in a pond of blood. All the while close gunfire, Tenzin's horrible scream and the explosion cutting through his head. 'I'm sorry – I'm sorry,' he whispered repeatedly the first two nights, staring into the dark. The third night, he just stared like he could transmit apologies into the dead if he just stared hard enough.

Sitting there flat-rocked barely knowing what to do with himself, he suddenly felt older, sadder and tireder than ever. He asked himself, What's happened to the heart of a man who can murder an old monk and an old woman – an old monk so adept at communicating great warmth in the simplest gestures, an old woman still full of fun and empathy and interest in the world? What sort of poison runs through the head of such a mongrel bastard? 'So it goes,' Kurt Vonnegut wrote more than a hundred times in *Slaughterhouse Five*. Is that all that can be said of such barbarity? 'And so it goes,' Joe mimicked – his throat going tight like a hand had seized it and squeezed. The Stakna massacre was a

Wordsworth 'spot of time' too, as horrible as the day Sara was diagnosed, as the day she died. His head drooped. He crossed his arms tight over his chest as though they might drop off and cried until it hurt.

'Tap's leaking.'

'Yeah.'

Wiping his face finally and getting his emotions back in order, he looked around and saw three young schoolboys approaching, their high-pitched chatter drifting into the lonely space.

As they passed, they offered him smiles, one clasping his palms together in front of his face.

'Hello,' Joe said.

'Hello, sir,' they responded in harmony – slowing, smiles widening. 'Day good for you, sir?' the closest one asked, unclasping his hands.

Barely readers, so they'd know only what they'd overheard or nothing at all about the killings. In their eyes, by their manner, he was just a random tourist involved in some solitude time. Happy, happy? he recalled being asked on the Leh bus after returning from his wondrous climb that day. 'Yes, day good,' he answered, nodding. 'School good for you?'

'Yes, sir, good, good,' the boy spokesperson answered.

They waved goodbye and continued their 'good' day.

An oft-used word was 'good' in these parts. He'd come out of retirement given the opportunity to teach students like those in their high school years. In truth, 'fair' might have been the more accurate reply in one-wording his day. Not great to start, but brief encounters with an old donkey and the students had improved it – as had the fit-for-purpose rock he was on and what surrounded him.

He listened to the silence and thought about contacting Ahchook in the next day or two, and with some Singay-bought food return to Stakna and spend time at the new viewing site, walk out to the river, share a word or two.

Quickly, mid-afternoon, he set off again and an hour later arrived back at the Gomang better for the outing. At his door a folded note with his name on it, a bag of chocolates and a packet of tablets. On the packet a note saying, 'If want good for sleep.' Instructions written in three languages, including near-perfect English said, 'Swallow one tablet at night to make good sleep.'

Two thoughts: had he told someone he had the sweet tooth of a schoolboy? And of concern that his night terrors must have gone audible, spilled out and woken people up, though the people could only have been staff. He was the only guest there now. The hotel was due to shut down soon for winter.

He opened the note. It was from Ahchook:

Deer Joe. Two England climers want to go to Manali in my taxi not bus. Thay want to go in 3 days. I know you want to leeve soon Leh. I can take you to Manali for cheep cheep. Dolma want to cook spesial food for you tonite. I come get you okay. Call me. Ahchook

He walked out to the balcony and sat rubbing his knees as though they needed polishing. In minutes, tea and cakes arrived. Tea poured, he looked out over Leh. Was there any reason to rush back home just to resume his little life – walking to the shop, weeding the garden, sweeping the footpath, watching the news? And coffee at Nima's, good as it was, could wait another week or two. The torturous flight home would be just as torturous whenever he did it. And though he'd once vowed to sit on a fuselage if there were no plane seats available back to Delhi, the way he felt now, after a last Stakna visit he would welcome more mountain time to 'think higher, live deeper' on the high passes, on small climbs to huge vistas of emptiness.

And the Manali walks, the aromas of honeysuckle and jasmine, coffee at outside tables like the ones he passed weekly in Battery Point and Salamanca might help him in transitioning back from Stakna to Moonah. Besides, he'd worked and suffered for his Himalayan-standard lung power. While he had it, why not take advantage of it for a little while longer?

He swigged his tea, ate a cake. And there was this as well: he and

Ahchook shared a history; granted, a very brief one, but it covered the emotional poles from familial highs to the most tragic of lows, so was rock solid as any history, any relationship could be. Why not avail himself of Ahchook's good company a little while longer? As Tenzin and Lobsang had been, and would continue to be, he was special.

Buddhist saying: 'You can't step in the same river twice.'

Maybe not, but you can the mountains.

Suddenly he felt grateful for the opportunity.

It would help to have a smartphone at his disposal now, he thought, mumbling away and shaking his head at the turns and ironies of life. He finished his tea and headed down to reception to use their phone and computer.